## Praise for *You Can't*

"An elegantly-written novel, this is a com,
which explores brilliantly the relationship between pain, memory,
our bodies and ourselves. An absolutely gripping read which comes
together with a neatness that is both satisfying and chilling."

**—Ellery Lloyd, author of the *New York Times* bestseller *The Club***

"An assured debut that is as fresh and exciting as it is dark."

**—Lisa Ballantyne, bestselling author of *Everything She Forgot***

"Exploring the ways our closest relationships can destroy us and the
dark downside of ambition, Emma Cook's tightly woven thriller *You Can't
Hurt Me* proves that the worst pain isn't caused by physical wounds, but
by the emotional harm we inflict on one another."

**—Tara Laskowski, Agatha Award–winning author of
*One Night Gone* and *The Mother Next Door***

"An exceptional debut: tense, taut and thrillingly original. Emma Cook
writes beautifully."

**—S.J. Bolton, award-winning author of *Awakening***

"A slow-burn, atmospheric and literary thriller full of menace and
secrets with some killer twists—loved it."

**—Catherine Cooper, *Sunday Times* bestselling author of
*The Chateau***

# YOU CAN'T HURT ME

*a Novel*

## EMMA COOK

HANOVER
SQUARE
PRESS

HANOVER
SQUARE
PRESS™

Recycling programs
for this product may
not exist in your area.

ISBN-13: 978-1-335-43048-9

You Can't Hurt Me

First published in 2024 in Great Britain by the Orion Publishing Group, an imprint of
Hachette Livre. This edition published in 2024.

Hanover Square Press
22 Adelaide St. West, 41st Floor
Toronto, Ontario M5H 4E3, Canada
HanoverSqPress.com

Printed in U.S.A.

Louis, Evie and Amelia

# 1

I am a ghost in the room tonight. A shadow no one will notice, exactly as it should be. Guests arrive, flowing toward the heat and hum of the glass atrium at the back of the bookshop. Turning my back to them, I retreat farther into the deserted aisles of Anthropology, reach for a slim volume, inhale the flutter of air as my thumb zips through the pages. I wait for that aroma, dry and sweet, biscuits and sawdust, to work its usual magic, a sensory hit that never fails to reassure me. Until now. Books used to be an escape. A window to another world that for a short time might alter me in some unfathomable way. But I've been too close to them, seen how they can taint and twist the truth.

I slip into the atrium packed with a hundred or so more guests. It is easy enough to lose myself here, hovering at the back behind a pillar. I've been paid to melt away into the ether, but I doubt they'll be looking out for me.

So why risk coming along at all, what will it solve? His book is displayed on a table next to me in a tower of carefully spiraled spines, a DNA strand to show every angle. On top, a hardback copy is perched upright, his name embossed across the front in glossy black. I imagine teasing out the bottom copy, watching them topple to the floor. The cover is luxuriant, creamy, a lily in one corner. It could be a bereavement card.

In a way, it is. Loss in fifty shades of vanilla. In those pages resides a version of his wife, Eva, much-loved, much-missed, much-constructed, packaged up for public consumption. The other ghost in the room tonight.

It is his back I see first as he walks through the crowd. Briefly he turns around and from my vantage point I watch him, this stranger who only three months ago I thought I knew so well. He pauses to chat to someone, draws his fingers through the back of his hair, letting his hand rest at the nape of his neck, something I know he does when he's tired or anxious. He looks a little older this evening, a little grayer, a scattering of salt at his temples, a silvery haze of stubble at his jawbone. I see now, or is it wishful thinking, how the past few months have punished him too. He is leaner perhaps, his face more angular. His brow bones protrude a little, lending him an almost hawkish glare.

From my vantage point, I spy an attentive young woman as she approaches him, offering up an open copy of the memoir, the shadow of a smile as they connect. Even from here I can see she is transfixed, caught up in whatever he is telling her, that way he has of diverting the conversation and channeling it elsewhere.

He pauses, bites his lip, and I see something new in his expression, a tentativeness perhaps as he excuses himself from the guest, disappears into his public persona. Slowly he climbs the spiral staircase to a gallery that circles the room and by the time he's at the top, he has become Dr. Nate Reid, any shade of hesitation vanished.

Priya, his editor, is already there, smiling down at the

crowd. Everything about her is sharp and precise, the cut of her pale silk dress cinched at the waist, the razored line of her dark glossy bob tucked neatly behind each ear. She taps her ring against a champagne flute and the clamor subsides.

"Hello, everyone. Thanks so much for coming tonight. I'd like to start by saying what a privilege and an honor it has been working on this book." She turns and raises her glass to him, her hand touching his arm.

"Nate's instinct for storytelling is rare and inspiring. Many of us are used to hearing about Dr. Reid as a distinguished neuroscientist and TV personality, so it has been even more impressive to discover his gift for personal writing, his unflinching honesty and extraordinary ability to let the reader in."

As she hands it over to him, there's a peal of applause. Unflinching honesty? Here's to fantasy fiction.

He clears his throat and steps toward the balcony edge.

"I'd like to return Priya's compliment and say how deeply satisfying it has been collaborating with her." He touches her hand. "One silver lining in my journey is that it has brought me here tonight. To be here with so many friends who have given me their unstinting support. In a strange sort of way, it's like Eva's last gift to me. I feel very loved."

He falters, falls silent for a moment.

Priya passes him a glass of water and there is a tingling anticipation as the silence stretches.

"When I started this book, I was overwhelmed. My first thought was, why would anyone do this? Then I realized here is a golden opportunity. My chance to help others in a similar situation. There are more of us around than you'd think." He looks down at us, as if seeking out other grief-stricken souls in the crowd. "No one can really bear the truth that every minute of our life hangs by a thread. However much we think we can script our own existence and try to ensure nothing bad can ever happen to us, it does and it will. To each and every one of us. Tonight, tomorrow, at some point."

His index finger silently strikes the iron balcony rail, in sync with the rhythm of his words. "Of course, that's why memoirs about grief are so popular. They're a window to a world that one day we'll all inhabit, if we haven't already. It's only a matter of time." He grips a copy of the book, raising it up.

"Eva was an extraordinary person, someone who radiated optimism, a hunger for life. As many of you are aware, she was best known as a sculptor, her work was widely regarded. She also made headlines around the world when I first diagnosed her with a rare medical condition, congenital analgesia, the inability to experience pain. But pain is nature's alarm system helping to protect us, or as C. S. Lewis once put it, 'God's megaphone to rouse a deaf world.' The value of pain is only evident when you see its absence. Which was why Eva was the most fearless person I ever knew, but the most vulnerable too."

Guests lean in, heads tilt and crane. One woman tucks loose hair behind her ear in the hope of catching more. That voice. Gentle, well-spoken. Articulate and low. Gravel and smoke. He's lectured around the world, been interviewed by the *New York Times* and doorstepped by the *Sun*. As his reputation grows, his words became quieter, loaded with a particular power.

A waitress passes with a tray of champagne and reluctantly I shake my head. It's been months since I touched a drink. Months since that night at Algos House. Now I can't help wondering if everything would have turned out quite as it did if I'd kept a clear head the whole time. I sip on a flute of orange juice, watch as he effortlessly ramps up his performance.

"I wanted to examine how you carry on after something like this, how to accept the horror of it. To come back home one evening and discover, in an instant, that my wife had died. How do you begin to make sense of it?"

How indeed.

"Death is the great leveler, even for those who appear to be invincible." He pauses, eyes shining. "Because it shows us who we really are, and reveals how much we truly love the person we have lost. Here's to Eva. Tonight is for you."

He raises his glass as a tide of rapturous applause swells. It takes a moment or two, as the clapping subsides, to identify another noise in the crowd. A shriek. Like a contagion it spreads through the room, palpable and urgent.

"Murderer! We know what you did!"

I swallow hard. There are ripples of movement close to the door, security staff swarm, a scuffle ensues. "Justice for my sister!" she shouts, saying something else inaudible before she is bundled outside and removed from the event, leaving the crowd murmuring in her wake. I know I should leave but I'm frozen to the spot.

Back up at the gallery, Priya steps steadily in front of him. "Well, I guess grief affects us all in different ways," she says. "And hopefully Nate's book will offer comfort and understanding to anyone who's suffered great loss. As a publisher, I couldn't ask for more. Nate's on his way down now to sign copies so do buy one and see what all the fuss is about."

He appears, unphased, unflustered, his enigmatic reserve intact. There is nothing like the fury of a scorned woman to add intrigue, allure even. Priya knows this, so does he. Scandal swirls around him, somehow raising his stock rather than dimming it. I watch as he works the room.

"Well, that was all highly entertaining, wasn't it?" says a woman next to me, her breath ripe with wine and crisps. "Who *was* she?"

"I'm not sure," I lie. "Eva's sister, I guess?"

"Ah, the disgruntled sibling desperate for the true story to be told. Delicious." She regards me for a moment and there's a flicker of recognition in her eyes. She seems familiar, but I can't quite place her.

"Maybe a bit misery memoir for my liking," she says, her tone conspiratorial. "But a great idea. Whoever got him to do it was completely on the money. Even more so if the sister doesn't like it. I'm Jane. Jane Burton by the way. And you?"

She swooshes the bubbles around her mouth and studies me as if I'm a puzzle to be solved. There's that familiar glint in her eyes that I have grown to recognize down the years, a precise and very familiar brand of curiosity, watching from the sidelines, prying, insinuating, picking away. It's part of the job, until it becomes part of you.

"So you're covering the book," I ask.

"Yes, we ran first serial last Sunday. Triumph over tragedy, the usual." She shrugs lightly. "Still, if you cry, you buy, they say." She smiles briefly, moves in a little closer so I can see a smear of fuchsia lipstick on her front tooth. I'm repelled by something in her that feels too close to home. I shudder slightly, step away from her, but she inches closer, as if we're both coconspirators.

"Good-looking, isn't he? In that rather obvious way." She crooks her head to one side, her eyes slide over him.

"I guess, I hadn't really noticed."

"What a horrible thing to happen. I don't think you ever get over something like that, do you?"

"I hear he's doing pretty well."

"I wonder if he wrote it all himself?" Her steady look unnerves me. "A lot of them get help these days, don't they?"

"I wouldn't know. If they choose to have a ghostwriter, it's usually kept a secret." A flush prickles my neck and spreads upward.

I make my excuses and head for the exit, via Memoir &
Autobiography for old times' sake. The siren-call of those glittering lives on display spilling all—fame, grief, misery and
addiction. "Read all about me, me, me," they seem to echo,
screaming for attention. I walk to the end of the aisle and stop
in my tracks. There he is with Priya, standing just yards away.

Something in me deflates, and I know that it's all over. He
talks quietly, rapidly, and Priya nods in affirmation, her head
dipped.

They carry on, deep in conversation. As I walk briskly past
them toward the door, he looks up and our eyes lock. Priya
reaches for his arm, but he pushes her away, starts toward me
as I turn to the exit.

"Wait, Anna," he shouts after me. But I don't turn back. I
have spent too long under his skin and now it's time to burrow out. I won't be another acolyte like Priya. I don't deserve
Eva's fate.

I take off my heels, stuff them into my bag and start to run.
Away from him. Still, I hear his voice, urgent and cracked,
calling my name. I turn a corner and break into a sprint, my
bare soles slap the cold wet pavement. *Keep going*, I tell myself, my breath ragged, my lungs burning. Only two questions keep circling.

*What did you do to Eva?*
*What could you do to me?*

*One Year Earlier—December 2021*

Renowned neuroscientist Dr. Nate Reid is tipped to land a "hotly contested and significant" advance for his memoir, say industry insiders.

At a post-award speech in Geneva last week, where Dr. Reid was the winner of the prestigious Ackerman research prize, he hinted that his next book project would most likely be a "personal one, close to his heart."

Bestselling author of *The Pain Matrix*, a guide to his work on the neuroscience of pain, Dr. Reid also directs the Pain Laboratory at London's Rosen Institute. His scientific research appears in journals worldwide including *Science*, *The Lancet* and *Nature*.

According to sources, this next work will be a radical departure, focusing on the loss of his first wife, Eva Reid, and how her rare condition still inspires his work to find a cure for pain. Two and a half years ago, his wife was discovered dead from a drug-induced heart attack on the floor of her riverside studio in West London.

"He has still never spoken about her death publicly and everyone wants to know what really happened," says another source close to Dr. Reid. The only mystery remaining is whether he'll require professional help.

"Writing of this nature has always been a struggle," he once admitted. "One I'm not sure I'm really born to."

While his previous works were solely scientific, Dr. Reid believes that "a personal memoir may require a more 'collaborative' partnership… It's just a question of choosing the right ghostwriter."

# 2

It is still early in the morning by the time I reach the river. Barges and boats are submerged in shadow, and the curves of Hammersmith Bridge are swathed in a silky mist. I love this hidden pocket of London, trapped between the flyover and the river where the city exhales, the sky expands and the rumble of traffic refines into birdsong. There are geese and herons, weeping willows and wildflowers, even a shingle beach of sorts when the tide is out. The water is higher than usual this morning, its dank breath hangs in the air.

No matter how I vary my jogging circuit, somehow I return to the same spot: Algos House, a riverside avenue of Georgian homes, grand and rambling, with ivy curling through high black railings and pretty manicured gardens that spill down to the water's edge.

I think back to the first time I saw the house, when reporters stood here solemnly delivering the news of Eva's death to the camera in forensic detail. As a journalist myself, I had watched intrigued, not only by the story but also by the views of her studio where she had died. Eva helped to design it, one simple story of floor-to-ceiling windows and cedar wood on the site of an old boathouse, perched on the river's edge. She told a design magazine how she wanted the building to play with the idea of what is hidden and what is on show through its playful use of mirrors and glass. "Spaces can be deceptive," she'd said (a little pretentiously, I had thought). "Even when those windows appear to be transparent, they're merely trapping the human dramas that take place within, reflecting them all back in distortions and imitations."

After her death over two years ago, of course, those words took on an extra significance and the papers were fond of quoting them, drawing attention to their uncanny prescience and how this riverside annex held the clues to what had happened to her. The detail that came to obsess the media was the destruction of Eva's signature glass sculptures, female bodies edged in blades at the waist like a belt. Five of these had been laid face up close to her body, deep crosses scored on each of their torsos with what was probably one of Eva's glass cutters. Like her iPhone, it was never found.

Part of this macabre fascination was the idea of a golden couple who fell from grace. At first the newspapers loved their story. "Has the King of Pain Met His Pain-Free Match?" ran one headline. But soon their interest turned judgmental. There were raised eyebrows that a scientist would marry the subject of his PhD research. After they became a couple, the press paid more attention to her "party lifestyle," the rumors of substance abuse and hanging out with glamorous art-world celebrities. Yet, they didn't really take her sculptures that seriously, or understand her reasons for training as a psychotherapist later. They wanted the sexy, libidinous woman who lived life recklessly, thanks to her genetic makeup.

When she died, of course, there was a sense that somehow she had transgressed, got what she had coming to her. In contrast, Dr. Reid was viewed as cold and uncaring, suspicious, responsible even for his wife's untimely death. Neither of them was cast in a flattering light. Googling them weeks afterward, I wondered how he could continue to live on in a place so inextricably linked to her.

I think about how I could somehow cover all this in my magazine, how I would pitch it to Jess, my editor. There is the small detail I would have to slide around, that I'm not an entirely objective observer here. If I'm honest, I was drawn to Eva for additional reasons beyond my professional curiosity, a more personal one. I had spoken to her once before she died. It was only a short phone interview for the arts pages of a broadsheet, spiked in the end because another paper got there first. But our encounter, brief as it was, now took on for me a special significance, knowing that one minute she had been there and the next, inexplicably gone.

We talked about her work, how she hoped being a therapist would give her fresh emotional insight as an artist, how excited she was to complete her training and see her first patient. I told her how much I loved her sculpture and she had invited me to visit her studio for a follow-up interview. I remember her soft cut-glass vowels straight from a B movie washing over me, her voice a little husky as if she had only just woken.

She was genuinely curious about me, at least it felt that way at the time. I had never seen a therapist before, but I could see why her patients would like her, how much they could gain from her unique perspective about pain. I found myself telling her about my frustrations as a journalist, that I longed to write books, screenplays, real, lasting work. She had urged me to keep going, saying, "If you don't turn your life into a story, you'll just become a part of someone else's." I didn't have the confidence then to really believe I would one day find my own voice, but her words of reassurance stayed with me.

When I read about the rumors of her husband's memoir,

I began to think how unfair it all seemed, given her advice to me that day. I couldn't imagine her ending up in someone else's book, a story that she would have no power over, that would inevitably be more his than hers. She would have hated that, I'm sure. But the dead don't get a chance to answer back, do they?

As I sprint away, Eva's voice drifts back and with it that sense of my own potential she alluded to. Maybe this could benefit both of us.

I run a little faster, an embryonic idea forming. The best way to cover it would surely be an interview with Dr. Reid for my magazine, *The Londoner*. I'd impress him with my skills, maybe I could be in the running as his ghostwriter. Unlikely but at the very least it's a good idea to present in our next features meeting. I polish the outline in my mind, exactly how I'll sell it to Jess. Their love story, her inability to feel pain, his obsession to find a cure for it. Eva deserves better than to be the silent wife, a footnote in her husband's narrative. Just thinking about it makes me angry on her behalf. If I were working for Dr. Reid, I would never let that happen.

# EVA'S SELF-REFLECTION JOURNAL

*14 January 2019*

*Welcome to the self-reflective, analytical, navel-gazing new me!*

*Janet, our psychotherapy lecturer, told us we have to record our thoughts and our patient sessions to "facilitate learning by exploring our inner feelings."*

*She assured us yesterday that it's for our own personal development, not for anyone else to read or assess.*

*Okay, so here are some deeper feelings. Confession number one. I'm the shitty one here. The faker. I'll never be like them.*

*This morning we sat in a circle in an airless basement of the clinic, taking it in turns to think about what attracted us to train. People talk about their natural empathy, their listening skills, how they want to help others to avoid the same terrible mistakes they've made. On and on they go. Caught up in their own worthiness, their own smug sense of how bloody good and helpful and caring they are, how they want to use their own suffering to help others.*

*When Janet turned to me, I froze. Watching their eyes slip-slide over me, I was convinced they could spot an imposter in their midst. What was my reason for being here? I told them about my diagnosis of congenital analgesia, how my mutation prevents me from feeling pain or anxiety. Maybe this was why I sometimes felt closed off, empty, as if nothing really mattered.*

*Someone asked if the two were really connected, the physical and emotional. Janet suggested that maybe it was down to language; how experiencing pain allows us to express and inhabit emotional pain too. In this way, our bodies and minds are intricately linked. She talked about Finnish researchers who have mapped the body for different types of emotions, locating grief and heartbreak in the chest, anxiety and fear in the stomach, anger in the arms and, in contrast, love as an all-over body sensation. They were fascinated by all of this, but somehow none of it chimed for me. Fear, anxiety, anger, depression: my body lacks an atlas for it all. I'm Teflon-coated. How can you be truly brokenhearted, for instance, without feeling the physical ache inside?*

*Of course, I'm curious about the extremity of other people's emotions. I've always wondered if I lack what it takes to be a real artist. Would Frida Kahlo's boundless creativity have existed without her chronic pain? One was almost certainly a condition of the other. To make real art is to know how suffering truly feels. Where better than a therapist's office? I see and hear it all around me. On the faces of the other trainees when they talk about their messy lives, painful divorces, neglectful parents, addictions, recovery. It's emotional torment that I cannot comprehend, food that I will never taste. But perhaps being up close to all this will help to unlock me, to find out how it really feels to hurt.*

# 3

In the end, Jess was keen on my pitch to interview Dr. Reid for a cover story. What she really wanted, like any magazine editor, was to get inside his mind, find out who he really was and how he felt about his wife's death, living alone in that sprawling riverside house without her. And, of course, what this meant for his research. I crafted an email to his publicist, reassuring her that my interview would focus mainly on his recent guide to neuroscience, *The Pain Matrix*.

I wake early on the day I'm due to meet him, just to make sure I have everything I need. The pens must be blue fine-tip rollerballs, the batteries Duracell, the printed list of questions bolded up. The wrong font or a battery that has already been used, even once, is enough to derail me. My mind has always been a little bit obsessional, seeking out patterns and rules that protect and comfort me. These are the rituals that shore me up before every interview. Although this time, there's more to lose.

It will be a delicate balancing act, steering him toward territory that he will instinctively want to avoid, risking his hostility but, at the same time, inviting his admiration too. It's a line I've become an expert at toeing, over the years. If there is

a memoir in the pipeline, I want to seem like the perfect can-
didate, the right choice. Every detail will need to be just so.

I scrutinize myself in the hallway mirror, wipe away the
sheen of lip gloss and the blusher too. Nearly there, except for
the hair scraped high in a tight ponytail. Too austere. I let it
down so it falls onto my shoulders, do up the next button of
my shirt so only a glimpse of neckline is exposed. I dab away
a smudge of eyeshadow with the pad of my thumb. This display of effortlessness has taken me over half an hour. I test out
my quizzical gaze, open my eyes a little wider. Tilt my head
to affect empathy.

My strategy is always the same: ease my subject into conversation, feel the satisfaction as they uncoil, revealing everything.
I can't help envying that moment when they let go without
intending to, how that freedom must feel. The less you offer
about yourself, the more they really talk.

Over the years I've heard it all. The personal revelation in
all its tawdry detail. They've had an affair; their marriage is
over; the tumor is malignant. The subjects of their confessions
vary. But it's the kick of reeling them in, question by question,
letting them think their decision to speak openly is entirely
voluntary. A lot of it is also timing, knowing exactly when to
drop in that deceptively simple question: "Why?" The shortest
word that can often elicit the longest answer. Then I sit back
and say nothing, knowing they will be compelled to speak.
The less self-assured they are, the more they feel a lingering
silence is their responsibility, their problem to solve. So I circle and return. Navigate the push and pull of disclosure, how
we fly back and forth between the need to be hidden and the
desire to be known.

The thrill for me always comes in breaking down their
defenses, watching them let go without intending to, until
I discover what I'm there for. How consuming curiosity can

be, without any of us ever really knowing why. An itch and a drive, and for me, one that also happens to pay the bills.

My phone vibrates, the cab is waiting.

I check my handbag for everything one more time before I leave. Outside it's about to rain, the air is swollen and damp. The driver sets off and West London slips by, comforting and familiar, dry cleaners and kebab shops, barbers and money kiosks. I close my eyes, lulled by the warmth in the back of the car, the sweet smell of plastic seating and vanilla.

I visualize the interview, imagining Dr. Reid's wary demeanor. I'll make him comfortable, let him seduce himself with the power of his own words. Be the mirror that reflects his expertise back to him. Then follow his fault lines; pick at the edges of his discomfort, like the newly formed skin around a scab. I never flirt or use feminine charm. I've found that simply by being a woman, a male interviewee assumes you are there to listen, to be deferential, grateful to absorb the details of whatever their arcane specialism may be. It's not about tricking them, but playing with their assumptions. Beware the sympathetic female ear.

But, in the long run, it's the writer who has the final say. Deciding how they come across is down to me.

The car picks up speed, its tires hiss on the surface of the Westway, vertiginous and exhilarating, a strip of road that rises like a Scalextric high over the streets of Paddington and north Kensington. Rows of elegant stucco terraces line up stiffly like piano keys. The market stalls along Portobello and garish letters of street graffiti flash below us before we're tipped down into the gridlocked traffic of the Euston Road. Eventually, the taxi stops outside the Rosen Institute, a Gothic Victorian building in Bloomsbury, darkened by centuries of grime.

"Ah, the Rosen, I've always wondered what goes on in

there," says the cab driver, peering upward at its turrets and towers spiraling into a granite sky.

"The Pain Laboratory." I smile. "It's the only one of its kind in Europe."

Deep in that basement lies a state-of-the-art research lab. Designed by Dr. Nate Reid, dedicated to observing human pain in all its infinite variety. Here, I know, volunteers offer themselves up to be physically hurt. The more extreme, the better. Willingly they are prodded and poked, scalded and scraped, burned and pierced. Precisely how they suffer, the state of their neural responses, has been scrutinized and reported upon, peer-reviewed and published around the world, making Dr. Reid something of a celebrity beyond the world of neuroscience. It was the *New Yorker* profile that originially crowned him the King of Pain.

He met his wife, Eva, six years ago when he began researching her rare condition known as congenital analgesia, or congenital insensitivity to pain (CIP). It's a rare disorder where the sufferer can walk on hot coals, place their hand in fire, walk on a broken limb for weeks and feel nothing more than a light tingle or a dull ache.

As he once wrote, pain defines our quality of life, its presence can wreck the activities that make us most human: thought, sexual activity, sleep. If Dr. Reid could identify the gene that "switched off" certain receptors in her brain, he could be the first to find a universal cure, crucially, one that wasn't addictive, that was opiate free. She became the focus of his research paper, and then they fell in love.

"Can you give him ten minutes, please?" his assistant asks, motioning me toward a reception area at the end of the corridor, spare and bland.

The room is preternaturally quiet. I focus on the small

courtyard outside where water pools on the mottled paving stones in the rain. The voice of the city seeps through a half-opened window. On the pinboard opposite me, there's a poster inviting sufferers of trigeminal neuralgia to join a research group. It's a condition that can, apparently, feel like someone's inserting crushed glass under your skin. I remember that one from my interview research. I can recite the symptoms of several others too. I like the words, the chewiness of them and how they resonate. Postherpetic neuralgia, the searing nerve pain that can follow shingles. Ilioinguinal neuralgia—a stabbing pain that radiates to the genitalia. Cluster headaches, sometimes known as the "suicide headache" for the extremes to which they drive their sufferers.

It takes several days for me to read around my interviewee. I will have forgotten every detail about them and their work by the time the article is printed but, for a short while, I am fluent in someone else.

"Dr. Reid will see you now."

His assistant has come to fetch me. I follow her into his office, arid, white and windowless. I wait and I wait.

I hear him before I see him: brisk, urgent footsteps along the corridor that proclaim self-importance. He stands in the doorway, talking into his cell phone, and turns away from me. "We don't need to overcomplicate this. Those reports are pivotal and we can't wait any longer on the results. What's the hold up?"

I take him in, a wall of defensive energy, tapping his fingers on the door frame. Impatient, not quite at rest even when standing still. He talks rapidly, as if he wants to wrap up the conversation but can't resist prompting more questions, as if to assert his authority.

I have spent so many hours like this. Out of sight. Waiting, observing these unconscious displays. You could say it's an early calling. As a child, I'd consume Agatha Christie novels and treat my home life like a mystery to be solved. No one told me anything so I was the detective searching the dust for fingerprints. I was always the mouse in the corner, watching everyone, from the neighbors across the street to the arguments between my parents and my brother. Mining details from a distance, inferring meaning from sighs and glances, from the sort of silences that seep under doors and settle like layers of snow, what's left behind in the room long after the adults have left.

"Sorry, with you now," he says, his tone shifting as he slips his phone in his pocket, walking toward me. "Nate Reid. Dr. Nate Reid."

"Anna Tate." I stand up and extend my hand, aware of that visceral jolt whenever I meet a stranger who is highly recognizable. His photo has stared back at me from the paparazzi shots, the portraits in broadsheet profiles, TV shows, TED Talks. His hair is short, still dark except for that one distinctive bolt of silver at his temple. He glowers a little, heavy dark eyebrows knit together in appraisal. A fleeting tension ticks away below the surface, the muscle working in his jaw. His eyes are dark brown with specks of amber.

"Pleasure to meet you, Anna."

"I know how busy you must be. Thank you for meeting me."

He shakes my hand, assessing me before turning away. "Okay, let's go. Follow me." His accent snags on me. English private school flecked with the odd drawn-out mid-Atlantic vowels.

"Go? Where? I thought we were doing the interview here?" I look back to where my recorder and notepad are laid out on the table. I want to scribble all this down, hold on to my early impressions.

"Oh, you can bring them with you. We'll walk and talk."

I scurry into the room to get my things and follow him, irritated by the way he's taken charge and my hardwired eagerness to comply. He strides ahead of me, oblivious. "My postdocs are excited they've got you as a volunteer this morning. You're the first journalist to try them out—I've never let reporters inside here before. We have some interesting tests lined up for you."

This was the part of the interview my editor had insisted on when we talked through the angle it should take. I agreed, reluctantly, to subject myself to his techniques for measuring pain to add an "extra dimension" to the profile, an idea I still hadn't really warmed to for obvious reasons.

"But we are coming back afterward to talk alone?" I say, quickening my pace to keep up with him. "Your book PR Rhik agreed I'd get at least forty-five minutes…"

"Your hair," he interrupts, his dark eyebrows shooting up in a sideways glance at me.

"My hair…?"

"Is it naturally red or do you dye it?"

"Oh, it's natural."

He peers more closely at me as we walk, and for a brief second I think he's about to pick up a strand of my hair and roll it between his fingertips.

"Redheads generally tend to be more sensitive to pain," he says, looking at me thoughtfully. "Although their pain threshold can be impressively high. I'm doing a study on it, and these tests will provide valuable data."

"Well. Glad you're getting some use out of me," I say dryly, which he doesn't seem to register.

We reach a set of stairs that take us down into a maze of corridors. Exposed steel pipes run along the low ceilings. The doors ahead of us are molded aluminum with small glass port-holes, like the bowels of a wartime submarine.

He stops under a sign that reads Strictly No Entry, and below that I notice someone has scrawled No Pain, No Gain in black marker pen.

"You should put that on a T-shirt."

"One of my hilarious students." He rolls his eyes, pressing a small buzzer next to the door. "Welcome to my lab," he says, and I follow him inside.

# 4

The room is saturated in a pale blue fluorescent glow. Machines blink and bleep. Behind a glass screen at one end there is a bank of computers and, in the middle, a large hollow cylinder with a motorized bed poised to glide inside it.

"Please, do sit down," he says as I glance anxiously at the MRI scanner.

One of the researchers hovers at his elbow, brisk and efficient, and asks me to roll my sleeve up, smears some gel on my arm. Dr. Reid sits on a chair next to me. There's an acuity in his gaze, a focused energy about him that unnerves me. I'm experienced, I remind myself, prepared to the very last detail. Yet, for once, my preparation rituals haven't quite worked their magic.

"Okay, so I hope I can give you a little insight today into what we're doing here at the Rosen."

"Right," I say crisply, trying to avoid looking at the gleaming instruments neatly lined up on the trolley next to him. There are fine needles of varying sizes, tweezers, pincers, forceps, tubes of gel and a metal box attached to two electrodes. As a couple of other researchers flit in and out of the lab room, his hand hovers over the tools, as if unsure which to select first. My instinct is to keep him talking.

"And what exactly are you trying to find out?"

"For us neuroscientists, pain always presents an intractable problem. It's a universal experience, one that creates misery for millions of sufferers. It's also utterly private, in that only you're going through it. A bit like dying," he muses. "Nearly all people feel pain. Yet we still struggle to describe it, words often run out, as you'll discover."

I grimace. He smiles.

"So," he continues. "How can we treat a patient who's unable to define what they're feeling? What we need is measurable data. When I inflict a unit of pain on you, I can see exactly how your brain reacts and I can give that a measurement. This creates data. And data is hope." He pauses for effect. "The hope of easier diagnosis and more effective treatments."

"Sure," I nod, wondering when the longest needle is going to come into play.

Nate hesitates, grins briefly as he sits back. "Sorry, you've got me on my favorite subject and we should be focusing on you. I'd like to ask a few questions too before we start. You do bruise quite easily, don't you?"

His gaze shifts as it travels down my bare legs, settling on the mauve crescent rising above my left knee, and I swallow, reflexively tugging at the edge of my skirt.

"Corner of the kitchen table yesterday. Yes. Very easily."

"Tell me about the last time you were in real pain. The symptoms, how it felt."

"Well, I suppose last year…"

"Describe it to me."

"How to describe the pain." I sigh, finding myself strangely inarticulate. All his assumptions coming true. "I guess my mind goes blank when I try to think of the right words. I cut my finger. Badly. I was slicing garlic."

He waits for me to carry on. I take a deep breath, wincing

at the memory, particularly the phone call last year that preceded it. Where do I start? If Dr. Reid really wants to hear about pain, we could be here all day.

It was a silly argument with my brother. Tony had wanted to meet my new boyfriend, Dan, and I had been putting it off, pretending I was busy. He had even suggested a double-date with whoever his newest girlfriend happened to be. I had refused, instantly hurting his feelings. "But why not? We always have fun together," he had reproached me gently. "And it's what Mom would've wanted. I'm here to protect you. It'll be fun."

After the call I had felt distracted by the usual cocktail of emotions Tony provoked in me, irritation, guilt, regret over hurting him. I peeled off the pink papery skin of the garlic, tipped back a glass of wine, angling an oversized knife through the small kernel. Why can't I be a more decent sister? Another gulp of wine. Another slice. Then the slip, a cut that was deeper than a usual knick. I think about that exquisite hiatus, less than a second or so, between the act of harm and its effect. How do you tell a pain expert that on this particular occasion the sensation was weirdly satisfying, clean and uncomplicated, obliterating everything that came before?

"It was agonizing," I say instead, because it's the straightforward answer, the one he expects. "I felt sick, frightened too."

"Of?"

"Of what would happen next." I shrug. "It was all fine in the end. A&E. Four stitches, acetaminophen." I hold up my hand and he touches the ivory ridge of scar tissue at the top of my finger.

"Well, I promise you that nothing here today will feel as bad as your contretemps with a sharp knife. These are simulations, acute but brief. Shout and I'll stop." He pauses, his expression growing intensely serious. "So, we're going to stick some electrodes on you to monitor each region of your brain and they'll flash up on those screens over there in different colors, depending on how you react."

"I think I can guess."

"Doubtful. No one knows how they'll respond to pain until they're up against it…"

"Can we just get on with it?" I interrupt.

He looks at me quizzically. "You look worried, why?"

I see all sorts of assumptions flicker in his eyes. *Female. Red-haired. Oversensitive. Likely correlation with low-pain threshold, higher-complaint score.*

Nate's directness unnerves me, a clinical candor. It's not that I'm afraid of pain. But the idea of being studied as I'm experiencing it is unsettling. The last person I want gazing into my brain and drawing conclusions, I realize, is Dr. Reid. I'm not sure he'd like what he found there.

"No, not all." I try to sound bright. "I'm fine. Let's go."

"Okay. What I'm going to do is rub some capsaicin here, a chemical that you find in the hottest chili. It's the part of the pepper that gives you the deepest heat." After outlining a circle on the inside of my arm, he lathers it on, scrutinizing me as the gel starts to tingle. "You're okay?"

I grip the chair as a burning sensation ripples through me, aware that he's noting my reaction.

"It's intense, right? Capsaicin is one of our most efficient conductors, it reacts with the nerve endings really well."

He presses what looks like a metallic circuit board, the size of a SIM card, onto the gel.

"This will help to kick it up a bit and give us more control, like a volume button. I want you to rate what you feel out of ten. So zero is nothing, five unpleasant and ten pure agony. We'll try not to go further than five."

"Try?" I echo, as a flash of pain shoots along the inside of my arm.

"Too much?" He turns it down instantly, but the volt of his smile disconcerts me. "Okay, now? Out of ten?"

"Er, four?"

He increases the power and I flinch, terrified now that he'll ramp it up further. I want to tell him to stop.

"You're sure you're okay?"

I nod, gritting my teeth.

"Score?"

"Eight." Mercifully the pain begins to recede and I compose myself, determined to steel it out in front of him. "Out of interest," I ask cooly, reaching for a glass of water, "has anyone tried this experiment and not responded at all?"

We both know there's only one person who was oblivious to these simulations, however agonizing. I remember reading in one profile how he'd brought Eva here soon after she agreed to take part in his research. He probably couldn't wait to entomb her in the scanner so he could peer into her brain, all those neurons firing up for him to see.

"You're referring to my work with CIP patients?"

I continue looking at him until he breaks eye contact.

"Believe me, watching someone unable to respond to these tests makes one profoundly grateful to experience any sort of pain," he says, with maybe more feeling than I'd anticipated. He glances down at his tray of implements, briefly lost in thought.

"But finding a cure for pain, rather than helping those who can't feel it, has that always been your aim?"

"I guess the answer to one lies in the other. Pain is more complex than other senses because unlike, say, taste, hearing, smell, vision or touch, it's a warning sign—a distressing sensation with real or potential damage involved. Someone once described it to me as the white-hot core of human experience, and I think that's accurate." He pauses, checks his watch. "Okay, let's try the next test."

"Needles?"

He nods. "They're superfine, more like acupuncture," he says neutrally, selecting a couple from the trolley that look anything but superfine to me. "Now I'll need you to raise your left leg slightly. We want to get to the fleshy part of your calf."

I roll up the side of my skirt, grit my teeth and look away. The sensation feels like a hot knife, as if my nerves are fizzing. "Eleven!" I cry. "You said you wouldn't hurt me."

"That was unexpected." He hands me a small circular ice pack, holds it to my calf, and the relief is almost tear-inducing. A wave of nausea rises in my stomach and my back arches.

"It was more than unexpected. You promised," I say, shaking. My breath feels uneven, as if all the air has vanished from the room.

"Some people barely notice this test but it really depends on the lateral peroneal nerve. Unusual that you had such a strong reaction," he says, evidently pleased. "You see, the peroneal nerve winds around the outside of the fibula and it can be exquisitely painful if you catch it. It's an easy one to stimulate. In fact, yours appears to be particularly sensitive. I told you, it's all subjective."

Nate notices my teeth still chattering and looks as if he wants to say something, but then he shakes his head. "Right, so Kate, our researcher, will pop you in the scanner and I'll be checking your reactions on-screen over in the corner."

He walks away while she takes me through a list of instructions. Slowly I slip into the machine and a small screen above me flashes READY in green lettering before each sensation is administered. Yet again I picture Eva, trapped like me in this rattling metal tube, blissfully safe from whatever agony was about to be inflicted.

A series of red flashes and I feel an acute burning like a blowtorch deep within the muscle of my arm. Another needle slips into the skin around my ankle close to the bone. I think of all those useful adjectives the pain specialists devised back in the '60s. Throbbing, shooting, drilling, lacerating, crushing, sickening.

The problem is that these are only lame explanations. Once pain strikes, language shatters. Memory makes it difficult to describe precisely since we try to block it out, but so does the sensation itself. I see and feel it in colors more than words. Shutting my eyes, I focus on the orange patterns at the back of my eyelids, morphing into silver shards.

The scanner vibrates and an alarm sounds. My bed moves slowly into the light and I open my eyes. I try to stand up but my legs are unsteady. He walks briskly back over to me, checks my pulse, the tips of his fingers pressing into my wrist.

"So how did I do? Do redheads really perceive pain that differently?"

"They appear to," he says, his head tilting as he studies my scans. "But in conflicting ways. Their pain tolerance can be higher and yet they can also require more anesthetic to be sedated. So I'm not surprised you're a complex respondent," he reflects. "Resilient at points I wouldn't expect, but then over-responsive at others. On the whole, unpredictable as far as the data is concerned."

He flips through a series of images where regions of my brain glow orange and red like a forest fire. "It's a fascinating start and, if we had longer, I could talk you through all your results, your pain profile, but I'm afraid we're out of time. Is there anything else Kate can help you with for your article?"

I realize I am being dispatched. The interview is over.

"Is that it?" I say, still jittery from the tests. "What happened to my interview?"

He shrugs, polishing his reading glasses.

"No." The pitch of my laugh takes me by surprise, and I touch the tender skin inside my arm. "It's been great hanging out in Room 101, being poked and burned and prodded. So you get what you want and I get nothing?"

"Not exactly nothing. It will add to your profile, surely?"

"Amazing," I say. "But you haven't really kept to your side of the deal."

"I disagree. As I said before, you're the first journalist to set foot in here. You've had a unique opportunity to see my work, to experience it firsthand for yourself. Anything else, background, facts, more quotes, I'd be happy to follow up by email."

"That doesn't work for me." I stand up, aware that my face is hot, my hand trembles as I grab my bag off the floor. "It's a cover story. Readers will want to know more about you, a bit of background. We can talk about your work, but there needs to be a personal element to my article too, for color and context."

I inhale sharply, instantly regretting my show of impatience. This was meant to be a charm offensive but now I've sabotaged all that. I've let my emotions surface, disaster for an interviewer, let alone a prospective ghostwriter. "Look, I'm sorry. I think those tests may have thrown me slightly." I massage my arm, laugh awkwardly.

"No, you're right." His tone softens too. "The truth is I don't do interviews, but Rhik is very persuasive, and there is *The Pain Matrix* to promote, so I gave in. But I value my privacy above all else and, as I think we both know, there are good reasons for that."

"Okay, well, how about I send you a list of questions first

so you know exactly what I'm going to ask you? Could that work?" He considers this for a moment and I press on, "You don't have to answer anything that makes you feel remotely uncomfortable, I promise. Completely up to you. I trusted you and now—"

"It's my turn?" He looks faintly amused. "Okay, fine. But I may as well say now that I won't answer the really personal stuff, particularly what happened in the past. I'm not keen on raking through all that, not yet." He picks up his phone and scrolls through the diary. "I'm away for a while from next week so I can do…this Friday?"

"Fine. Do you have a home office?" I suggest, as casually as I can.

He hesitates. I see a small pulse in his jaw line. "Yes, but—"

"Well, that sounds ideal," I say, jumping in before he can change his mind about the prize that's being dangled in front of me, an open invite to Algos House that has always been very much off-limits to journalists.

"Just to clarify, Anna, my home office, not an at-home interview. You do understand? I don't want to disappoint you on that one."

"Of course. Absolutely." But we both know it's a compromise, an unpredicted win.

"I'll get Rhik to email you and confirm the details and address. My niece is staying there at the moment while she's on a research placement and she'll be around if I'm delayed here for any reason," he says and then he's on the move again. I follow him back along the acres of beige corridor until we reach the elevator, facing each other. "Thank you for coming along today, Anna, for being so game. There's something about seeing an authentic response to my work that is always such a privilege."

He gives me a small, secret sort of smile as the doors close.

# 5

Back out on the street the world seems spikier, as if the volume button is turned to high. Colors are savage, noises shriller. It takes a few seconds for my eyes to adjust to the clarity of light pouring into the garden square opposite. The tree branches are paper cutouts spread across a buttermilk sky, the black railings that encircle them sharpened spears. Heading for the square, I register a dull ache behind my eyes along with a strange bitter taste in my mouth. I sit down on the nearest bench, take out my phone and tap away furiously into Notes.

Details swim before me as I replay the experience, how the interview I had taken so long to research and prepare for was ambushed by Nate. How it was me who wound up placed under the spotlight, not him. At least I hadn't given too much away, except apparently my pain tolerance.

Still, hadn't I won out with an invite to Algos House? I couldn't help smiling to myself. Who had been more persuasive in the end?

I get the rest of the facts down as I remember them, and then sketch in my initial impressions of him, how contradictory and clinical he can be. There's a lot I won't include, because I'm not sure I have the words quite yet for the intensity of those sensations in the lab, the peculiar intimacy of the whole experience, the way that it all made me feel.

I reach down to touch the back of my calf, still painful, perforated like a pin cushion and bruised. The inside of my arm all the way down to my wrist is blistering. I want to go home, replay and analyze this scene in my head many times over. But I promised to meet Amira for lunch. I drop my phone in my bag and walk briskly to the subway.

At Oxford Circus, I weave my way south toward Lexington Street where a sliver of Georgian Soho still lingers between the bubble tea bars and independent coffee shops. The sludge-green restaurant facade looks like it should sell antiques. The blackboard outside is chalked, *Old Spot pork chop and mash.* Downstairs in the gloom of the basement, the walls are lined with a print of Hogarth's *Gin Lane* and old *Punch* covers. While I wait to be seated, a man in a paisley silk waistcoat at a nearby table orders a second bottle of Châteauneuf-du-Pape. And then I remember why I've always loved this place. Barely 1:00 p.m. and it already has the louche air of a lost afternoon on the run from the office.

I see my friend and editor, Amira, at a table in the alcove. She waves.

"Anna." She stands up to kiss me, her face clouding with concern. "Are you okay? You look...washed out."

"Honestly, I'm fine," I say, sitting down and studying the menu. I know Amira well enough but can still never quite work out if her inquisitiveness is born of sympathy or prurience, or most likely a combination of both. "I'm starving."

I look at the wine list, stalling for time while I work out what I'm going to tell her about the interview. I will need to break the news that I let it slip through my hands today, spin it to manage her expectations. *Delayed but not lost. All to play for.*

"Come on, tell me what happened."

I try to catch the waitress's eye, avoid the beam of Amira's interest, always shining a spotlight into corners one would prefer to remain in shadow. It's been something of a relief to me over the years that she's much better at asking questions than truly listening to the answers.

"He was interesting," I say, carefully. "The Rosen is such a weird old place. Like a time warp really. Miles of corridors and these dusty old laboratories. Except for Dr. Reid's, which is like a high-tech lair." I pause, registering a shade of panic in her eyes.

"So definitely interesting enough for next week's cover story, do you think?"

"That soon?" It's my turn to panic now.

"Jess is desperate, our lead interview has just fallen through."

"I guess I could turn it around but I'd need a few more quotes. I've pretty much been a lab rat for the last two hours; it wasn't exactly the interview I expected."

"Well, we may have to make it work as it is," she says as the waitress starts to hover at our table. "Let's get the drinks in first."

Amira and I studied at the same journalism course and since then we have slipped in and out of each other's lives, drifting apart until someone or something snaps us back together, remaining close through it all. She's Jess's deputy editor and commissions me to do most of their cover interviews. A year ago, I lived in her loft room while my apartment was being renovated and now I'm returning the favor. Amira recently finished with her boyfriend, so she's about to move in with me for a month or two.

The second bedroom was originally my older brother Tony's—we bought the apartment together ten years ago with our parents' inheritance, not a life-changing amount

but enough to cover a decent deposit. He's a freelance photographer for travel magazines and websites, spending much of
his time away. When he's back in the country, he stays at our
apartment. I know how difficult it is freelancing in this business so any rental income we get from the extra room, I tend
to give him. It's a mixed blessing really, owning a property
and yet never being able to enjoy the freedoms it should bring.

"Nice bag," says Amira, as if reading my thoughts, eyeing
a fake Celine that Tony bought me from Hong Kong.

"You know how he is." I wave it off. "Dropping in without warning, always with the gifts he really shouldn't be able
to afford."

"Such a hardship." Amira eye rolls. "Balenciaga from Milan,
an iPhone and AirPods from New York. He never bought me
anything like that, fake or otherwise."

Amira had a disastrous fling a few years ago with Tony,
which ended when he met someone else. She was devastated
at first but eventually they became friends. Sometimes I suspect she still finds the idea of him intriguing.

Tony and I have always been close, so I avoided them as
a couple as much as I could because I didn't want her to feel
excluded. Amira often made comments about our relationship. She once told me that as an only child, rattling around
a sprawling Edwardian house on the edge of Ealing, she had
yearned for a younger brother or sister, all that volatility and
emotion and bickering and love.

"He *adores* you, Anna," she would say. "He talks about you
all the time."

"Does he?" I'd scoff. Love, yes, but also it was something
else. After our parents died, Tony and I were all each other
had. He always looked after me and protected me growing
up. But I never wanted to dig back into that time of our lives.

I preferred to look forward, unlike him. Secretly, I was relieved when Amira and Tony's fling came and went quickly.

"We're cursed," I remember her saying after the breakup. It was during one of our many wine-fueled lunchtimes and evenings here, counseling each other through various crises, from work to mortgages to men. "I choose the wrong type, and you don't choose any type at all. One serious relationship after college and then singledom ever since."

"Superficial dating never hurts anyone," I said defensively. Tinder was perfect. Fleeting, transient, under the radar. My love life had been much more manageable this way, skimming the surfaces and avoiding the depths. "Here's to never being hurt again," I had said, raising a glass.

The waitress disappears and returns with our wine. I dissect the menu, seized by indecision while Amira orders a pint of prawns, chips and a Caesar salad. The thought of anchovies makes my insides roil, so I just order some olives and pita.

Amira's mouth opens in bemusement. "So? Tell me more about Dr. Reid."

"They put me in the machine and did all these scans of my brain, which was kind of amazing, seeing different areas light up like a Christmas tree depending on what they did to me."

"You could start on all that. You in the chair, him like the mad scientist in his torture chamber. So was he playing ball?"

Her chin tilts up and she purses her lips, expectant for more. Thankfully her focus slips as the food arrives. She rips her prawns apart, squeezing out the soft pink flesh from their shell, sousing them in a bowl of aioli and popping them into her mouth. I reach across for the jug of water, my shirt sleeve slipping back to my elbow as I lift it up.

"God." Her hand reaches to touch my inner arm, tilting

it toward her over the table lamp to get a better look. "That looks nasty."

I grimace. "It's not that bad. His researcher did a lot of it. I've got sensitive skin. Apparently, redheads feel more pain."

"That old cliché."

"No, really, he's doing a research project on it." She looks at my arm again and I pull my sleeve down.

"So was it worth it?" Her eyes glint.

"What do you mean?"

"Come on, I know you, Anna. Scheming away. I can't remember the last time you were so keen to pitch an idea to Jess. I saw that piece in *The Bookseller* too."

"What piece?"

"Dr. Reid's potential memoir? You're always saying you're bored of journalism. I get it. It's a good plan. So…are you in, do you think? Did you pass the test?"

I redden, but I know it's useless to pretend. Amira can read me too well, able to provoke me more than anyone.

"He didn't even mention it. We stuck very much to his obsession with pain."

"Bit creepy. What a bizarre job, spending your life doing that to people."

"Not that bizarre," I reason. "He's about to get a prize for his research. He's a world-class scientist trying to find a better cure for chronic pain, not just some sadistic freak doing it for pleasure."

Her face breaks into a grin.

"What?" I protest. "I'm only saying what you used to tell me. He's *interesting*." I remind her about Nate's TV documentary a few years ago and how I would tease her about her crush on the enigmatic researcher popularizing neuroscience.

She shrugs. "After his wife died, it was all a bit of a turn-off.

But clearly you're willing to give him the benefit of the doubt. You really believe that stuff about Eva? His version of events?"

"Well, the evidence is that he wasn't there at the time. The inquest said it was death by misadventure."

"Except there's a second inquest, isn't there? So clearly not everyone accepted the evidence."

"You mean Kath?" I nod, remembering the public statement she made about her sister soon after she died, how the media were too obsessed with the salacious details and indifferent to the real story. She accused the press of "postmortem misogyny," how they focused on her sister only as "the woman behind the King of Pain." She felt, justly or not, that no one was defending Eva's corner, least of all Nate, and she wanted him to be more accountable. "She's pushing for a second inquest," I confirm. "But until then, it's all rumor that he or anyone else was involved. I can sympathize with Kath, how you'd want someone, anyone, to blame. And as Eva's husband, Nate fits the bill."

"Except didn't reports say that Kath's daughter was there living with him? Why would she allow that if she really thinks he's responsible? Wouldn't she be worried?" She shrugs and barrels on ahead. "Anyway, you did ask him about those rumors that he had something to do with it, I hope?"

"Not exactly, no. But my feeling was that he'd have shut down the interview instantly. I had to play the long game. He was incredibly defensive."

"Ah, the long game," she muses. "That's the real point, isn't it? You can't afford to be too critical in case it jeopardizes your chances of being his ghostwriter."

"That's not true at all—"

"I wondered what happened to that insatiable curiosity of

yours. I thought you'd maybe try to do a bit more digging, at least for the sake of the article."

"So we're a tabloid now, are we?"

"You're the one who's obsessed with the case, Anna."

"Of course I'm still skeptical. I'm not stupid. I just like to get all the facts. So far, I'd say he's genuine enough, maybe a little nerdy and strange, if you can call that a crime."

"So what else did he tell you about *her*?" She shifts forward in her seat.

"Well, he didn't exactly…" I hesitate.

Amira looks at me and I see my own anxiety mirrored in her features. Her face falls, her mouth opens in disbelief. "Did you actually get a proper interview out of him?"

"I've got bits and pieces, but after the experiments we ran out of time."

She shakes her head in disbelief. "Anna, no. I've been working on this cover for weeks, ever since you first mentioned it to Jess last month. Now, somehow, I've got to explain it to her this afternoon that you let him weasel his way out of it."

"Amira, listen. It's not that bad. I'm trying to tell you there's good news too."

"Really, how?"

"Well, after the tests, he basically gave me the cold shoulder, asked me to follow up any other questions via email and, regardless of what you might think, I got snippy with him. I told him that he'd got it all his own way but now he had to play by my rules. Guess where he invited me?"

She shakes her head, unconvinced, but opens her mouth a little. *"Go on."*

"Algos House. This Friday. Only the first journalist to get into his home since Eva died there."

She squeals, claps her hands, her faith in me restored. "Brilliant. But will you have enough time to file?"

"I'm sure I can. He's promised me it's all on. I'll work on it over the weekend and file first thing Monday. He owes me—I've got the bruises to prove it."

"Just don't let him ply you with coke." She half smiles at me, retrieves her card to pay the bill. We both laugh, any tension between us dissolving. We chat about next Saturday morning, the logistics of her moving into Tony's box room, the small amount of possessions she'll be bringing. She looks at me, her expression clouding.

"It won't be too weird, will it?"

"In what way?"

"For Tony, I mean. The thought of me staying in his room—would it upset him?"

"He's not like that at all. He'll be pleased you've got somewhere to stay."

She looks relieved. "Thanks again for putting up with me. I'm sorry for being a bit stressed over this interview. Jess must be getting to me."

"Apartment rule number one. No talking about work at home." I smile at her as we both get up to leave, knowing if anything I'll be the first one to break it.

As we walk out there's a queue of people waiting to be seated. Diners lean in closer to hear each other above the rising clatter. The man in the paisley waistcoat is reclining in his seat, sipping cognac and digging in for the rest of the afternoon. No one except us is in any rush to leave.

"So promise to file Monday morning?"

I nod. "Of course. It'll all be fine."

"Don't give him an easy ride, Anna." She winds a pale pink cashmere scarf more tightly around her neck. "And take care," she adds, almost as an afterthought as we hug each other goodbye.

★ ★ ★

When I get home, I lie on my bed, a biblical weariness washing over me. I stare up at the rain streaking the attic windows and think back to the knife cut I had told Nate about, the memory of that day. The physical pain had been fine, eventually, once Tony drove me to A&E. Just a simple mistake. Reflex reactions beyond my control.

All this will pass, I tell myself, if I don't let it break the surface.

Falling asleep, it's her face I see. Eva's. She reaches out to me, brushing a blade across my skin, and I feel…nothing. It is exhilarating, euphoric even, watching it move across my flesh. Is this how she felt, how she wants me to feel too? I wonder as I drift in and out of consciousness. How easy it must have been for her in so many ways to be protected from pain.

The endless freedom to push yourself to the sharpest edge, never afraid of what may happen if you fall.

# EVA'S SELF-REFLECTION JOURNAL

*25 January 2019*

*Oh, the joy of group analysis this morning. In the windowless basement room of the clinic, we sat and we stared at the circle of floor between us, as if it was a mirrored pool that held the secrets to our poor frayed psyches. The silence skewered me.*

*The usual suspects cracked first. The woman with oversized red specs and waist-length silver hair sighed and told us about her narcissistic, alcoholic mother, the long shadow she still casts in her life, the father who walked out when she was a baby. I stifled a yawn, pitying the undeserving patient who ended up paying her for wisdom.*

*"You know it's difficult sometimes," she said, her wispy, querulous tone rising with a glance at me. "Sharing so much when others don't share at all. It doesn't feel…supportive?"*

*"Silence can stand in for so much," said Janet, agreeing with her.*

*Boredom, chiefly, I wanted to say. I was feeling nothing. But* the new self-reflective me decided to play the game. I offer, "Silence can feel like a judgment, I guess."

I wanted to tell them about myself, I really did, but I wasn't sure where to start. One tabloid described me once as a "medical mutant" and maybe they were right. At the age of ten, while eating a pizza, I bit off the tip of my tongue without even realizing. I remember a moment of alarm, the crispy pepperoni mixed with blood. Unpleasant but not remotely painful. I once cut myself with a knife, and to stem the bleeding, cauterized it on the stove. The smoky aroma was like barbecued pork.

Is it that surprising I find the emotional stuff alien? I'm wired up differently. I'm a house with no alarm system, doors and windows flung open to the world. Set fire to me, break my bones, cut me open, make me bleed. Please, be my guest. I can assure you, I'll feel precisely…nothing.

If I'm not going to confide in them, what the hell am I doing here? Why do I even want to be a therapist?

Briefly, I had entertained the idea as a way of finding inspiration for my sculpture. Artists need pain, it's their fuel. But on reflection, such logic was never going to sustain me through this. I needed to really believe in this new process, as a way of finding new ways to feel, to empathize and understand.

Nate's agenda for me was different. When I first suggested it, I could see a glimmer of hope in his eyes, that maybe I could change back to the person he fell in love with. In a therapeutic setting, given time, I could become a nurturing empathetic wife, even. "You're not like the others," he used to say, by which he meant the (very) few other women he had met. Bold, risk-averse, restless for novelty, immune to consequence, he loved that in me. Until he didn't. How quickly we are repelled by what we once desired.

When Nate diagnosed me, he told me I was one of less than a hundred people in the world known to share the condition. Once *he isolated the gene, SCN9A to be exact, he was convinced it was a blueprint that could unlock the key to pain. Whatever is inside me, he said, could ease the suffering of so many lives.*

*Was it only because of this I fascinated him? I began to wonder. He examined and studied me, wrote papers and gave lectures about me. For too long, my uniquely flawed, fucked-up brain became his calling card.*

# 6

It is less than a twenty-minute walk across the park to Dr. Reid's riverside home, but it could be a different country. Instead of screeching sirens, there is the shrill, insistent pitch of birdsong. I pause, crane my head. Shutterless windows stare back at me. From the outside Algos House looks the same as the others, nothing out of place, an elegant Regency facade with sash windows, a gravel drive, a gleaming black front door. Now, finally, I'm about to find out how much that's really the case. I had doubts the interview would happen at all until last night when Rhik finally texted.

Nate can do midday for the interview and an early slot for the photographer, around 10am if that suits? His niece Jade will be there to let you in—need any more directions?

No worries. I'll find it.

Of course, I will. Anyone like me familiar with the story knows exactly where Dr. Nate Reid lives, the sort of neighborhood where nothing bad ever happens. Except that, not so long ago, it did.

Two and a half years prior, to be exact. It was a Friday

evening and Nate had returned home, according to news reports, and walked into Eva's studio to find her collapsed on the floor. The pathologist gave her cause of death as a hypoxic-ischaemic brain injury—lack of oxygen to the brain—after a drug-induced heart attack. A high level of cocaine was discovered in her bloodstream, which could indicate an overdose, although there was no evidence Eva wanted to take her own life in the days leading up to her death, and no note was left. Still, that was the theory Nate had offered to the investigators.

The type of heart attack that reportedly killed Eva was the deadliest. Known as the widow-maker, it causes a total blockage in the left main coronary artery, meaning the heart stops beating almost instantly. An early indicator in cases like this is often severe chest pain, a crucial sensation that, tragically, Eva would have been unable to feel because of her genetic condition.

In the end, the jury's verdict was open, meaning they were unable to draw any strong conclusion since evidence was lacking. Questions remained with no black-and-white answers, only endless gray. Who inflicted small bruises discovered on her upper arms? Who vandalized her sculptures and why? Who took her cell phone? And where was Eva's glass cutter, the tool she relied on most for her sculptures?

Inevitably, Nate was viewed in a suspicious light even though he denied any wrongdoing. He told the police the last time he saw Eva alive was the morning of the day she died, that he had spent the day at a work conference in Manchester and stayed overnight, only returning the next day. His alibi was watertight—his speech was well-received by a large audience and afterward he went out for drinks with colleagues. There was no sign of forced entry at their home, and only Nate's fingerprints were found at the scene.

While her sister, Kath, battled publicly to reopen the inquest, Nate chose to vanish from view, burying himself in his work at the Rosen, trying to ignore the media's interest in the tawdry details that portrayed his wife as a vulnerable-but-reckless figure. Kath was adamant this wasn't the sister she recognized and loved, the woman who dedicated herself to helping others by training to be a psychotherapist.

With all this scrutiny, it wasn't surprising that Eva's art had increased in value since her death, selling steadily from a small gallery in Whitechapel. She had established her style early on, sculpting female torsos in mottled bronze. What set them apart was their generous forms, wide-hipped, curvy and soft-bellied. These weren't idealized female figures, far from it. At the waist they would taper to a fine edge where she would spike them with an array of razors, knives, nails, crushed glass or barbed wire, depending on the scale. The female body weaponized.

Visceral and urgent, the critics agreed her work was a powerful comment on female anger and self-expression. I followed her art on auction sites and was even tempted to buy one of her smaller pieces, until I saw the prices. Definitely out of my league with my journalist reporter's salary, along with a brother like mine to support.

I check my watch and repeat my name into an intercom. I hear footsteps inside, stand a little straighter and step forward. Showtime.

A young woman answers the door. "Hi. You must be Anna," she says, shaking my hand. "I'm Jade." I notice a tiny blue swallow tattoo on the inside of her wrist. She wears a long box pleat skirt in eau de Nil that shimmers as she walks.

"Come in. Your photographer left around an hour ago, they spent most of the time in the garden," she says, turning, and I follow her down a dark paneled hallway completely at odds with the bright white galleried atrium at the end of it.

A balcony runs around its edges with a floor above and, at the top, a ceiling of glazed glass throws off a pale mint light the color of swimming pools. It's a bit like stepping inside a giant glacier mint.

"Nice place," I say, affecting polite indifference. Maybe it's journalistic instinct to avoid too much excessive enthusiasm when it comes to wealth, a fear we have of appearing too sycophantic, or worse, envious.

I'm well-aware of that nasty scratch of longing whenever I visit homes like this, the reflex to find my own lifestyle lacking. It goes with the territory this, nose pressed to the window, an invitation to observe but never belong. Amira started out as a travel writer, one of the reasons that she clicked with Tony early on when I introduced them, but after a while she couldn't hack the press trips. "You're chauffeured to a ski lodge in St. Moritz for a few days, then dumped back at Gatwick, and it's a bus home to your apartment-share. Sometimes it's better not to know how other people live." Soon after, she took a desk job instead.

My show of mild indifference becomes more of a challenge as we walk into the open-plan living room with double-height windows. The floor is gray slate scattered with bright Moroccan rugs in electric pinks and reds. Two low sleek sofas in turquoise velvet face each other. Every blank space is an opportunity for color; bold abstract canvases hang alongside bright decorative collages. No surface is unadorned, all wrestle for space and attention. There are floor-to-ceiling shelves lined with books, arranged by color. It is cluttered but also highly ordered and obsessively arranged.

Beyond that is a dining space with an oval marble table like a sculpted egg. Over it hangs a crystal candelabra complete with fuchsia pink candles. The dining space is framed by a wall of glass sliding doors that are open with a view of manicured lawn that runs straight down to the river. At the end, where the grass slopes down a little, there is a row of cypress trees and through it I can see Eva's studio, a cube of slatted wood-and-glass windows that gleam back at me. I stand transfixed by it, her inner sanctum, the place where she took her last breath. For so long I've been an outsider staring in and I am here, at last, an insider looking out. So, this is what it feels like.

"Are you okay?" Jade's voice makes me jump.

"Sure, yes. Sorry." I turn around to face her.

"Well, I think Nate wants to do the interview in his study," she says, sliding the glass doors firmly shut and directing me back toward the kitchen area. "I'm Nate's niece, by the way. You've probably seen my aunt in photos?" The lilt in her voice is brittle rather than friendly. Kath's daughter, of course. I wonder why I've never read about her before.

"So you're working for Nate?"

"Not exactly working for him. I get lab credits for helping out with his research until I go back to uni next term."

"Sounds like a good arrangement," I say, noticing her worried expression. "I guess it's been pretty tough for you all, with the new inquest and everything?"

"Yeah, well." She shrugs. "Hopefully it's happening in a few months' time, if my mom gets her way. It's pretty much all she talks about."

"I don't blame her." I think back to the pictures of Kath in the papers after the first inquest. Standing on the courtroom steps, Nate had looked gaunt and quietly devastated while his sister-in-law had appeared undefeated, fighting for Eva's name.

"You must be proud of your mom still campaigning after two years. Is Nate behind it all too?" I say, watching a subtle shift in her features. She folds her arms, raises her chin. I can't help noticing the family resemblance in Jade's wide-set eyes framed by black bangs.

"Of course, he wants justice as much as she does."

"I'm sure, yes. It's only that I saw your mom's name in the papers and not Nate's. I wondered…"

"He prefers to stay out of the media, and I don't blame him for that." She gives me a fierce look and I'm not sure what to ask next without causing offence. I turn away from her for a moment, step closer to the pictures above the sofa as if I'm admiring them, feel her eyes bore into my back.

"You're not going to quote me, are you? About this, I mean."

"About what you've told me so far?" *Maybe if you said something remotely interesting, I might*, I say inwardly. "Of course not, it's completely off-the-record and I'd always ask your consent first. Anyway, it's not that kind of piece. Just a profile, an interview with Nate. I'm sure he probably told you about it?" I find myself mirroring her defensive tic, making answers sound more like questions.

She shakes her head.

"I wouldn't worry. It's a really positive take on Nate's resilience, what he's drawn on to get through his grief and his tireless commitment to work, of course." I repeat the soothing phrases I have perfected over the years, designed to reassure angsty interviewees and PRs. "And of course there's his new—"

"Good. The press has been pretty awful to Nate so far," she interrupts. "But I suppose you know about that already."

I know Jade's right about the press. When the story broke, they were brutal, camping on the pavement outside, asking him intrusive questions. At first, they were generous to Nate, casting him as the grieving scientist devoted to curing his wife's condition. But others were more vicious, preferring to portray him as overly absorbed in his work, remote, imperious. I remember thinking there was something in his manner that had been unlikable, an arrogance that didn't inspire much sympathy. One particularly bad scuffle with a photographer hadn't helped his cause.

"Okay. I'll check and see if he's off his call." She hesitates, glancing down at my feet. "Shit, sorry, I should have said earlier, would you mind taking your shoes off? It's a Nate thing."

"A Nate thing?" I repeat. "Are there any other Nate things you want to tell me about?"

She shrugs. "Well, he doesn't do small talk but I guess you know that already." She picks up a sleek silver gray cat, who purrs in her arms, surveying me placidly with its burnished orange eyes.

"He's pretty obsessional about this one too."

"Really? He doesn't strike me as an animal person." I reach out to stroke it.

"You'd be surprised. Her name's Nico." Jade smiles, barely. "She belonged to Eva. A present from him for her last birthday. She must never go outside, or upstairs in the bedrooms. Welcome to Nate's world."

I look around their kitchen area next to the living space, all gleaming surfaces, pristine if not a little soulless. I run my finger along the smooth gray marble of the kitchen island and peer into a bin—empty. Even their rubbish is nonexistent. I wonder if it's Nate's fastidiousness, or the design itself that dictates this way of living. Perhaps it makes sense. When something unpredictable happens in your life, you'll do anything to take control, create a veneer for yourself of stifling perfection where nothing bad can ever happen again.

Jade's phone dings. It's from Nate. "He's still a bit delayed but I can take you down to his office in ten minutes. Tea?"

"Sure, thanks." Turning, I notice the wall behind her, the only one that's bare with a row of ghostly square outlines where pictures must have once hung. "So where have they gone?" I nod over to them. "Another Nate thing?"

She flicks her hand in the air. "You'd have to ask him. I think they were Eva's drawings and sketches. There was so much of her stuff lying around, he's decided to give some of it away. He's starting on this floor and working his way up to the bedrooms."

It's a pointless task: however much he tries to remove all traces of her creativity, her presence is everywhere like a tangible energy. I catch sight of one of her sculptures near an archway that leads into a smaller space.

I get up and walk over. "Would you mind?" I sound tentative, even though I'm already stepping through. "Just for a bit of color."

She wavers, checks her watch. "Go on, then. I doubt you'll find much in there, but fine, if you're quick."

I can tell immediately that Jade is right. It is lackluster and gloomy, as sterile as roses wrapped in cellophane. I touch the chrome ridge of one of the mid-century leather chairs that face each other, glance at the requisite box of Kleenex on a table between them. What exchanges must've taken place here, the many stories that Eva heard? Above a low divan are shelves lined with books. Freud, Jung and Klein all present and correct.

Reading about her online, I couldn't help thinking that Eva's decision to become a psychotherapist didn't quite make sense. It didn't seem as though helping other people was a calling. If anything her work had reflected a certain level of self-absorption, along with a recurring theme of seeking out extreme sensation, neither of which seem ideal traits for a career in counseling. It was hard to imagine she was motivated by guilt or selflessness and yet somehow it didn't matter. Her honesty was refreshing. When I had chatted to her that time,

I wanted to dislike her but I couldn't. I expected a dilettante but she was surprisingly serious about her pursuits.

Wikipedia didn't give much away about her background except that she grew up in Cornwall where her father had been a local councillor. He and her mother still lived in the farmhouse close to Padstow.

I spot a small framed photograph on her desk, Eva from a different time. Her jet-black hair is shorn into a pixie crop that accentuates her cheekbones. She leans back on an old Triumph motorbike, slim and tanned in cut-off denim shorts and a faded pink vest. Behind her stretches an epic landscape of sand dunes and sky.

It's all there in that one expression; defiant, completely free and very much in control. I can't resist. I have to take a picture of it. Jade has her back to me, making tea in the kitchen. I discreetly pull out my iPhone and focus on the image of Eva. As I drop the phone back into my pocket, I sense movement in the doorway behind me. I swivel around.

"You don't waste any time, do you?"

"Hi." I flush to the roots of my hair and look down as if I've been caught red-handed in the headmaster's study.

"It really is such a privilege to see journalistic curiosity in action," Nate says, a subtle shimmer in his eyes. He pauses for a brief moment in the open doorway, turns on his heels and walks away.

# 7

I rush after him and he stops, turns to me with a stony expression. "I'm so sorry," I say, taking out my phone again. "I can delete it if you want." He doesn't say anything, his silence cuts in reproach.

"I feel bad, I can explain. It's not what it looks like."

"Oh, and what does it look like?" he says evenly.

"Look, it's only for a visual prompt for background color when I'm writing it up. It helps me to remember. Honestly, that's all." Words spill out in a guilty rush and he gives me a wary look. "Honestly, I'm happy to get rid of it." My finger hovers on the bin icon.

"I guess if it's useful for your piece…" he says, finally. "And if you want to know, it was taken in Morocco on the edge of the Sahara."

"She looks lovely," I say, glancing down at the screen image in my palm, the way she smiles directly at Nate in a secret sort of way, their two helmets at the edge of the picture. "Was it an amazing place to visit?"

He gives me a strange look. "I wouldn't know. I didn't take the picture. Motorbikes aren't my thing."

"Ah, I see. Sorry, I assumed…"

"Well, I trust you won't be publishing it." He sighs. "Come on then, let's get into this."

I follow him out of Eva's study back through to a small featureless meeting room off the hallway. A copy of Nate's book lies on the table. Neatly laid out are two notepads and two glasses of water. There are also two printouts of the interview questions I sent over, as requested. He sits down opposite me, scans the list and glowers.

"Before we begin, how were you after the tests?" He studies me, a flicker of curiosity returning to his eyes. "Any late-hitting headaches or dizziness?"

I think for a moment back to that morning in the Rosen, the cold scientific scrutiny in his gaze as he observed my discomfort. But something else too. The subtle enthrallment, pleasure even, that had unsettled me.

"I guess I found it quite educational playing lab rat for the morning."

"Really? Well, I'm glad it wasn't too painful an experience for you after all."

"Are you? I thought that pain was sort of the point."

"You coped admirably, nonetheless. I guess now it's your turn to make me suffer. I'm curious, how do you think your intro will go? Something like, 'Nate Reid rests his elbows on the table, looking anxious and uncertain, completely out of his comfort zone,'" he parodies.

"That's really how you feel?"

He runs the tip of one finger across his jawline. "I'd prefer to be exactly where you are right now, asking the questions."

"We can ease into it. Why don't we start with your favorite subject: your book *The Pain Matrix*? Where did the idea come from?" I press Play and watch his shoulders soften as he leans back.

No one really cares, obviously. But it's a classic warm-up,

indulging the interviewee as they talk up whatever product they're plugging. It's that time when you can let them enjoy the sound of their own voice before you go in hard with the real questions. I hmm and aah in all the right places as he explains his groundbreaking research into the brain's "pain-modulation circuit," the key to understanding how we all have power to control our responses.

He relaxes into his subject. They always do.

I'll let him go on as long as it takes to feel that his ego is sufficiently stroked. Then I can lead him to riskier territory. But, for now, I nod attentively as he talks, try to observe the small unintended clues and micro expressions he is giving away. I write down my observations in shorthand. *Japanese denim. Designer linen shirt. Jaeger-LeCoultre watch. Vintage trainers. Works a little too hard on his appearance.*

"And what about you? Did you enjoy the book?" He gives me a long assessing look.

Way too dry, I want to say, too much terminology. What would have saved it was a ruthless editor. Maybe he's learned he needs a little more help for his next writing project.

I enthuse about it anyway, ready with a specific detail I rehearsed earlier. "I found it fascinating, that bit where you talk about Catholics reporting less pain if they're exposed to religious imagery before you test them. The idea that our worldview can affect our threshold was intriguing. I liked that quote you concluded on too," I say, only to imply I'd reached the final chapter, which I hadn't. "Nature has placed us under two powerful masters. One is pain, the other pleasure."

"Almost. Nature has placed us under the governance of two sovereign masters. Although my interpretation is that pain is something we should celebrate as much as pleasure."

"Celebrate? Really? Not quite the word I'd use to describe those threshold tests."

"Maybe you should," he muses. "Pain is a better friend to humans than pleasure in many ways, making sure we've survived down the centuries."

"You seem to feel strongly about how much we should appreciate pain. I wonder if all your patients feel the same?"

There is a brief silence and the room feels somehow smaller and more airless.

"I mean, those patients who were unable to rely on that reflex to protect them? How did watching them firsthand impact your conclusions?"

He nods imperceptibly, looks into the middle distance for a long moment. "You mean Eva. Yes, it was incredible luck, really, that we met at all."

I pause, wait for him to go on, a bit. It still surprises me how you can drop in a question that you dread asking and yet meet so little resistance, as if it's almost a relief for them to confront whatever subject has hung over them.

"An anesthetist introduced us. Eva came into A&E after a bike accident, only because her boyfriend at the time forced her. Her arm was fractured in two places and yet she refused an anesthetic, insisting she'd never taken a painkiller in her life. Eva always knew she was different to other people, so did her family, but they never knew exactly why. My colleague realized at once she was a unique case and referred her to me."

"So you invited her onto your research program?"

"She was happy to get involved. It was great for me because the newspapers jumped on it. I got more attention for my work and ultimately enough funding to carry on. But really, it was her they wanted, or the mythology around her. The woman who seemed invincible, who could thrust her hand into the fire and not feel a thing."

"How did she react to all that attention?"

Nate shifts in his seat, looks down.

I smile, cross my arms. *Your move.* He only stares, the silence stretching interminably. I check my watch, fidget. My usual trick has let me down. After a moment of hesitating, I add, "I mean, maybe she saw it as a sign of strength, her superpower even?"

"Yes. At times, Eva would often forget about her condition, assume she was invincible."

"So you had to be her pain reflex, remind her of her limitations?"

"You could put it that way. Protect her from herself mainly," he says, carefully. "Eva was a risk-taker; even after living with CIP all of her life, she still didn't realize how easily she could harm herself. She didn't process danger in the same way as—" he pauses "—you or I might."

"How did you feel, witnessing that struggle in her?"

The muscles under his skin tighten. "Feel? You like that word, don't you? For neuroscientists, it doesn't hold much weight."

"How can you ignore that word when pain and feeling are inseparable?"

"That's not how a scientist views it. We prefer our language to be objective."

"Okay," I sigh. "How did you react?"

"That's better. Really, I just wanted to help her."

"Of course." I nod. The air traffic controller in my head starts to scream directions. *Keep him talking about Eva. Keep him on track a little longer. Bring him into land.* "You know, Jade was telling me earlier that Kath is pushing to reopen the inquest over Eva's death."

He slowly looks up from the table.

"I'm curious, what are you both hoping to prove in a new inquest, if it happens? Are you worried you'll be implicated again?"

"Implicated?" His voice is low, eyes flashing darkly as he points to the printed questions in front of him. "This wasn't on your list, was it?"

"It was a follow-up question. You can't expect it to be a straight Q and A," I say, reasonably, but instantly regret my words as his features harden into contempt.

"No. You're done here."

I freeze. The atmosphere is charged, ugly. The way he turns on me is so unexpected that, for a moment, I wonder if it's really happened. He looks as if he's about to lash out, stands up too abruptly and knocks his glass of water off the table. It smashes to the floor and he curses again, rifles through his jacket to locate a crumpled pack of cigarettes and strides out. "You lot are all the fucking same, aren't you?"

I sit for a moment in shock, now alone in the study.

How dare he? All he had to do was decline the question. My hands tremble as I bend down to pick up the broken glass. *My default setting*, I think bitterly, always forced to navigate the periphery of male volatility, sweeping away the evidence. Nothing to see here. I tut, impatiently pick up the shards, but as I do, one of their edges nicks me. Beads of blood ooze from the cut, small but deep, on the pad of my thumb.

Slipping into the kitchen, I spot him through the open door, his somber outline a mass of negative energy hunched over a lighter. Jade is with him too. She must have heard the commotion and run to his aid. As if he is the one in need of help. How familiar their body language seems from this distance, her slim arm looped around his shoulders.

Nate turns around and catches my eye, steps away from Jade and rushes in. He glances at my thumb, the steady drip of blood down my inner arm.

"Christ, what happened?"

"It's nothing. I was trying to clear it all up and..." My voice wobbles imperceptibly. "Have you got a plaster?"

Jade disappears and Nate instructs me to hold my arm up to stem the blood, fetches a first-aid box, plasters, antiseptic. I study him as he carefully applies a dressing.

"You know," he muses softly. "I remember Eva standing here in almost exactly the same spot once after cutting herself badly. A broken wineglass, her foot was bleeding but she didn't even notice..." I nod, make a mental note of this for my piece, as he passes me a glass of water and some acetaminophen. "You won't need stitches, a minor laceration, we can safely say."

I nod, relieved. His phone vibrates.

"Excuse me, I need to take this," he says, walking back outside. I wait a minute or two before I follow him, slipping my recorder into my pocket. The smell of burning embers drifts over from a neighbor's garden. He's finished his call and leans back against the glass door. He offers me a cigarette.

"No thanks," I say reflexively but immediately change my mind. "Actually, go on." I haven't smoked for years but something in me is tempted by the illicitness of it, the spontaneity.

"Anna, I'm sorry I lost it back there, it was unprofessional. You're probably thinking, does he always lose his temper so easily?"

I look at him levelly. "And do you?"

"Never. It was a mix of a lot of things. It's been so long since I've gone over all that. I—"

I let him finish but he can't seem to find the words.

"I would have walked out of the interview," I say, shaking my head slowly, "but I didn't, because I assume that's what you would have wanted. An easy way out. I wasn't going to let you off that easily." I pause. "You know by answering some of these questions, it could put you in a better light? I think if you're honest, our readers will respect you for it. I imagine you're not just doing this interview to sell this book, but maybe there's another in the pipeline. Makes sense. Try to engage with the public again, regain their sympathy?"

"Impressive, Anna." He smiles ruefully, then continues before I can protest. "Okay, well, let's start again. You asked earlier if I'm on Kath's side. The answer is, yes, absolutely, although I'm not sure she's on mine." He holds up a hand. "Actually, scratch that."

"Sure. But if she isn't, why is Jade here and helping out in the lab?"

"It's something she agreed to a while back before—" He pauses. "Before I decided to write a memoir. It sounds like you've already put two and two together."

"I think I read something about it," I say, vaguely.

"It's a new project, something my publisher and I are working out at the moment, but it's about Eva, and a personal account of my grief, our relationship, lots of things. But Kath sees it as a huge betrayal, I think." He shrugs lightly. "At least she and I are in agreement over the next inquest. Neither of us think the investigation was thorough enough. We still don't know what really happened to Eva."

"But we do know she died of a heart attack—"

"It's not as simple as that. There are too many loose ends."

"So what do you think really happened?"

"I don't entertain theories," he says, pointedly, flicking the cigarette end onto the damp earth where it glows and dies. I stare at a wall where a vine has spread across it, tentacle-like, suffocating the camellia beneath.

"The press seemed to wonder if someone else was in the house that day, even though apparently the inquest couldn't prove it."

"All speculation." His voice falters. "It was unimaginable

really, coming home and finding her, like something out of a horror film...those ruined sculptures around her. Not being able to save her."

Nate's features soften and he looks lost in his thoughts. I wonder how he can still live here with reminders everywhere, the shadowy outline of her studio through the cypress trees, lined up like sentries guarding a tomb.

He offers me another cigarette, exhaling a trail of silvery smoke into the damp air. I tilt my head over his lighter, cup my hand around the flame. I consider telling him about the day I spoke to Eva, but think better of it.

I remember it clearly. How my mood was jagged all morning. I hadn't slept. Tony was staying over before he caught an early flight to New York and his noisy nocturnal presence in the apartment kept me awake, as usual. The click of the light switch in the hallway, the metallic echo of his ring on the stair rail. *Clink, clink, clink* as he reached the top. Up and down, round and round, his footsteps, his tics and rhythms stalked my dreams.

I had sniped at him the next day for keeping me awake. He'd apologized but I could tell he was upset. He said he found it hard to live with me anymore, that I was always on edge. Then he turned from me, that familiar wounded expression in his eyes, a look that always skewered me with guilt. Before I could say another word, he was gone. I had sat on the sofa in the early morning light, sad, emptied out, and then my phone rang. It was her. Eva's voice instantly lifted me from my stupor. She had talked about her therapy practices, and I felt warmed by her enthusiasm, transported. I had hinted briefly, when she asked, about the exhaustion, some familial pressures still lingering in my life, anxiety, no more than that.

"You don't sound like someone in therapeutic need," she reflected and for a moment I wanted to tell her about my squabble with Tony. "But I can tell you're self-aware, thoughtful, the sort of person who'd benefit." A pause. "I really think you are. One session at the clinic where I train, if you fancy it. For a piece? They could do with the publicity."

My skin prickles and I rub my arms. Why is it that some people are so difficult to refuse? Nate looks at me again, pulling me back into the moment. I'm surprised by the concern in his gaze.

"Come on, let's get you back inside. You look like you've seen a ghost."

Jade throws me a sharp glance as we walk in. She tells him he has a 2:00 p.m. conference call with a professor at Columbia and he checks his watch. "Well, we've got around twenty minutes left, so I'm not sure what you—"

"I'd love a guided tour." Jade raises her eyebrows imperceptibly to Nate and walks away. He hesitates. "It would be so useful for context. No photos, I promise." I hold up my phone, conspicuously switch it off.

"Alright," he says finally. "Not her studio though. But I can show you the house." I follow him down the glass stairs into the basement, which feels entirely disconnected to the space above. The ceilings are lower and it's darker down here. Even the smell is different, a mix of old carpets and wood chippings.

"We kept as much of the Victorian cellar as we could." He pushes open the paneled door of his study. One wall is exposed brick, the rest of the room is a dense burgundy, the floorboards are painted black. There's a couple of Persian rugs and a worn-looking leather sofa facing a marble fireplace. "I'm the only one who worked in here," he says, catching my expression as I notice a lock on the inside of the door.

"Ah, the man cave," I say, looking at papers piled on a battered antique desk, dirty mugs on the floor.

"Eva loved the idea of styling everything like a glossy magazine." He makes a face as he turns and sits down on the sofa. I place my recorder on the coffee table in front of him and press Record. My eyes flit around the room, hungry for detail. Over the mantelpiece is a row of macabre cat portraits. I've read about Nate's passion for collecting Louis Wain, an Edwardian artist.

"Bit weird," I say, stepping forward to take a closer look.

"Not really, once you know more about him," he says, standing next to me, absorbed by the anthropomorphized creatures staring back at us, wild-eyed and garishly psychedelic. "I put them up last month. I like the way they capture the artist's turbulent state of mind."

"Schizophrenic?"

"Possibly. Specialists could never agree. But if you look at an MRI brain scan that's tracking, say, physical arousal, the way the colors light up look weirdly similar." He points to one of the more abstract florid prints, saturated swirls and curlicues.

"Sorry, before we continue, I just need the washroom."

"Of course, second door on the left," he says, scrolling through messages on his cell phone.

I don't need to, really, but a bathroom break is a chance to gather your thoughts, retreat away from the watchful eye of your interviewee. Their surroundings are more likely to give them away than anything they'll ever tell you.

Leaving my recorder on while they're alone is another old ploy. If I'm lucky, it might pick up something in my absence; a flirtatious compliment from an aging actor, an intimate phone call, a spat with a book PR over an indiscretion they shouldn't have let slip. Always worth a try.

I lock the door and wash my hands, catching my reflection in the mirror. My pupils look dilated, my cheeks glow, as if I'm running a fever. The room is windowless and opulent, shimmering like a dark gem; the walls are jewel-toned and the taps are burnished gold. Coppery mosaics line the floor, glittering like coins. It's like stepping inside a Fabergé egg.

Above the sink is a small vintage medicine cabinet; *Apotheke*, it says in italics that curve across the frosted glass. I lift the latch. It exudes the faintest medicinal aroma, musty and antiseptic.

There's Nurofen, acetaminophen, earbuds and antihistamines. So far, so regular. On the shelf above is a black leather glasses case. I take it down, snap it gently open and inside, find a slim strip of pills with a printed label.

Dr. Nate Reid. Fentanyl. Prescribed in May 2019.

I've written stories about fentanyl, how dangerously addictive this synthetic opioid can be. What chronic pain could the King of Pain be suffering?

I rattle the blue discs in the blister pack and replace them, thinking about his behavior earlier, how it had flared up from nowhere. At the Rosen that morning he had seemed completely in charge, as if nothing could phase him. But his unpredictability today, an inability to self-regulate, suggests something else is going on. Vulnerable, fragile, someone struggling to cope.

In the end it is Jade who sees me to the door while Nate excuses himself to take his work call. She stands on the step and watches me as I leave.

I look back at the house, buttery in the afternoon sun, and toy with precisely the right adjectives to bring this to life in my profile. Usually, I savor these moments when the interview is over and I can take stock, reflect on how I'll write it up, but now intrusive images flicker cine-style through my mind. The color rising on my cheeks, the clumsy way I'd almost tripped over my bag in my haste to get out of there. All the time I could feel his eyes in my back.

Worst of all, I wasn't able to go deep about the publishing rumors, whether he'd drawn up a shortlist of ghostwriters. For all I know, thanks to the excruciating outburst that robbed the interview, he's writing it on his own.

It starts to rain, a steady drizzle darkening the pavement. I take in the row of terraces opposite that stare back at me, their windows like lidless eyes. The sky is ashen, the real world is a shade grayer after Dr. Reid's interiors. Time to go. I check my phone. A few work emails, a voicemail alert from Tony asking me what I'm up to and when is a good time to call, but then another notification flashes up:

*Dr. Nate Reid is following you!*

I click straight through to his X profile.

Nate Reid
@natereid100

Neuroscientist at the Rosen Institute, *Sunday Times* bestselling author, host of BBC's *Grey Matters*. Latest book: *The Pain Matrix*.

10 Following 480k Followers

Instinctively, I follow him straight back. Now, at least, I have his attention.

# EVA'S SELF-REFLECTION JOURNAL

*4 February 2019*

*I am writing in my studio this morning, staring out at ragged clouds chasing across a low gray sky and wondering where to begin. Janet told us yesterday that when someone trains as a therapist, it can leave their partner feeling insecure. Naturally you become more analytical about yourself and those around you. It's easy for loved ones to feel scrutinized, dissected, wary of your new insights and perspectives.*

*Is that how Nate feels? We barely spoke last night over supper. There is so little we can discuss honestly anymore. It's as if he's on an island getting smaller and smaller as I sail away from him, until one day he'll vanish on the horizon like a tiny speck.*

*Why is it the longer you live with someone, the more of a stranger they become? So many landmines. I watched him as he finished his meal, his knife scraping the plate, his jaw clenching as he chewed. Even the way he breathed began to enrage me.*

*My phone buzzing on the table made me jump. He glared*

at me when I took the call. Of course, I'd almost forgotten about the phone interview.

"Eva. Is now a good time?" she asked me. Nate's eyebrows shot up and I left the table, walked over to the window.

"Hello," I sparkled. Nate pushed back his chair, almost knocked it to the floor. These volatile displays are nothing new but they're ramping up since I've started my training. "No, don't worry. It's perfect timing, really. Fire away."

Cutlery clattered, cupboard doors rattled, he was registering his presence, making a point, a pass-agg habit of his. Meanwhile the journalist asked me all sorts of questions. Her curiosity was a balm. I demurred while she told me how much she loved my work, flirted with her to punish him for ignoring me. That's how it started anyway.

As we talked, I slipped deeper into the conversation. I told her about my therapy course and, for the first time, I felt…engaged. I admitted I was nervous but also looking forward to seeing patients on my own, unsupervised for the first time. And I realized that I meant it. I've been so resistant to this course, to really opening up. But perhaps my inability to feel my patients' pain will bring a sense of objectivity for them, help of a different kind.

I asked a little more about her, shared some advice about pursuing her passion for writing, even found myself offering her a free therapy session at my clinic. "Try it," I suggested, catching Nate's eye. "Keep in touch."

"Who was that?" asked Nate, after the interview ended.

"Oh, no one," I told him.

# 8

After leaving Algos House, I head to Shepherd's Bush. Once on the subway, I check my WhatsApp to make sure the photo of Eva in the desert is there, which it is. Suspecting Nate would make me delete it, I'd sent the picture to myself as soon as I took it.

Those two motorbike helmets. Who did the other one belong to, if not Nate? A friend's? I file that question away for another day. Retrieving my recorder, I hold it to my ear and press Play to make sure all our conversations are there. Inevitably, the interview will be toe-curling to listen to, it always is. Embarrassing interjections from me, superficial reflections. No interaction is ever quite how I remembered it. What I do know for certain is that you can never predict the dynamic of two people in a room.

Hearing the remnants of our conversation makes me feel queasy. Why didn't I see what he was doing, the way he dodged me, channeled the subject away from him like water? Did he always have the upper hand all along?

But I know that's not the root of my revulsion. That came earlier when he lost his temper, the crack of the chair legs on the slate tiles.

I text Amira that I'm on my way in. I promised her I'd come

into the office to write up my piece so we can edit together and the subs can start working on it more quickly.

The carriage is empty. Fixing my eyes on the Underground map above the doors, I look at the Central Line, bleeding its trail east, ending in that loop. The names are still oddly memorable, like anagrams: Theydon Bois, Hainault, Fairlop, Roding Valley. In my head I am sixteen again, counting each stop along the Central Line that took me away from home and deeper into London. The farther west and beyond that I traveled, the closer freedom seemed, meters and meters away from where Tony and I both grew up. We never return to that place. Back then, I was the baby of the family and after our mother died, Tony and I looked out for one another. When my dad—his stepfather—died a few years later, he was there for me all over again. We were alone, our family unit shrunk to two.

Whenever I try to recall that time with any clarity, memories fragment and dissolve. Not for the first time I wish I could replay the past like one of my interviews in all its digital verity. Everyone has their own illusive version of the truth. A recording is more objective. Until it's written up, transcribed and morphed with my own subjective observations. A memory is no different, nothing more than a palimpsest, layer upon layer altered and modified by yourself and the perspectives of those around you. After my father died, the narrative of that night, the responsibility and panic it placed on my shoulders, still weighs me down. This is what happens when you're forced to depend on someone else as much as I did.

I shut my eyes, trying to stem the feelings that threaten to resurface. Deadlines, interviews, writing, this is what occupies me, distracting me from who I used to be. Most of the time it works well enough. I put on my headphones again. Here is Nate's voice, telling me about his research, the developing brain of a newborn, how the tiny intricate branches and cells grow into a rich, interconnected tangle of connections. Leaning back in my seat, I let his voice wash over me. The carriage seats around me fill as we reach Marble Arch. I skip to the part where I leave Nate's study, recorder still on, to visit the washroom.

Silence. Then, footsteps approaching the table. A muffled, rustling sound as he picks up the recorder. He clears his voice.

"You're doing well, Anna, I'm not used to being the one under scrutiny, although I may get my own back yet. By the way, I really hope you're not rummaging through my cabinets." I rewind and play it again to catch his tone, dryly amused. "Please try not to jump to any wild conclusions."

Was that a guess? A shiver of unease runs through me, how mercurial his moods can be. Furious and lashing out one minute, cool and calculated the next. When is he truly himself?

My magazine company occupies an office block in Portland Place. In the foyer, the walls are marbled and windows stretch from floor to ceiling. There are mirrored lifts and a statue of the newspaper tycoon who founded the company back in the '30s; his imperious gaze tracks me as I take the escalator to the second floor. All that hubris, along with newspaper sales and profits, vanished decades ago. Last year the title was bought out by a billionaire property tycoon who promptly sacked half the staff, slashed editorial budgets and down-paged the magazine. We all know it will close when the new owner decides to "de-invest."

Until then, it is death by a thousand cuts. The remaining few of us hang on by our teeth, working in a warren of stuffy windowless spaces with soulless strip lighting and coffee-stained carpet tiles that curl at the edges.

"Ah, Anna, how did it go?" says Jess as I follow her into a cramped corner office.

I give her all the right affirmations, tell her that he was hard work but I was able to charm him, eventually, and he opened up. She nods, her thin red lips part into the briefest of smiles. Jess doesn't do nuance. She's either nice or nasty, and I prefer nasty. At least it's more authentic. Jess moved over from *Vogue* a few years ago, bringing with her a pitiless brand of perfectionism. "I don't think that would pass the smile test," is Amira's wry response to most of my pitches.

Editorial assistants weep mutely in the washrooms, meetings are torturous and cover stories routinely spiked at the last minute. There is no gossip or banter, only the silence of people dying inside. It's really more morgue than magazine. I cling to my outsider status as a defense against the misery around me, but I'm not sure how much longer I can last here.

While Jess usually only opts for cover interviews with young actors from a London family dynasty, or salacious exposés of wealthy scions, Dr. Reid was an exception. We carry on talking about the interview and how much content I can work into the spread, when our art director walks in.

"How are the Dr. Reid photos looking, Elaine?" snaps Jess. Elaine wears a Ramones T-shirt and ripped jeans. The warm honey highlights in her curly shoulder-length hair conceal the inevitable tide of gray. As with most women's magazines, aging is celebrated in its editorial but studiously avoided in reality.

"We've got enough here to hold two spreads and a cover," says Elaine, fanning out the pictures of Nate across Jess's desk. There are several shots of him in close-up, standing in the courtyard of Algos House, his patrician features framed by the branches of a cherry tree. He faces the camera, his eyes staring off, suitably reflective and melancholic. They've gone full-scale wistful widower. Inwardly I cringe. The dark snark has been erased, along with that questioning glint in his eye that gives him edge. There's something so posed, so wooden about his expression. It doesn't look like him at all.

"This would be strong for the cover," says Jess, pointing to one of the images. "He looks defiant."

"He looks hot," Elaine corrects her with a smirk, and the chrome bangles on her wrists rattle as she points to one. "How old did you say he was?"

"Forty, and too young for you." Jess's tone is caustic. "This will need to be two thousand words. We'll do it over three pages and make the pictures smaller if need be. He's not that good-looking."

"I'll file first thing tomorrow morning," I say, walking out of her office to my desk as my phone vibrates.

Forgot to ask, can I please see the final edit before it goes to print? Just want to check for any inaccuracies or misquotes. I'm away after tomorrow, any chance you can send it through later this evening? Hope the thumb's bearing up okay. N

The phone pings again.

Still up for tonight Meet you there? Tony x

My heart lurches. I was supposed to go to a gig tonight in a small club in Camden with him. He's always trying to interest me in obscure indie bands and it's become something of a shared joke between us, how terminally uncool I am when it comes to live music.

I'm so sorry. Complete nightmare at work, can't speak right now. You'll have to go without me. Will call later to explain. A xx

I return to Nate's message. Every journalist knows the cardinal rule is never to show your copy to your interviewee, no editor allows it. If I did and Amira or Jess found out, I'd lose any future work. I reply cautiously.

Thumb's just about bearing up, thanks. Re. copy, you can only query errors, none of my reflections or descriptions or quotes, unless what you say is factually incorrect.

"Sooo?" Amira appears behind me, in search of an entertaining debrief. I turn my mobile over so she can't see my screen and repeat, briefly, what I told Jess about the interview, but of course that isn't enough to satisfy her. "Check out the pictures," I say, throwing her a bone. "Elaine fancies him."

"Come on, give us a quick listen," she says, removing my AirPods, but I grab them back off her.

"No way."

"Come on, Anna, tell us how did you really feel about the charismatic, brooding Dr. Reid?" She drops her voice dramatically.

"Feel? That's such an overused word." I roll my eyes, find myself echoing Nate.

"Okay, did you like him, then?"

"Not articularly." I affect a dispassionate expression, staring at my screen while my heart hammers. I couldn't quite bear Amira to hear Nate and I chatting about art in his basement study.

"You don't fancy a drink after work?" she says, catching my distracted expression. "Looks like you need one."

I shake my head. "Wish I could but—" My phone vibrates. She gives me a suspicious glance, but thankfully Jess's door opens and she calls Amira into the meeting.

I take longer than usual writing up the piece. It needs to be more sympathetic, but not so bland that Jess and Amira might question it. I leave out the tantrum, the insights too that I would normally read into something like that, how controlling he seemed, volatile and unpredictable. Looking back I wonder if the dismay he expressed about losing his temper was no more than an attempt to persuade me he was really a good guy. Reflections that Amira would have loved me to include but I've come this far, I can't risk upsetting him.

Instead, I ramp up details about how eloquent he is, how charismatic and smart. It feels like I'm writing a puff piece but I also know this profile needs to be my calling card. By 8:00 p.m., I'm done. As I leave the office, I text Nate.

I've finished—I'll email it through now. If I don't hear from you by midday tomorrow, I'll assume all is good with it. Thanks, Ax

I read it back. All good, except for the *x* at the end. I delete it and press Send.

When it goes to press a couple of nights later, I find myself unable to sleep. As I drift off, black italicized words and quotations swim in front of my eyes. I wake up to an ashen dawn light seeping around the edges of my blinds, quickly dress for work and head for the newsdealer at the end of my street.

There's something about seeing my words in print that still exhilarates in an old-fashioned sort of way. The thrill of something that exists in a vacuum, blissfully free from the online trolls. I pick up a copy of my paper, piled up on the floor between the *Telegraph* and the *Times*, and my pulse quickens at the sight of us in print on the cover, our names so close to one another:

> *King of Pain reveals personal agonies:*
> *Anna Tate interviews Dr. Nate Reid*

I peel away the different sections like layers of an onion. Sports. Travel. Arts and Culture. Until I reach the magazine, a slim glossy prize at the center. I turn the pages until I see his mournful gaze staring out at me, a quote emblazoned above his head.

*"I came home to find my wife dead. It was like something out of a horror film seeing her surrounded by those sculptures..."*

My heart plummets, knowing how he might react. What felt like genuine disclosure looks brutal blown up like that, slapped brazenly on the page. Maybe they beefed up the headlines because the copy was too kind to him. If only I could get a chance to explain.

On my way to the office, I scroll through my phone, check the reader page views. Three-hundred-and-forty-thousand reads and rising, median attention three minutes, best read on the website.

Who was it that said the death of a beautiful woman is unquestionably the most poetical topic in the world? Some stuffy old Victorian author. It may not be poetic but the sentiment still stands—it is perfect click bait.

Over the coming days, there's a small-scale swirl of attention, tweets and comments, hero emails from Amira and even Jess. A brief high followed by a rapid comedown. But nothing from Nate.

His silence makes me uneasy. I try not to think about his contempt for journalists, how I could be another one to add to his list of most hated, my chance of being a ghostwriter ruined. Untrustworthy, sensationalist.

I throw myself into researching my next interview with an infamously bad-tempered but innovative Scandi chef, and it's his voice I plug into my ears; his TV shows, his memoir and his documentaries I immerse myself in. The strip of mauve on my arm has faded.

Within a week, I persuade myself that I've banished Dr. Reid from my thoughts entirely. It is a Friday afternoon and I'm about to leave the office to meet my chef in a converted courtroom in Shoreditch when the email lands.

Priya James
Request re: Dr. Nate Reid

A bolt of anxiety crackles through me. Fuck. A libel. I click straight onto it, convinced it's from his lawyer until I see Priya James's signature—Grayson Inc. Publisher of Non-fiction. His publisher.

Dear Anna,
I do hope you don't mind me dropping cold into your inbox like this. Rhik, Dr. Reid's book PR, passed on your contact details.
Nate was thrilled with your magazine profile and asked me to make contact. I worked with him on his recent book about neuroscience and we're in the early stages of his next project, something very different which I'm excited about—his memoir. We do have a few potential names in the hat but I wondered if you'd like to come in for a chat so we can tell you a bit more about the book, ideally next week? I look forward to your reply.
Best wishes,
Priya

Something fizzes inside me like static. I feel charged, alive. He liked my interview, although reading between the lines, she's less than underwhelmed.

I feign a poker face as Amira walks up and stands behind me. It drives me mad when she sneaks up on me to read my emails, as if they're her property, even though I know it's just Amira gleefully fishing for gossip. I click out of the mail but it's too late, she's seen the subject line and the sender.

"Priya James, eh? She did that memoir two years ago; you know the surgeon with the inoperable brain tumor we extracted for the mag? *New York Times* bestseller for months."

I make a noncommittal sound, avoiding her gaze.

"I've heard she's ruthless. A friend of mine knew someone with stage one cancer who got in touch with her about a book idea, only to be told she wouldn't consider a cancer memoir from anyone with less than stage four, for maximum sales." I grimace, Amira laughs. "I'm not sure we'd be interested in profiling her, if that's why she's in touch?"

"Not exactly, no."

Amira raises her eyebrows. "It's nothing," I say. "An informal chat about a book idea."

"Is this about the memoir that Nate hopes to publish—you're in the frame for it? See, I knew you had this all planned out." An annoying grin spreads across her face. "Makes sense that you were so bloody nice about him in the interview. Seems like it paid off. So is anyone else in the picture or just you?"

"They're lining up a few ghostwriters to interview, by the sounds of it."

"Ah, the beauty parade. I've heard about those, where they meet you in a hotel and get to decide which one they'll choose."

"Beauty parade," I repeat, trying to block out the nightmarish image of a line of us in blue satin sashes shimmying down a catwalk while Nate and Priya hold up score cards.

"I wouldn't get your hopes up about this. Even if Nate wants you on the job, I'm sure Priya has her own favorites lined up.

I've heard she can be quite…possessive…about her clients. Nothing gets by her."

I can no longer contain my curiosity. "You mean there's something more going on? They're a thing, seeing each other?"

"It's only a rumor, but something to bear in mind for the interview." She scans my expression, suitably neutral for her benefit.

"Well, maybe that will be for the best, if I don't get the job then," I say. "I'm not even sure I'd want to get inside Dr. Reid's head. That's what you'd have to do as a ghostwriter, isn't it? I really don't think that would be a good place to go."

She opens her mouth, another question forming on her lips, but decides better of it.

"Well, see you tonight back at the apartment," she says cheerfully. "Have fun with your chef."

"I will." I smile back at her as she leaves.

I don't tell her I ordered two books on the art of ghostwriting weeks ago and replied to Priya that I'm free all next week. In the cab I check my phone, idly search for her Instagram. A gallery of corporate profiles pop up. *Priya James takes the reins as head of publishing at Grayson Inc.* There's a wide-angled shot of her across the boardroom table, poker-faced, intimidating.

I can't help looking at her through Nate's eyes, it's not hard to figure out the appeal. That itch of competitiveness flares up in me again, of wanting what can never be mine. Their easy, comfortable lives and careers. It's a heat that I try to ignore. But it's there anyway, leaving its bitter aftertaste.

# 9

The Temple Court Hotel in Southwark is bland, functional and anonymous—in other words, the ideal setting to interview a bunch of ghosts. I take a glass elevator to the seventeenth floor and stare out over the city. The sun casts a metallic light across the Thames, turning it into a gleaming ribbon of steel. In the reception area, a middle-aged man in green tweed and jumbo cords sits on a mustard L-shaped sofa, a copy of Nate's book—awash with Post-it notes—in his hand. I imagine there are a few of us lurking around the building with well-thumbed copies of *The Pain Matrix*.

A woman walks up to the reception desk and I recognize her immediately from the boardroom picture. She raises her perfectly manicured eyebrows.

"Anna?"

"Yes. Priya?"

She offers her hand, cool and dry in mine. There is the discreet sparkle of expensive jewelery: diamond studs in her ear, an opal solitaire sparkles at her throat.

"So pleased to meet you," she says, flashing me a smile. "Nate's already here." She shows me into a meeting room at the far end of the corridor. He sits at a small circular table framed by a vertiginous panorama of Blackfriars down to London Bridge. The glass windows lend a muffled quality to the room as if all the sound has been dialed down.

I sit down opposite both of them.

"Hello again, Anna," Nate says, holding my gaze for a second too long and I find myself having to turn away, focus my attention on Priya instead, who begins speaking.

"Can I start by saying how much I enjoyed your interview with Nate. He's not easy to get at but somehow you managed," she says, smiling at Nate as if this is entirely for his benefit. "And you were spot on in your observation that he fidgets like a child, that way he chews his pens. Drives me mad in our meetings." She eye rolls and Nate's dark eyebrows shoot upward in mock indignation. "Trust me, Nate, you really do."

He tips his head toward her, clearly familiar with this well-worn dynamic. I find myself fixating on their body language, the way a micro movement in one is mirrored by the other. Priya regards me intently.

"You certainly seem to specialize in opinionated, high-achieving men. Is that because you get on with them better than women, would you say?"

I laugh but she looks deadly serious.

"Well, I've interviewed a lot of famous women as well; I really don't have a preference. My editor usually decides, and I guess she thinks I get good copy from difficult alpha-male types. Maybe there's just a lot of them around."

Nate is studiously looking down at another cutting that I recognize, an interview I did two years ago with José Mourinho.

"You certainly got under that guy's skin," Priya says, tapping the close-up of Mourinho's face. "He walked out on you. But somehow you managed to talk him round. Is that a well-rehearsed habit of yours?"

I wonder if she's alluding to Nate's meltdown with me, but

he doesn't look particularly self-conscious. I can't help thinking he doesn't really look as if he's here at all.

"How your interviewees react under pressure can be revealing." I stare at Nate across the table. "When someone turns away and walks out on me, I know I've broken through. I've touched a nerve and hit a deeper level. It's a promising sign."

"So would you say as a ghostwriter you'd try to push your interviewee to the limit?"

"I'm not sure either of us would benefit from that, would we? Ghostwriting Nate's memoir would be an entirely different process because, of course, he would have all the control."

"And that wouldn't bother someone like you?" Nate asks.

"Someone like me?" I echo, smiling. "I don't see why it should. I'd be paid to write your truth, the one you want to reveal, and I'd be happy with that."

Nate flashes a glance at Priya. They exchange a look, too brief to decipher and yet again I find myself feeling like a third wheel.

"So, Anna, everyone reckons they've got a story to tell. I'd be interested to hear your thoughts on why Nate's would stand out in such a crowded marketplace." Her hand rests lightly on her latest raft of titles; the female MP who grew up on a council estate, the doctor who worked in war-torn Syria, the writer who spent seven years of his life locked in a cellar by his mother. If Nate is the King of Pain, Priya is the Queen of Confessional Memoir. The perfect match. She taps her pen on one of the book covers. "What makes his different, do you think?"

I'm ready for this one. The answers I rehearsed in the mirror roll through my mind.

"People want something with more substance. Nate's story has huge potential and, crucially, it's very relatable. Love, despair, grief and hopefully transformation. It's all there. Nate is in a unique position, being able to analyze all of it from a point of expertise. I'd like to explore that further." I pause for effect. "His work is a bridge between two worlds: the emotional pain of his loss and his passion to measure the immeasurable. Physical pain. And, at its heart, of course, is Eva. A love story that threads all of it together."

I've noticed the energy shift between them, the sound of her name somehow makes them stiffen. Or am I imagining it? I reach for a glass of water; the ice cubes set my teeth on edge.

Priya begins to scrutinize my application letter once again, her smooth forehead ruffling. "There's nothing at all about science here. It's all arts and culture. Would the lack of a track record in science writing present a problem for you, do you think?"

"Actually, I see it as a distinct advantage. Part of my job would be to transform Nate's complex ideas into prose that everyone can understand," I say, warming to my theme. "Disarming candor is what makes these books bestsellers. The alpha brain surgeon who feels sick with anxiety before an operation, or the country's top forensic pathologist, terrified that he can never be totally certain about an unnatural cause of death. That's what I'd want to tap into. You need to let the reader in, make them feel that they're mainlining Nate's feelings, downloading his darkest fears."

"Excellent," says Priya, glancing over at Nate.

"And do you have any questions for us?" he asks neutrally.

"I do have one actually. Why, really, do you both want to publish this memoir? Nate is clearly a very private person, understandably so. Why expose him in this way?"

That strange energy again in the room. Nate opens his mouth but Priya steps in.

"Well, I'm not sure he wanted to initially. But then we—I mean he—could see it made sense, for Eva and for his career."

"I do think the book could help other people as long as it has the right science behind it," says Nate.

For an instant, I can't help picturing Nate in Eva's garden studio, standing over her body, an image so piercing I try to push it from my mind. I want to believe more than anything that his motives are genuine. But isn't it quite convenient that he's so keen to tell the world about his love for Eva, his devastating grief, just as there's another inquest in the pipeline?

Priya, I'm sure, couldn't care less, too busy thinking about the royalties and another "narrative nonfiction" bulldozing its way into the bestseller lists.

I think about my old friend, Karl Bauer, a retired ghostwriter I chatted to on the phone yesterday, hoping to glean some insights before my interview. He told me a ghostwriter needs to know the real reason someone wants to expose their story to the world, in the same way a barrister needs to know exactly how guilty their client is to defend their corner. They have to tell you everything, said Bauer, no subject can be off-limits. "There will always be something you can't name. The elephant in the room. Work out what that is as soon as possible and confront it. Otherwise, it taints everything else."

I look up at Priya then.

"I just wondered, if I did end up on the project, I'd want to know nothing would be off-limits. How would Nate feel about that?"

"Legally, *if* you did get the job," Priya says, "Nate and I would want you to sign a nondisclosure agreement, so whatever he does tell you about Eva is completely confidential. You couldn't go spilling to any of your newspaper contacts."

"Eva isn't a taboo subject," chips in Nate. "It can still be difficult talking about her, but I'm sure with the right person, the right approach, that could change. All I really want this book to be is my way of immortalizing her, so I know I won't forget her. Anyway, are we nearly done here?" He starts shuffling his notes together, suddenly self-conscious.

Priya swerves in. "Just one more question, Anna, before we wrap up."

"Sure."

"You've built up a distinctive style, a regular interview slot with your name on it. Why would you want to give that up to be...invisible? There'll be no glory, no mention of you at all. Experienced ghostwriters don't do it to seek the limelight. All your work would be in Nate's name."

Her chin tilts up. It's clear that she doesn't want me anywhere near Nate or the book.

"Actually, no, that's not the case. It's frankly a relief to lose my name for a few months," I say with conviction. "I feel strongly that Eva was an amazing woman and her life fascinates me. It helps that I enjoy the cut and thrust of the creative process, and I get the impression Nate does too."

They nod, talk to me a bit more about timings and deadlines, while my mind drifts. I think of that house, the boundless possibility. How stunning it all was, Eva's history right there. The voice I could craft for her, the storyline she deserves, so different to the lies that were written.

I agreed with Kath's concerns in that respect, how unfair it is that a woman in the public eye who dares to live a full and complex life, messy, honest and unfiltered, will be punished for it. Naively, perhaps, I'd like to challenge that.

"Well, that went well," I say, dryly, as Nate walks me back to the lift. I know I probably shouldn't let on how I feel about the interview, but I can't help it.

"Don't read too much into Priya." He holds back a rare smile.

"Well, I can understand if she wants someone with more experience in ghostwriting. When do you think she'll decide?"

"She?" He frowns. "Why would you think it's all down to her?"

"Er, she's the publisher?"

He shrugs. "Don't assume anything," he says. As I step into the lift, it crosses my mind that this is the second time in a fortnight I've left Nate feeling more perplexed by his behavior than when I started.

Crossing the foyer on my way out, I spot another man, almost indistinguishable from the earlier one, in a pink button-down shirt and olive chinos. He reclines, his legs straight but crossed at the ankles, flicking through *The Pain Matrix*. He looks up, assessing me, trying to work out if I'm the competition.

Unexpectedly I am high, reeling, this high-voltage surge of...what exactly? Confidence, arrogance even. Nate's world is familiar to me after all, a twisted world of smoke and mirrors where nothing is ever as it seems. No one else could navigate it but me.

# 10

I spot him as soon as I walk in, sitting up at the bar reading a book with his back to me. From the deflated slope of his shoulders, I can tell this place bores him. Tony's never been a fan of gastropubs like this, selling ten different types of craft IPA but no draught Guinness. This particular one is shaped to the comforts of the well-heeled residents from across the park, the earthy smell of coal dust and wet dogs is more Chipping Norton than West London.

I walk up behind him, touch his shoulder.

"Sorry I'm late," I say, as he swivels round.

"Hey, stranger," Tony says, placing a large glass of red in my hand. I take him in, this skewed mirror image grinning back at me. A small republic of two, Tony likes to call us. More totalitarian state than democracy, as I frequently joke to him, but he is all I have. Our biological mother, my father, his stepfather, his own father; all gone, one way or another. It's for the anniversary of our mother's death that we're meeting up tonight to spend the evening together.

I pull up a stool next to him and pick up his book with its pristine, uncreased spine, give a small snort of disbelief.

"So you're pretending to read David Foster Wallace."

"I'm enjoying it, actually."

"Good luck finishing it. Even the endnotes have endnotes."

"Have you read it?"

"Of course," I lie. "You'll never get to the end, you never do."

He opens his mouth, pretends to look offended.

Secretly I've always envied Tony's dilettantism, the way he just skims through life only ever dipping a toe. First chapters, first episodes of Netflix dramas, opening scenes of plays and films. Dabbling, tasting, always moving on, the least effort to appear the most erudite. Friendships, relationships, all manner of passions and pleasures, he's never in it for the long haul. There have been flirtations with transcendental meditation, bookbinding, even taxidermy. Who cares about endings when there are so many new beginnings to enjoy?

Somehow Tony makes me feel that it's cowardice, not tenacity, that makes us stick out our life choices long after the novelty fades.

He bags a table next to the fireplace over which hangs a framed Victorian map of Oxfordshire, while I order a bottle of house red, watch him from the bar as he pointedly glances at the couple next to him. Both wear quilted gilets, his in navy, hers pale pink, while their Labradoodle laps from a water bowl close to Tony's feet.

Tony, in stark contrast, is dressed almost entirely in black. His leather jacket is undone, just low enough to reveal the insignia of an XR T-shirt *(There is no Planet B)*. He looks like the bassist from a '90s Brit-pop band that recently reformed.

"This place! What happened to real pubs?" He shakes his head as I sit down, glancing at me for affirmation.

"Don't start," I say, and he leans back in his chair. Tony is easy most of the time, but he gets like this occasionally where everything is fodder for a sneer or ridicule. It grows worse around this time each year, near our mom's anniversary, and it's down to me to make him feel better.

"Why do they have to bray? Can't people just talk normally?" Tony stares at two young men at the table opposite, speaking loudly with plummy exclamations and guffaws. He tops up his glass again and doesn't fill mine, then reaches for a menu. With a flourish, he takes out and puts on a pair of oversized designer glasses, which lend him a rakish, academic air.

"I never knew you were long-sighted. They suit you." I reach over and tap the frames.

"They're not real," he confesses. "Clear glass."

"You old fake," I say, pushing them a little farther up his nose. "So how long are you back for?"

"Just a few weeks, staying with an old friend who owes me, then I'm off to Tangier and Marrakech."

"Tough life." I smile.

"I'm doing a picture story while I'm out there," he adds, a little defensively.

"That's great, Tony. Who's it for?"

"Some crappy corporate magazine, but still." He looks down and I try to appear encouraging. I'm always worried his photographic work will dry up and he'll flit to the next pursuit. Before this there was travel writing; next it will be film, judging from the TV script that he's been working on. I make a point to take an interest as he tells me about it, wide-eyed, nodding, knowing it's another project that most likely will never see the light of day.

"Hey, why don't you put in a good word with your company and we could finally work together? It must be pretty easy," he says, his hand brushing mine. "It's not like your magazine is even a national title," he mocks. I pick up my drink to avoid his touch, force a brittle smile.

He leans across the table to reach for my arm, a conciliatory gesture but one that provokes me all the same. "Only teasing," he says. I look at his unlined face, piqued by his youthful looks, the absence of a furrowed brow or purple shadows beneath his eyes. How does he manage to look younger than me when he's six years older? Perhaps his levels of self-absorption have a protective effect, never worrying about anyone or anything beyond himself. Narcissism does have one distinct advantage, I think, observing his flawless complexion. If only they could bottle it.

"Come on then, what's been happening? Where have you been hiding?"

"I'm sorry. I kept meaning to get back to you. I've been up to my neck in work—interviews, deadlines..." I trail off, hoping to avoid more unnecessary questions. Tony's chin tilts up so he looks down at me through heavy eyelashes.

"Stop being so evasive. You got it, didn't you?"

"Got what?"

"I bumped into Amira last week at an old mate's party."

"Really? She didn't say anything."

"Maybe she forgot."

"Maybe," I say, finding this unlikely.

"We had a long chat. She told me all about you and the memoir. So, Dr. Nate Reid and my little sister writing the big book together."

"Well, I wouldn't get too excited," I say, refilling our glasses, my tone clipped. I'm not sure I'm ready to tell people anything about this project just yet. "I was asked to apply along with lots of other people. His publisher got in contact with me."

"I'm not too excited, don't worry," he says, frowning a little. "Just interested. Quite a big-shot job for you."

"I'm sure I won't get it," I lie again, rolling the stem of the wineglass between my thumb and forefinger. I always find myself doing this, play down my ambitions to make him feel

better about his unfruitful ones. The effort of tiptoeing around
my career, downgrading it to a series of lucky accidents, is ex-
hausting. He needs to maintain the illusion that we're equals,
orphans together struggling in the storm.

Tonight, however, I'm struggling to suppress my jubilant
mood. A few days after my interview, Nate texted. They, although he didn't mention Priya, wanted me to start the job
straightaway. I couldn't think of a better outcome. Life away
from the office, away from the confines of my work pressures,
my cramped apartment.

"You're smiling," Tony accuses.

"Am I?"

He leans back to study me. "You'll get it, you know you
will, you're brilliant. Although I'd think we should maybe talk
about it before you got into something like that."

"I don't need your permission." I force a laugh, embold-
ened by the wine.

"Sure. Only after seeing the newspapers, I'd worry about
you working for someone like him. I remember reading about
it all—the whole situation sounded screwed up. I don't like the
idea of you going anywhere near Dr. Nate Reid." He shivers.

"Well, don't worry. Another drink?" I say briskly, eager to
change the subject.

"Maybe a bottle?" Tony replies, pushing his chair back.
"Snackage?"

"Go on." The pub begins filling up with the clamor of a
Friday-night crowd. They push their way to the bar, knock-
ing our chairs. My nerves jangle, my own mood darkening
by the minute.

Next time I won't drink, I vow to myself. I know where
this can lead. Tony returns and sits down, pouring dry roasted
peanuts into a bag of salt-and-vinegar chips and shaking it, a

little trick he devised in the pub gardens of Essex when we were kids.

"Dinner is served." He rips the packet open and places it on the table between us, pours us each another glass and raises his to mine. "I'd like to make a toast. To Mom."

"To Mom," I echo and he chinks his glass with mine. We always meet up around the anniversary of her death, and each year I dread it, the grief it brings out of us both. His hand reaches across the table, long slender fingers like our mother's cover mine, his voice softens.

"It'll be twenty-three years on Tuesday."

"Twenty-three years," I echo, conscious of the weight of his hand on mine.

"I thought we could do something special. Maybe go to her favorite spot, that pub on the river back home in Essex."

"I'd love to, but we'd have to find a time when I'm less swamped at work."

"I understand," he says, his eyes raking my face. "Just thought it had been a while since you last visited her grave?"

I open my mouth to say something, then close it. He gives a theatrical sigh, watches me take a long swallow of wine and glance out the window. "Mom loved this time of year, didn't she?" I offer, inadequately.

"What are you on about? She hated winter, always moaned about the cold."

He gets up to go to the bar. I pretend to read the news on my phone but the headlines blur. The room swirls a bit, my eyes lag, the clatter of voices and background music rises up around me.

I wonder, sometimes, how can two siblings grow up in the same family and turn out so differently, feel our grief so differently. As soon as I moved to London, I did my best to forget about the past and move on, more or less successfully.

But Tony has become stuck in that time, unable to move forward emotionally, incapable of sticking to a grief counselor or therapist for more than a few weeks. Traveling around the world looking for new adventures is his coping mechanism, not a particularly effective one. When we meet, he drags me back to my younger years with the gravitational pull of a black hole. Armed with anecdotes that he repeats over and over, they are the only version of our childhood I seem to remember. Sometimes I think siblings are like a mirror reflecting back a twisted picture of who we believe we are.

At times it can feel that one's family history is like a Wiki entry, allowing you to go back in there and edit your details whenever you wish. The trouble is so can other people.

This is what I remember still about Tony, my half brother. He was five when his father died from a heart attack and a year later, my mother remarried. She met my dad at the local school where they both worked as teachers and, within months, I was born. I've always wondered if it was a marriage of convenience, or some sort of reaction to grief. Tony maintains she was only ever in love with one man, his own father. The perfect union that created Tony. My father was highly insecure about my mother's first marriage. There was a tacit understanding that her husband was never to be mentioned, no photographs, all memories of him extinguished.

Perhaps that's why my father went along with my mother's suggestion to adopt Tony. For him, I suspect, it was one more way to erase evidence of that first marriage. If the surname was gone, so was her husband. In defiance, of course, Tony resolutely hung on to his original surname, Thorpe, once he left home.

I can still recall the precise shade of her chili-red sundress that she wore each summer, the cinched drawstring waist and spaghetti straps. The smell of her favorite nail varnish as it dried. Toasted almond. How on warmer days the veins stood out on the back of her hand, eau de Nil green, as she held mine. I remember her fingertips in my hair, the soporific feel of them grazing my scalp, how even now the memory of that particular touch makes me drowsy.

I treasure these fragments, no matter how small or fleeting, because I alone own them. No one can steal or reframe those recollections. I have never told anyone, not even Tony, that I visit my mother's grave at least once a month, when I have her all to myself.

From the outside we functioned well enough. There were family camping holidays and theater trips to London, birthday meals out together. But hovering below the surface was a simmering tension between Tony and my father. After the adoption, there was no acknowledgment that we were a blended family, patched together with a stepparent and stepsiblings.

In the end, that turned out to be the least of our problems when my mother went for a routine checkup that revealed a small shadow on her left lung. A stage four tumor, secondary breast cancer. A year later, on an unseasonably bright sunny January morning, she died peacefully in the hospice with us around her. I was eleven and Tony seventeen.

Maybe it was grief or loneliness, the responsibility of caring for us as a widower, but my father began to change. He always had a temper, but looking back, I realize that without my mother there to mediate, his behavior grew more extreme. Tony started out as the target of his anger, but I could never take for granted that he wouldn't turn on me. An innocuous remark, an unfinished meal or muddy shoe marks on the stairs: all these could trigger the molten heat of his rage.

It was verbal at first but quickly escalated. The soundtrack of that time still stays with me: the crack of knuckle on skin, the pop of bone on slate as the back of Tony's head met the flagstone floor. I would cry and plead with my father to stop but he wouldn't listen. Then there were those moments, short-lived, when he tried his best to make up for the bad nights, teaching Tony how to use a camera for the first time, making a skateboard for him.

I could never predict what would push him to extremes, why Tony was the catalyst for his outbursts. Did he recognize a part of himself that he found unbearable? Or did he look at Tony and see my mother's first husband staring back, perhaps the only man she ever really loved?

Tony's reading of our childhood, in those rare moments he pauses for self-reflection, is that his upbringing was as deprived as mine was privileged. I was the indulged one and he witnessed me being indulged, he maintains, yet I see it differently.

For me, my childhood was more like a series of isolated moments that I never understood at the time, standing alone outside closed doors, speculating what was happening on the other side. Violence pulsed at the edges, nudging closer each day. Growing up, Tony and I quickly learned to read the temperature of a room. Like a seasoned weather-watcher, I was hyper alert to signs of potential conflict ahead; storm clouds gathering on the horizon.

I look up, try to focus on the neat rows of malt whiskeys behind the bar, the animated faces of other drinkers, the fuzzy halo of light encircling them. I take an enormous breath, steadying myself.

Tony returns. "One more for the road?" He looks unsteady as he plonks himself back down.

"More?" I say.

"Come on. It's a special occasion."

"Any excuse." I realize how much effort it's taking not to slur.

"So come on, what's this Dr. Reid really like?" He swerves us back to the here and now, his eyes glinting for the gossip like a shark at feeding time.

"He's...you know, normal. A bit up himself..." I shrug, trail off.

"You can do better than that, surely."

I sigh. "I guess, supersmart too. Obstructive, wary of journalists."

He takes out a pouch of tobacco and rolls a cigarette. "Interesting. What did he say about Eva? The rumors?"

"He's pretty guarded about her—so far."

"But you're going to work your magic on him?"

"Something like that."

His smile is vaguely twisted, his mouth weirdly distracting. His lips are stained a mauve from the red wine, his front teeth ashy gray. We regard one another for a moment and I recognize that look in his eyes: hollow. Numbed by grief, and now by alcohol. I let the dig slide.

"I want a cigarette." He screws up his mouth. "Let's get out of this shithole and go somewhere else."

Outside, he stumbles slightly on the step and steadies himself for a moment in the doorway. I feel my phone vibrate, check it quickly. A single text from Priya lights up the screen.

I know it must be about the job but I don't check it for now, decide to stay in this moment with Tony a bit longer. "This way." I let him lean on me, steering him away from the pub. He lights his roll up, which we share as we sway across the park, the sky dark and velvety. My shadow, my other half.

"I'm sorry for being an arse about everything," he says, and I can tell his regret is heartfelt. "You know I only want to protect you," he says, softly.

"I know," I echo. "I know."

# EVA'S SELF-REFLECTION JOURNAL

*15 February 2019*

*Today, six months from the start of my training, I sat face-to-face with my first patient. For the record, I'll refer to them as patient X (Janet advises us to avoid real patient names, and even gender, for reasons of confidentiality). Unsupervised. No more trial runs, simulated setups or role-playing. After weeks of almost quitting, convincing myself I shouldn't be on the course, I felt like a fully fledged therapist.*

*I started with my rehearsed preamble, how I could work with them, what I hoped they could take away from our session, but I needn't have worried about formalities. The patient knew everything I could possibly say, having already been familiar with my work, my condition. They were fascinated with my capacity to absorb and objectively understand the pain of others is potentially greater, simply because my brain is wired in a different way.*

*Within minutes of hearing their full story, listening and reflecting back my thoughts, we both knew we were a suitable match. By the end of the session, I could already see the hope of change—in me and them. When they said goodbye, they told me how different they felt, as if a weight was already lifting.*

*Later on, at home, I told Nate how promising my first session had been and he barely looked up from his book. I assumed that my reflections on pain and emotion, how it can be of benefit in a therapeutic setting, would be of interest to him. Instead, his eyes flashed with irritation and all he could say was, "I've never seen any clinical data on that," before sloping off to his study. It's as if he's shutting me out, closing me down. Understanding pain is his domain, his empire. Am I only of value as data for my condition?*

# 11

"He's running late again," says Jade when she answers the door to Algos. She turns quickly and I follow her in. "He called and said you can go straight down to his study. There are some background notes on his desk, he says, which you can get started on."

She shows me downstairs, hovers in the doorway as if reluctant to leave me alone. I feel her eyes on my back as I sit down at his desk but when I turn, she has closed the door silently behind her.

The walls are lined with reference books. One theme dominates. *Pain: The Science of Suffering*; *Why We Hurt*; *From Prayer to Pain in the Nineteenth Century*. I spot an old copy of Virginia Woolf essays *On Being Ill* and a collection of poetry by Emily Dickinson. Idly, I remove it from the shelf, curious—is it Eva's or Nate's? I turn to where the spine has been bent open and begin to read.

*Pain has an element of blank; it cannot recollect*
*When it began, or if there were*
*A day when it was not*

I flip back to the opening page and see an inscription written five years ago on Nate's birthday.

*Thank you for putting up with my element of blank. Yours forever, Eva.*

I find myself checking the door again, wary that Jade could be watching me. I sit for a moment in his swivel chair, feeling his authority resonate as I examine the piles of clinical notes on the floor, the old papers and discarded ink cartridges. Next to his computer is a small anatomical model of a brain on a white plinth. I draw my hand along its bumps and ridges, the network of red veins running along its surface. An A4 file is placed neatly next to it, a Post-it on the cover.

*Here are a few notes and reflections I've been working on over the last week or two. I'm keen to weave them in somehow, if you think they're suitable. Speak shortly.*
*Nate*

There're only a couple of pages, no more than a thousand words of thoughts and reflections, and yet somehow it seems longer.

I stifle a yawn as I read through it. Paragraphs pile up, dense and impenetrable, swimming before my eyes. How best to distinguish acute from chronic pain? What are the long-term benefits of spinal cord stimulation? I search for anything that hints at a glimmer of personal insight, self-awareness. As an introduction to neuroscience, it's passable. As the seeds of a personal memoir, it's a disaster.

I do a word search. Eva's name lights up only once. Buried in the last chapter I finally locate her, hoping for a glimpse of emotional complexity.

*Eva was lying on her side, her back exposed, where I observed little blood but a deep staining of the skin, indicating a passive distention of the inert vessels which takes place within an hour or two of death.*

I draw breath, shake my head, press my fists into my eyes. So your wife dies and your first observation of her in a memoir is *a passive distention of the inert vessels.*

Anxiety curls through me. Does Nate really have the emotional intelligence to drill down that far? I glance up at his books. Philosophy and art and cinema. Travel and medicine, memoir and biography. All those words that should connect him to raw experience. Yet, somehow, it's all so lacking in these reflections, as if he buried his emotions long ago. Even the best ghostwriter is only as good as their raw material. I have to try to get started on something.

*Every dead body is trying to tell us something. It's there waiting for us to listen, if we look carefully enough. What was Eva trying to tell me? We know that she died at approximately 4:00 p.m. on the Friday, before I returned home to discover her body the next morning. The truth is I don't remember a great deal about the rest of the day. I know I called the police and later, after they'd gone, I felt numb, unable to process the reality of what had happened.*

I look at the picture of her on Nate's desk, her face angled away from the camera, oddly beautiful. I want to let her tell her own story but, for now, Nate is her gatekeeper, the only connection I have to her past, the only hope of ever knowing the truth. And yet his memories of his own wife are about as passionate as a lab report.

★ ★ ★

"Good to see you're deep in concentration."

Head in my hands, I jump at the sound of his voice, his looming presence behind me. How does he do that?

"Hi, Nate. Didn't hear you. Sorry."

"The power of good prose," he says lightly, picking up the textbook lying open next to me. "You must be desperate if you're reading *The Oxford Guide to Neuroscience* as light relief."

"What? Oh, that. Translating some of your terms."

He pulls up a chair next to me, apparently ready to get to work. I tie my hair back up in its band, assemble my features into something that reflects enthusiasm.

"I see that. You found my notes too heavy going?"

"No, not at all. There's some really useful stuff in here," I say awkwardly. I shuffle the pages together and place them next to me as if I am laying something dead to rest. Above us I can see the light and shadow of Jade's movements through the square of glass bricks in the study ceiling, hear the reassuring clatter of lunch being prepared, dishes being stacked. How I wish I were up there. Even Jade's froideur seems preferable to this.

"Nate," I hear myself say, "I really think we need to talk. It's my turn to tell you something, before we get started."

He looks at me, expectant.

"I should have said it when we first met but somehow it didn't seem relevant. You see, I actually spoke to Eva once. I interviewed her. Over the phone, not for very long at all. I mean, she was amazing." I pause, try to gauge his reaction, but his expression is set, inscrutable.

"What exactly did you talk about?"

"Oh, nothing, really, and everything. Her sculptures, how she was training to be a therapist. The piece never ran in the end. She invited me to go to one of her exhibitions, but I couldn't make it. I always felt bad about that…" I trail off, bite the inside of my cheek.

*Tell him. Don't tell him.*

"That's a shame. You'd have liked her if you'd met her properly. Everyone did." The shadow of a smile plays on his lips, and I find myself relieved that this hasn't triggered a stronger reaction. "Eva could be difficult to refuse, whatever she asked of you."

"I sensed that, yes," I manage. "I just thought you should know. No secrets, right?"

The early afternoon gloom of his windowless study draws tighter around us as we sit side by side. He switches on a small brass reading light and I glance at him in profile, the tips of his mouth sloping downward, his eyebrows drawn together like a battle line as if bracing himself for combat.

My notes twist angrily through his text, in brash shouty capitals: *MORE OF YOU HERE, TOO CLINICAL. CLICHÉ ALERT!*

His head leans one way and then another in an attempt to decipher my thoughts, his features darkening by the minute.

"Yup, okay. Got it. You want more gush, more emotional honesty." He crowns the words with ironic commas.

"Right. The reader will just keep wondering, what are you really feeling here?" I turn my chair to face him.

"That magic word again. I *feel* fine. But I don't really get your problem with—this." He taps the paper with the back of his fingers. "I've outlined everything I witnessed when I came back and found Eva. It's accurate and truthful. I don't really understand what more you want?"

I flinch inwardly as his indignation rises, that old habit of hypervigilance ever present. Does it signal another meltdown, are these red flags I should recognize?

"Well, I guess the point is it's factual and it's not badly written. But—" I pause with the effort of being delicate "—sometimes the facts alone make it feel less accurate. They can be...alienating to the reader."

"So you're saying you want me to exaggerate, give a sensational account of what happened?"

"I'm simply outlining what I know Priya will want."

He nods dismissively, keen for me to finish so he can speak again. "As I see it," he says, that tone again, "I write down the facts, my life, my work and what actually happened. You warm it up if need be and I'll say if I like it or not."

"I'm not sure if that's how it really works. Can I ask, have you ever talked to a psychotherapist about her—I mean, about your loss?" It's a swerve but I need to shake him up a bit, get to the heart of the issue. He looks indignant.

"Why would I? I've got my own inner therapist. I'm good at processing my feelings. I know myself better than anyone." I try to suppress a smile. "What's so amusing?"

"Nothing, I guess. Except I've heard a lot of men say the same thing about therapy."

"Women have it all worked out, right?"

"That's what you think?"

"I think you sound like a convert."

"It's not a religion," I retort.

"Well, a cult then."

"You really are resistant. There's nothing wrong with seeking professional advice. It can help to talk it through."

Nate sighs, shifts in his seat and leans forward. "Okay, the truth is, I tried it for a month or two actually, but it wasn't for me. The goal of therapy is to work on change, but perhaps I don't want to. I'm quite happy the way I am."

"If only I could be that sure. I mean, who doesn't want

to change in some way, isn't that the whole point? I know I wish I could."

He shakes his head firmly. "Trawling through the past with someone, all that endless navel-gazing, it isn't my style."

"Much safer to stay the same and give nothing away." I tease lightly.

"Not quite what I meant."

"Little do you know, you're already shedding clues the whole time, giving away more than we ever really realize."

"Really? Surprise me, then," he says, sitting back and folding his arms, his forehead furrowing.

I hesitate for a moment, wondering how accurate I should be. A consuming interest in someone is never a good look.

"Okay, for starters, appearance is important to you. During our first interview, I noticed how you checked your reflection in the glass door on the way down here. You had a haircut earlier that day too because you knew you were going to be photographed before I turned up—I could tell by the red skin on the back of your head where it had been shaved."

His hand instinctively strokes the back of his neck. I plow on, secretly pleased.

"My feeling is you spend your life studying other people's brains so you don't have to turn the microscope on yourself. We're all guilty of that in our jobs, I guess. It's the way we like to stay in control." I pause for effect. "The smoking was a surprise though, I didn't expect that."

He sits up a little straighter. "Okay, my turn. You're an introvert masquerading as an extrovert. You like attention more than you care to admit, feel you can be overlooked in certain situations, so you reassure yourself that's a benefit in your line of work. But I'm not sure you really believe it." His eyes hook into mine and I struggle to muster a smile. "You're pretty allergic to the therapist's couch too, aren't you? You preach about it, may even have tried it but, like me, you decided it wasn't for you."

*If only you knew*, I want to say. Instead, I brush strands of my bangs across my forehead, suddenly worrying that my complexion is giving me away.

"I don't think you were too worried about experiencing pain. In fact, you displayed high tolerance levels in the lab. What you really don't like is feeling exposed."

"Touché," I say. Here I am, proving his little theory right, making my excuses to take flight.

"I'm sorry if I touched a nerve." He looks amused and entirely unapologetic.

"Sure. It's funny, if anything," I say, unconvincingly. "I'd happily talk about myself and bore you with my vanilla childhood, but we have work to do."

Satisfaction twitches at the corners of his mouth. "Nothing about you, Anna, strikes me as vanilla."

As another hour passes, I'm aware of the proximity of his foot close to mine, restlessly circling the air. I register the urge to kick him, hard, so he'll finally engage, stop treating whatever I say as irrelevant white noise.

"You missed this chapter. No red ink. What did I do right?"

"Sorry." I smile. "I just ran out of time."

"Or maybe red ink?"

At least there's humor in his eyes again, a self-deprecating lightness. Something that I imagine Eva would have found charming.

"Look, I know this is a trial for you. Emotion isn't something neuroscientists exactly embrace. Maybe we can even mention that in the opening chapter, an admission to the reader that this is a different medium for you?"

He nods, unconvinced, his fingertips tap on the back of his phone.

"I mean, not wanting to talk about emotions is something the reader would respect you for admitting to. We could explore it from a neuroscience perspective, how we use different parts of our brain to compartmentalise?"

"Sounds like pop psychology to me. Wrong discipline."

"But it's not the point. What I'm trying to say is that your science shouldn't be the most important thing about your book. You're excluding the reader. Do that and they won't read it. I don't blame them, I wouldn't either. You have to challenge yourself, aim higher."

I toss the notes I've been holding in my hand onto his keyboard. Some of the pages miss and fall in his lap. He stares at them for a moment or two, says nothing. Sweat prickles my palms. Will this be a confrontation? For a moment I think he'll explode but, he doesn't. Instead, he looks at me properly for the first time today and his mood shifts.

"Anna, look, I'm sorry."

I bend down to pick up some of the papers that have scattered to the floor. "I shouldn't have thrown them. I—"

"Seriously, you're right. I do rely on jargon, terminology, to hide behind. You're not the first person to point it out, or probably the last. I spend my life absorbed by the brain, the very place where emotions reside. I, of all people, can see the irony in that." He lets out a hollow laugh.

"If you can, then there's potential to change. As long as you trust the questions I ask you, and you're not defensive, we can do this."

"Right. A fruitful collaboration." He smiles, his features relax. Without warning he gathers up his chapters scattered on the desk, opens up the bottom drawer and throws them in, shutting it with a theatrical slam.

"Happy?"

"Not exactly, but it's a start," I say. "Let's begin with interviewing you. From now on, the only person asking questions will be me." He nods, and for the first time I sense he respects the steely finality in my voice.

I let myself into my apartment and hear the telltale signs of company. Amira is home earlier than usual, which explains the delicate scent of saffron and lemon permeating the hallway.

There's the suck of a fridge door opening, a man's gentle murmur I assume is her ex-boyfriend, Alex, followed by the distinct peal of Amira's laughter. I wrestle off my coat, absorbing a certain flavor of intimacy in the rise and fall of their conversation. I'd rather not intrude and head for the bathroom instead. Amira has always been more of an extrovert than me. Where she seeks out noise and company, I am a born scuttler, heading for the safety of an empty room. After four hours in Nate's study, pushing back against his iron-clad will, I need to recalibrate.

I turn on the hot tap to full, undress and step into the bath while it's still running and watch the steam turn the walls wet and glossy. I think of the flawless marble surfaces in Nate's bathroom where the bath, like a sculpted egg, takes center stage surrounded by mirrored mosaics.

By contrast, I am surrounded by flaws, cracks in the shower glass, the furred ancient taps, black spores of damp blooming between the tiles. The endless desire to compare is like a broken window where envy steals in. More of an impulse than a feeling, this longing keeps my mind focused. I sink beneath the bubbles until my skin feels suitably flayed and, finally, I decompress.

There is a rumble of knuckles on the door.

"Anna?"

I come up for air, open my eyes. "Yes? I'll come and say hello in a sec."

"I need a quick word." Amira's voice dips, a note of low urgency in her tone. I get out of the bath and wrap a towel around me, open the door and, even in the half-light of the hall, I can see that her cheeks are flushed. Her eyes gleam and the almost empty wineglass she clutches tilts at a perilous angle.

"Everything okay?"

"Sure. I just, I wanted to tell you something, before you came in and saw us."

"Us?"

"Us," she echoes, throwing a glance back toward the kitchen.

"You're back with Alex?" I offer. "That's fine. I knew it was on the cards. I've been there myself. On and off more times than a light switch. We've all—"

"Alex?" She recoils. "No way."

There's a moment of confusion before I make the connection. Her hesitancy, the guilt. A heaviness descends like rocks in my stomach. No.

"Tony?"

"He dropped by and I wanted to tell you before you found out. We've just started seeing each other again." She looks down, her tone gentle.

"What—?"

"Hey, sis," he calls from the kitchen in his crude singsong tone. I hear a cupboard door slam, the enthusiastic pop of another wine cork. Irritated, I wrap my towel tighter around me, dripping water on the floor, before locking my bedroom door.

I get dressed slowly, weighed down with a sense of foreboding. I felt the exact same way two years ago when they first met at my birthday party. There were twenty of us crammed around four tables in our local Turkish restaurant. The clatter of our voices bounced off the exposed brick walls and there was Tony and Amira sitting opposite me.

I tried to draw my gaze back to my friends, away from Amira's luminosity, her dark eyes and halo of curls. From Tony too, his usually pale skin tanned for once after teaching English for six months in Vietnam. He was supposed to be on the next leg of his journey, but he would never let me celebrate a birthday without him.

I had to admit there was something mesmerizing about the two of them, there always is when you see two relative strangers absorbed in one another, oblivious to everyone else in the room. Old friends nodded over at me with sly smiles and I shrugged, amused.

I was pleased for them, wasn't I? Why wouldn't I be? I tried to push away that old sensation, something slippery coiling in my chest. I love Tony, but I've never liked knowing about his affairs, nor him knowing about mine. It was better that way.

I think back to Dan, my last serious boyfriend, who I met on a press trip. Tony grew hostile toward him on my behalf when the relationship started to flounder. Over that final week, there had been vicious arguments between Dan and me, many of them Tony would have heard. He was staying over at the time after spending a month in Goa.

A month after Dan and I separated, I heard from an old friend that he'd recently come out of hospital after a serious bout of E. coli.

"He deserved it, didn't he?" Tony had said when I told him, giving me one of his strange wry smiles.

"Tony, nobody deserves a fortnight in hospital on an IV drip." I roll my eyes. "At one point they thought he'd need dialysis."

"Well, he shouldn't have been such a shit to my sister. I heard those things he called you. He needed a lesson."

"*Lesson?* Tony, what—"

He nodded, grinning. "He really should be careful where he leaves his toothbrush." He sniggers, delighted, letting the full force of it land.

"His toothbrush," I echo.

"I looked at it and thought, now, Tony, you're always up for a new experience. I wonder what it would feel like sticking that where the sun don't shine?"

"That's repulsive. He was seriously ill because of you. What the fuck?"

He shrugs. "Revenge. Come on, Anna, don't act so shocked. You're a master at that too," he fires back.

I was still cut up about Dan, but *that*? Bile rose in my throat. Growing up, Tony's appetite for practical jokes was tolerated by my mother as harmless signs of a restless, creative mind. Salt in my coffee, that sort of thing. Often she found these episodes amusing, the price you pay for an imagination, as she used to say to me. But this?

I considered telling Amira when it happened, but something stopped me, watching them so happy together. This was the reason for my initial foreboding, that a point would come when I would be implicated, blamed either for my silence or my honesty. So when I could tell Tony was growing bored with Amira, as I knew he would, I decided to step in to help them both.

Less than a month after my birthday, I invited Tony to a hotel launch in town, introduced him to Agatha, a fashion PR I had met through a recent interview. Her eyes were the palest sea green and the ends of her auburn hair were dip-dyed silvery blue. Tony told her, ever so charmingly, that she looked like a mermaid. Of course she did. That night I left them at the bar alone together, took a cab home early, and one thing led to another. If it wasn't her, it would have been someone else. I thought Amira had recovered, but clearly not, since here they were. Back together.

None of this is new to me down the years, the infidelities, the restless desire to seek the next conquest—Agatha, Amira, many others after them, the inability to commit. No different to him abandoning the first episode of a new Netflix show.

"Please spare me the details, save it for your newest therapist. You have major issues," I had replied, maybe a little too lightly.

"Everyone has issues, Anna. You of all people should know that."

A plume of steam rises as Amira sieves the rice. I help carry small dishes into the sitting room. There's lemon chicken and grilled halloumi, chickpea stew with crispy onions.

"What a feast, Am," says Tony, distracted, not really looking at the food at all. I sit down at the table, watch as he examines my desk, as if it's a crime scene dense in clues. Tony wasn't thrilled when I told him I'd been hired as a ghostwriter, but he'd tried to be supportive. I can see it's still an issue for him as he peers at my printer and its in-tray, where the top pages of my book contract lie. I meant to post it back to Priya yesterday. He picks them up and starts to read.

"Uh. Confidential, thank you." I swoop over to swipe them from his hand.

I notice how Amira's glances stray to him as he hovers at my desk.

"Does Nate know you took all these?" she asks.

"Of course." I swallow hard. "He saw me take one of them and was fine about it." The little white lies come to me more easily these days.

Tony nods, still staring at the photos. "I'm curious, is this normal for a ghostwriter?"

"It's called research. Immersing yourself in your subject.

Writing books demands that," I say, airily, aware of how pretentious I sound but riffing on it anyway. "You can spin so much around an image. There's a whole story in just one expression. You know that from your own work, don't you?"

He looks away, lets out a short contemptuous laugh. "Writing books? That's pushing it. You don't even get your name on it."

I open my mouth.

"What? I only meant you deserve better, Anna. A high-profile figure like him should credit you, at least."

I redden, angered, only because I've had the same thought. "Ghostwriting doesn't work like that."

"Doesn't it?" He lets the question hang as Amira walks over and they study a line of Post-its in yellow and orange that flutter on the wall above my desk. Below them is a small whiteboard on which I've felt-tipped two lines annotated with dates and details of their lives, one in green for Nate, the other red for Eva. They rise separately at first, meet and at their peak join together. After that, one dips sharply while the other carries on. It's a work in progress, still waiting to be fleshed out over the coming weeks. The undulating highs and lows of Eva's and Nate's lifelines.

"Come on, it's not that interesting. You're studying it like it's the Rosetta Stone."

"Poor old red line didn't stand a chance," he muses. "Still, getting to decide their fates must be fun."

"I'm mapping out the facts, not making it up. It's called a memoir," I remind him, frowning. "Apparently, they're based on true life?"

"I wouldn't bank on it if Dr. Reid's involved."

"Don't believe everything you read in the news."

"Don't believe everything he tells you."

"You two," Amira jumps in, infuriated.

Tony raises his hands in surrender. "Just playing around. She knows how proud I am of her, really."

He slopes away back to the table, holds up his empty glass for Amira to refill and asks about her day. She recounts another turbulent week at the magazine, a cover story pulled at the last minute, an actor threatening libel, the editor sacking a freelance picture editor who's six months pregnant. The usual dramas.

It's Tony's turn to talk about his week, a humblebrag very much for Amira's benefit, about the frustrations of preparing for his long-haul travel adventure next month: the visa queues, the reactions to various vaccinations, the malaria tablets that always make him queasy.

As he rakes through the remains of his rice, I catch a glimpse of the tattoo he got in Shanghai last Christmas. Four Chinese characters rising up his inner arm in blue ink. The tan is fading but Tony's other mementos endure, the leather bracelet wound around one wrist, the outsized jade gemstone on his middle finger, global traveler's code for spirituality and enlightenment.

He takes out a pouch of tobacco, rolls a cigarette. His fingertips brush Amira's arm for a second when he asks if she'd like him to roll her one. When he inhales, he tilts his head back and I watch as her eyes light up. I look down, shiver imperceptibly.

"You okay, Anna?" Amira looks at me.

"Just tired," I say, affecting to stifle a yawn. "Long day."

She picks up on my expression. "Of course. I meant to ask. Your first day ghostwriting."

"It was…interesting." I tell them vaguely about reading Nate's notes, breaking the news to him that his material wasn't working.

"So Dr. Pain's a terrible writer. No surprises there," quips Tony.

"It's all fine," I say and shrug. "He got the message surprisingly quickly actually. We're starting over on Monday, and I know I can get something good from him."

Tony and Amira exchange a look I can't work out and conversation circles back again to Tony's travels. His itinerary, his plans. Amira flatters him, and by the time we finish with more wine, he's scrolling for an Uber to take him back to North London where he's staying with an old friend for a few days. We stand up to say our goodbyes, but it's Amira who sees him to the door.

"So?" says Amira, walking back into the sitting room, a lopsided grin fixed to her face. "Why are you being so weird?"

"Weird?"

"About me and Tony." She kicks off her shoes, falls onto the sofa. "I saw you looking at us all evening."

I turn around and catch her looking at me as she sits down, hugging her knees to her chest. She looks beautiful this evening, her velvety teal top slipping from one shoulder, dark ringlets shimmering with gold highlights.

"I guess I worry about you getting hurt again, that's all. I'm allowed to say that about my brother. I think you deserve so much more."

"What is it about that word with you and Tony? *Deserve.* I'm not that naive, and I can look after myself."

"It's just—I know him so much better than you. He's not—"

"I get what this is about, Anna," she jumps in. "It's okay if you feel a little jealous. Tony told me—"

I snort. "He told you what?"

"He told me earlier he's worried about you. That you've become a bit…protective of him, or possessive or something.

No big revelation, but he thinks this is a pattern of yours—"
She hesitates, scans my face. "He says that's why he's been trying to travel much more lately. To encourage you to have your
own life a bit more?"

"I'm the possessive one?" I let out a whoop of incredulous
laughter.

"I knew you'd take it the wrong—"

"I'm happy for you both. Is that what you want me to say?"
My voice rises and I register a tightening knot of rage inside
me, one that will burn through me as I lie awake into the
night playing Amira's words over and over.

"I'm just saying he cares so much about you, Anna, and so
do I. And you've been so consumed with the Reid case…"
She shakes her head, assessing me as she pours the last inch of
wine into her glass. She's reached that dangerous stage where
she's drunk enough to feel sober again, to believe her insights
are acutely perceptive. "You guys have such a unique bond, it's
natural, I guess because of what you've both been through."

"Such a unique bond," I echo, unable to catch her eye.

"I know how difficult it was after your father—" She stops
for a moment. "He says how you both share all this stuff together but you never really want to talk about it."

"You two really have talked a lot, haven't you?" I say, coolly,
slamming the dishwasher door shut, waiting for the comfort
of its familiar purr to distract me from her needling voice.

"You know you can always talk to me about it, if you want."

I close my eyes a moment, rattled. Down the chute of memory I slip and slide. The smell of burned toast in my father's
kitchen. The obscene scream of the smoke alarm, the electrical
storm that followed. Tony's face when I returned that night.
The secret that binds us together. How much was down to
Tony, how much was down to me?

The blankness in my father's eyes is what stays with me. The sight of Tony smashing the smoke alarm with a broom until a tangle of wires spilled out. The noise stopped but it was all too late by then. Did it really happen? I have spent so many years perfecting the art of unremembering, unknowing what I really know. My mind flits back to the moment.

"Tony and I have talked about our parents many times," I say, neutrally. "I don't know why he's telling you all this."

I crave distance from her and yet she inches closer, close enough for me to see the fine dark hairs on her folded arms, how rapidly she's breathing.

"Look, I'm seeing Tony again, and we're happy." Her eyelids flutter closed for a second, her words feel stiff and rehearsed. "I want it aboveboard and open. It's important for both of us that you're happy about it too?"

Why would they care what I think? All I really want to do is leave. "I'm so pleased for you, really." I fold my features into the semblance of a smile. "For both of you. Welcome back to our fucked-up family."

When she hugs me, I feel relief flow through her, her limbs melt, soft as liquid. Quite suddenly she is languid, washed out by all this drama. She sinks back onto the sofa while I wash up the last of the dishes. My fingertips feel their way to the bottom, over the rubble of glass stems and cutlery. I read recently the most common household accident is cutting yourself on an upturned blade below the bubbles. A simple act of negligence. Only yourself to blame.

# EVA'S SELF-REFLECTION JOURNAL

*25 February 2019*

*Me: "Can you tell me a little bit about what happened to you today?"*

*Patient X: "Well, I was in a cab coming home and I began to feel...strange."*

*Me: "In what way strange?"*

*Patient X: "Terrified, I guess, without knowing why. I couldn't get enough air into my lungs. All the muscles in my throat con-stricted and I struggled to swallow. Later that night I woke up gasping, lying in the darkness listening to my own breathing."*

*Calm until now, Patient X appears agitated, arms wrapped across their chest, foot tapping the floor. Evidently, the expe-rience is still making itself felt, a memory trapped physically.*

Me: "It sounds to me like a panic attack. Sufferers are over-whelmed for no apparent reason with many of the symptoms you describe. But sometimes it comes from a deeper source. Why now? Can you tell me a bit more about what happened that evening, before you had your first one?"

Patient X: "I'd been seeing someone for a few months. We started fighting. They told me they wanted to end it. No warn-ing. It was all over."

Me: "Did they let you know why?"

Patient X: "Just being me, I guess. I wasn't very—I mean, I struggle to be open, to be real with anyone, after everything I've been through."

# 12

*All About You*

In classical myth, Poena is the personification of pain, deriving from the Greek word πoιví, meaning *penalty*. Goddess of divine retribution, she is sent to punish mortals who angered the gods, and for centuries afterward physical suffering continued to be viewed as a penance for sin.

Ancient cultures placed their faith largely in magic and ritual, votive offerings, sacrificial animals and scapegoats sent off in the hope of driving pain out into the wilderness.

Early modern thinkers such as René Descartes, the seventeenth-century French philosopher, scientist and mathematician, were the first to consider pain in a different way. Descartes, in his *Treatise on Man*, theorized that pain originated in the brain, a revolutionary idea that suggested physical suffering wasn't inflicted by an omnipotent external force. This raised the radical possibility of individual agency, if pain was created internally, then surely it was within our own power to find a cure.

"So, I'm thinking we need a bit more of your early life in here," I say. "Childhood memories, your mom and dad, recollections that make you relatable, that sort of thing?"

Nate stretches across the sofa, hands interlaced behind his neck, and I sit in the armchair opposite, tapping away on my laptop as he talks. Over the last three weeks, we have settled into a familiar routine. It's an absorbing process, working out how best to navigate his moods. If my questions are too direct he can often withdraw, other times he is animated by our conversations, springing up to elaborate on a memory and pacing around the room.

Very quickly the memoir has become a kind of refuge for me, an excuse to avoid the heat of Tony and Amira's rekindled romance, their smug couple status. In the evenings I escape to my room to transcribe and write. Tony's possessions are scattered around the flat. His presence lingers, the smell of his aftershave in the bathroom, his moldy running shoes in the hallway next to mine.

When I enter a room, they spring apart like guilty teenagers. The nights are worse since Tony moved their bed away from the radiator. Now the headboard pushes up against my wall, a thin partition that divides the original room in two. Their lovemaking seeps into my unconscious. I wake frequently from variations of a recurring nightmare, the sound of plaster splitting and their faces pushing through cracks in the bedroom wall, fingers poking through the holes, clawing to get at me.

I try to avoid Tony in the mornings. I am a stranger in my own apartment, tiptoeing from bedroom to kitchen, a spook hazing at the margins of their life. Ironic, really, that I feel more visible here with Nate, where my role is to evaporate on the page.

"Well, let's see," says Nate, staring up at the ceiling for inspiration. "My dad was a maths lecturer, my mom a history academic. When I was around ten years old, she told me I was going to boarding school in Edinburgh."

He catches my quizzical expression.

"My dad had died suddenly and my mom felt it was a good thing to send me away." He shrugs. "I got a scholarship and my mom wanted me to get on with it, not just hang around. The day after he passed away, my two brothers and I went straight back to school as if nothing had happened. We didn't discuss it again. I buried myself in books. We've all moved on."

"I'm so sorry."

"Don't be." He looks at me. "It was decades ago now, there's nothing to be sorry about."

"It sounds like a tough start. Losing your father when you're young is—" I shake my head, wanting to say more, much more, but a text suddenly lights up my screen. Tony.

I'm meeting Amira at a hotel launch tonight for some free booze. Wondered if you wanted to come along too?

An invitation to play third wheel for the night, no chance. I swipe it away rather than reply but I can see Nate looking, noticing the time.

"Sorry," I say. "A work thing. Your childhood. You were saying?"

I feel caught out but he doesn't seem to notice. "I was about to say it didn't feel so tough, but looking back, well, I've recognized how the adults didn't know how to handle grief. You weren't expected to talk about any of that stuff."

I nod in unspoken agreement. "Maybe a good place to begin is what happened after you met Eva. You said in our interview that a colleague told you about her case, how did you make contact?"

"Yes. I'd begun a research project actively searching for

people with Eva's condition, congenital insensitivity to pain, and my colleague put us in touch. I wanted to find out which part of her brain was able to trigger those responses, shut down all those sensations." He sits up now. "It's always been a part of my research. Do you know how many painkillers we pop globally? Fourteen billion and that's per day. If we can pinpoint that master switch, we can create a completely different kind of painkiller."

"Hugely profitable, I imagine."

"I didn't mean that." He gives me a look. "I don't want to be the next Sackler family if that's what you're implying. It's about alleviating so much misery with an alternative that isn't necessarily addictive."

"So you called Eva?"

He nods. "We spoke for a few minutes. Being Eva, she was open, receptive to the ideas, my research. Instantly, she could see how helpful it could be for other people like her."

"Except that it couldn't really help *her*, could it?"

"Well, no. I was looking at how to control chronic pain, not help someone actually feel it. But there was always a chance that the research could throw up other possibilities too. It was a million to one I'd find someone like her. I'd never seen a case before, only read about them. Often, they die young, many before they reach thirty, usually due to some unforeseen accident. Only the ones that are diagnosed early learn how to live carefully by constantly assessing the physical risks around them. The tragedy is their lives are often more defined by pain than people like us who are born to feel it."

"Even so, Eva survived unscathed."

"That's what made her case exceptional. But she wasn't exactly oblivious about her condition even if she wasn't diagnosed. Eva knew how much her life depended on being super cautious, and yet her nature fought against it. She yearned for the freedom that she perceived in everyone around her. That's where I think her hedonistic streak came from, partying hard to feel something, anything, that was memorable. When she first came to the Rosen, she told me how at the age of ten she managed to bite off the tip of her tongue. It upset her that she could damage herself so badly yet not feel a thing."

"She opened up to you in that first meeting? Can you remember how she seemed, what she wore, the chemistry between the two of you?"

He looks disapproving, his expression catches between a frown and a smile. "I see what you're doing."

"Do you? I mean, I think we need a hint of the dynamic, a sense of what was going through your mind, how this meeting would change your life."

He looks at me for a second or two, deliberating. He exhales sharply. "Okay, I suppose I have to go there. When I first saw her, what did I really feel? I guess all I could think was, imagine *being* her. Imagine not being wired up to the universal alarm system we all have, that enslaves us in fear, in so many ways."

"But you're always telling me it's what keeps us alive. That people like Eva are terribly vulnerable, unlucky even."

"Rationally, yes. And yet. As Eva sat there in front of me, I felt that I'd never met anyone more free. She wasn't tied down like the rest of us. Despite her diagnosis, she was innately fearless. I admit I envied that about her." He picks at the side of his nail while I tap away at my keys. As confessions go, it is hardly revelatory, but with a bit of work it could be a nice chapter opener, how he felt himself letting go, lifted and inspired by this contagiously wild, carefree woman. Nate leans forward.

"Actually, scrub that." He swipes the air. "I don't want people thinking I envied my wife."

"You've only said you envy her ability to feel so free." I look up from my laptop. "That's very fallible, likable even."

He looks unsure.

"We're onto something here. Eva had that unique ability to provoke strong emotion in everyone around her. It's part of who she was. Let's at least leave it in for now and move back to you for a bit. It would be good to have a bit of context, an early memory of what drew you to your work in the first place, perhaps?"

This relaxes him, the possibility of recalling his earliest personal ambitions. It always does for successful men, who've never had to question their limitless vistas. He tells me how he was instantly captivated by a science book he found in a friend's house when he was fourteen years old—full of vivid photographs of dissections through each of the brain's hemispheres.

"This strange mass that you can fit in the palm of your hands," he said. "That it holds our dreams, our memories, everything it means to be us. That everything happening to us in any given moment is right there."

"You mean it was love at first sight," I suggest, tapping away.

"Love at first sight," he muses. "You could put it that way."

I begin to sketch out the opening paragraph. "Perfect. Which brings us back to Eva. Now let's go back to that first meeting again and how you really felt."

He sighs, and eventually says, "What I think you're referring to didn't happen straight away."

"And what do you think I'm really referring to?"

"Attraction?" He leans forward, eyes honed on me. "Have you ever stopped to wonder what's happening in your brain, when you meet someone attractive, I mean?"

"No, not exactly." I waver, feeling as if I'm caught in the crosshairs. "Is it relevant?"

He leans forward, pushing his fingers through his hair, and I catch myself studying him. The tendons on his forearms, the shape of his throat as he swallows.

"The nonconscious you is the powerhouse of every interaction, every reflex and desire, even sexual attraction. Crack that and you can control any aspect of human behavior. What I'm trying to say is I had no intention, no conscious attraction, toward Eva at all. She wasn't remotely my type. I'm not sure I'd usually have been drawn to someone so…out there."

"You'd usually go for someone a little more straitlaced?" I suppress a smile.

"Who knows? What interests me is how little conscious control we have over any of this." He whisks one hand in the air, talking quickly. "Any attraction we feel toward anyone. Our brain's circuitry makes up its own mind, there's very little we can do about it."

"I believe we always have a choice, in the end," I say with more conviction than I really feel.

"You're sure of that?"

There's an awkward pause as he watches me. "So, tell me about her. Conscious or unconscious, what was it about your attraction, not what the science books say." I smile. "Describe her a little bit."

"Well, there's her photograph." He nods toward it but I don't turn around.

"I'm not interested in her photo. I need your own words, your own impressions of her."

He looks lost somehow, his features shifting uneasily. I let him sit with his silence until muscles in his face start to relax a little. "When we finished the research project, when the newspapers got hold of the story about Eva, it was big. People wanted to interview her. This gorgeous-looking woman, a hugely talented artist who only realizes her skin is burning when she smells singed flesh. One tabloid described her as a… sexy mutant." His mouth twists.

"She must have hated that."

He nodded. "She was a serious sculptor but they had a sort of voyeuristic obsession in her condition. The truth is, as an artist she felt like a fraud."

"Really? Her work was hugely respected."

"Eva's idol was Frida Kahlo, an artist who struggled her whole life with chronic illness after her pelvis and spine were shattered in an accident. Eva felt pain was intrinsically connected with great art. If she couldn't suffer, how could she create? Maybe she had a point." He thinks for a moment. "Scratch gorgeous, by the way," he says, abruptly. "Sounds naff."

"But how did you feel when you looked at her? Protective, perhaps?"

He lets out a short brittle laugh.

"I couldn't have protected Eva if I'd tried. When the project finished, I took her out. We drank a bit, and in the end, it was me and her in this bar. Somehow, we got around to talking about our greatest fears, and I admitted after all my research, extreme pain was mine. That, and losing your mind. She was quite drunk by this point and rolled up one sleeve of her jumper. 'Your real fear should be not feeling anything at all,' she told me, showing me her arm from where she'd accidentally cut herself. The raised skin was like a silverfish trapped in scar tissue. I'll never forget the way she looked at me, her face suddenly stiff and serious. 'How funny you fear pain when all I can think of is new ways to find out what it really feels like.'"

The sound of Eva's voice echoes in my ears. I type away. "So do you think there were other ways she liked to hurt herself?" He blinks, frowns a little. "I could unpack the question more, but—"

"The kinky angle? I should have guessed."

"Readers would want to know," I add, quickly.

"Well, you can check my wardrobe, if you want. No whips in there," he says, his tone playfully indignant.

"I had to ask. But back to what you were saying, she eventually grew sick of people seeing her as superhuman?"

"The more the media reported on it, the more she shrank away from it. I guess I felt guilty because I had courted the publicity. But I told her that the research I was doing was a stepping stone, and once we found the part of her brain responsible for turning pain on and off, we could help her too. If we could switch it one way, why not the other?"

"Is that true?"

"It could be, but no one would really bother trying."

"Why not?"

"Well, who's going to fund research into curing a condition that affects less than twenty people a year? No point. Drug companies are only interested in chronic conditions that impacts millions of us. One-off treatments aren't profitable; a lifetime of medication is what they like best. A condition like Eva's? No chance. But I didn't spell that out to her back then."

"And that fact didn't really bother you?" I can't help wondering how much he viewed Eva as a necessary sacrifice, a guinea pig to help in the pain race that he hoped to win.

"I thought about it a lot," he says, sharply, looking up at me. "But I didn't want to hurt her. Never tell someone everything they want to hear, only what they can bear." He stops himself. "On second thought, I'm not sure I want that in either. None of it makes me sound good."

"You're not meant to sound good. Good is bland. This—"

I nod at my screen "—makes you sound authentic. You felt for her."

"Yes. I emailed her after that night. I was concerned, maybe guilty, that I hadn't been as helpful as I could. I mentioned a few colleagues she should make contact with who could offer advice. She got back to me and after that we began to email each other a lot. We wrote letters."

"Letters. Really? How romantic. Her idea, not yours, I'm guessing?"

"Obviously." He smiles.

"Well, maybe we should take our cue from that. A series of reflections, like the letters you used to write. As I see it, this memoir is a love story above all else. Wouldn't you say so?"

I begin to type. Rather than answer me, he turns his face away instead, and for the briefest moment I think I see him flinch.

*Chapter 1*

Two years ago, I lost you, in the most upsetting circum-stances. And ever since, somehow your story, our story, won't leave me alone. When I first read newspaper re-ports about the night you died, I thought this must be happening to someone else. I always assumed tragedy only happened to other people. Until it happened to me.

The only way to make any sense of those early days was to get it down in words. Of course, part of it was a vain hope of somehow writing you back into being; that as long as I tapped away, conjuring you up from the past, it brought you closer to me.

Naturally, as a neuroscientist, I am aware of the chal-lenges—how flawed memory can be, no more concrete than footprints in the sand. Yet putting thoughts down on paper offers a permanence that appeals to me. I have tried to be a reliable narrator. It is so easy to idealize the person we have lost, focus on their perfections and forget their flaws, but I believe placing you on a pedestal, which would be so easy, would really be a cage.

I hope I've avoided this and created something that is honest; the essence of you.

This, my love, is what drives me on. Wondering, what would you say now? How would you feel if I told it this way?

# 13

The morning sun glares a little too harshly as I head for Priya's office, Grayson Inc., a sleek tower built in a curve of the Thames. Her text yesterday was abrupt, unexpected. She wanted to meet again but didn't tell me why, although I suspect it's about the early chapters I emailed her.

It is one of those pellucid days you get in the winter when the air is crystalline, the sky cloudless and sheer. Sharp light cuts across the river like a blade. My eyes ache. It's as if I have evolved to exist only in the crepuscular gloom of Nate's basement study, a liminal space where I'm able to keep the glare of the real world at bay.

Each day I sense Nate is a little more relaxed in my company, a little more confessional, exposing his more closely held thoughts. Yet on a relisten of our interviews, his responses are still somehow evading detail, so I'm forced to fill in the gaps. It's not that I'm making up quotes exactly, but scattering subtle reflection here and there to bring Nate and Eva alive. I convince myself that memoir is the art of persuasion, a magic act of smoke and mirrors, and, really, isn't that all I'm attempting? Now that his voice has almost become second nature to me, it only takes the subtlest of twists to make him sound more revelatory. I'm doing him a favor, helping him to be a better version of himself in print. But massaging can only get you so far, and the text from Priya gnaws at me.

I take up the elevator to the top floor and catch my reflection in the mirrored doors as they close, the crispness of my outline is reassuring. I've erased myself to such a degree in recent weeks I half expect to see a me-shaped hole where I used to be. The elevator shoots up through the bright light, London spread out extravagantly below me. The doors open and there is Priya's assistant waiting to take me to her corner office.

Priya doesn't look up or acknowledge me when I'm shown in. Elbows on desk, palms over her ears, she carries on flipping through the pages of a manuscript.

"Gripping read?" I blurt, instantly mortified by my tone. I sit down opposite her and she glances up at me, unsmiling.

"Yes, but it's not yours."

She retrieves mine from a pile, lets her hand rest on the opening chapter. Her voice is thin, stripped of the faux interest and sparkle that infused our last chat when Nate was with her. She appraises me properly, a small tight smile coiled on her lips. "So. Anna. How long has this taken so far?"

"Four weeks?" My tone falters.

"And how quickly could you finish by if, say, we needed you to cut all of this?"

I stare at the illegible scrawl of her upside-down notes, take a moment or two to digest what she's telling me. This is how Nate must have felt when he saw my criticisms.

"Sorry, you mean start again?"

"Yes, Anna, exactly what I mean."

Her eyes are stony. Only someone more senior than you gets to repeat your name twice in the first five minutes, and it's never a good sign.

"I thought it was along the lines we talked about. I thought—"

"It is nowhere near what we're looking for."

She sighs, leans a little closer to me across the desk. The room suddenly feels smaller. Her large tortoiseshell reading glasses magnify her stare. I want to look away but I can't.

"Oh," is all I can manage.

The first dizzy vertiginous stab of disappointment hits me in the solar plexus. Something inside me starts to crumble. I had entertained the thought of praise, perhaps constructive criticism, but not downright scorn. Her head dips down like a delicate bird as she flits through the pages, immaculate mani-cured fingers alight upon one page after another.

"Where's the brutally honest edge we talked about in our interview? The blood on the page? The forensic detail rather than the broad strokes?"

"But I thought it was all there, all covered—" I stammer.

She regards me for a moment. Her liquid brown eyes soften. "This is perfectly normal, Anna. It's a process. You have to write the wrong thing so I know what I don't want. It can be frustrating but I'm afraid that's how I work." She inclines her head, as if to apologize for such an adorably quirky streak. I glance down toward the river outside her window, the color of oily black tar. A tugboat no bigger than a single dot from up here draws through the water, vanishes under the bridge.

"I know how difficult he can be," she says. "I know what you're up against. He needs boundaries. But we need less about his research. We need him to be more expressive, to open up about the pain he's been through, the pressure of his career, feeling under suspicion after she died."

"It's not that easy," I say. "He closes down those conversa-tions pretty swiftly. So much so I'm starting to wonder why."

"You think he's got something to hide?"

"Whatever happened is private and personal, and I don't think he wants the world to know about it." I glance up at her shelves and scan some of the author names, mainly female, who have spilled their messy lives across the page. Addiction, abuse, bulimia, self-harm, guilt and shame. Priya's favorite ingredients. She's probably thinking right now about the ghost-writers that she should have chosen instead of me, that could have done a better job. She looks almost sorry for me.

"You'll get there, but we need more about Eva. She is the draw."

"I think Nate's worry is it could be too prurient, a bit low-rent maybe?" I pause. "Maybe if I were to get other voices who could share a little more about Eva, it would help. Like Kath, for example?"

"Kath simply can't be interviewed. She's off-limits for this book, given the recent inquest stunt she pulled. And remember, Anna, it's not prurience, but a responsibility to go there. We can't afford for Nate to turn a blind eye to Eva's story, she deserves our undivided attention."

I give a small sigh. "The first time I asked him about Eva's death, he got really upset, angry even. He pushed a chair onto the floor and stormed out."

"The infamous Nate temper," she says dryly. I suppose that confirms my suspicion that his outburst wasn't a one-off at all, despite his insistence.

"I know how Nate can be," she says. "But it's all bluster. You shouldn't be intimidated by him."

"I didn't say I was."

Priya's phone pings. I watch her manicured nails tap on a message alert. "Talk of the devil. I told him you and I were meeting, he knows there's something up. He wants to chat after we finish." She studies the text for a second, shrugs. "I'm not going to tell him what we've talked about. It's up to you how you play it. So, we're good?"

Slowly, I nod, give her a thin smile.

"Just don't be soft on him."

She returns my smile, clearly keen to tick this off her to-do list. What assumptions has she already made about me? That I shy away from confrontation, I'm too easily won over? Is it something she's discussed with Nate? I get the feeling they talk about everything, including me.

She tilts her head, a hesitant smile hovers on her lips. "You know, Nate originally wanted to work on his memoir with me. Of course, apart from the fact that I'm too busy publishing other people's memoirs, I felt he needed someone with more objectivity, someone who is new to the whole…situation." She pauses meaningfully.

"Less…involved?" I offer.

She removes her glasses, a strand or two of her sleek bob falls across her face, and really looks at me.

"Just stick to the task in hand, Anna. If you can." She shoots me a pointed look. "But, in the meantime, can't you be, I don't know, a bit more imaginative? Take him away from the house. Change it up a bit."

I think of Nate pacing up and down that study, both of us trapped in that windowless cell day after day. Her phone vibrates and I can tell from her expression that it's Nate. I shift uncomfortably. She slides her phone across her ear.

"Hey," she says. Her tone shifts, soft and girlish. She raises her palm to me. I'm excused. The razor-sharp line of her hair swings a little as she swivels her chair around. A hoot of laughter follows me as I leave the office.

Questions flood my mind. If Kath and Nate were really aligned on the inquest, why would she be off-limits for the book? And why would she admit that Nate wanted her to work on his memoir? Perhaps it's a way of letting me know how disposable I am if I don't give her what she wants. I was chosen, supposedly for my objectivity, my distance.

She's right about one thing. A different context couldn't do any harm. I can't help thinking that, freed from the confines of his study, the rising tension between us may dissolve. I remember reading about Romney Marsh in one of Eva's profiles, a desolate stretch of coast where she spent many childhood summers in her aunt's clapboard house.

Her words circle as I push open the door to the toilets on the ground floor, open my knapsack and remove my spiky ankle boots. I replace them with some squashy running shoes and wrestle a shapeless black hoodie over my silk blouse. Almost there, except for one detail. I wipe away the scarlet gloss from my lips and draw my hair back into an austere ponytail. Suitably erased, I head home. On my way to the subway, I text Nate.

Hello! Thinking instead of meeting tomorrow as planned, how about getting out of the city for some inspiration?

Nate typing…

Sure, Priya mentioned a Plan B, I think good idea

Nate typing…

Let me know where you decide to take me

I think I already have

I open my communal front door. Old cigarettes, fried food and a floral note of cheap carpet cleaner cling to the air, the universal aroma of every shared hall I've ever lived in. My keys fumble in the lock and I let myself into my own apartment. The sitting room is deserted but the air is still warm and musky. There is an empty bottle of wine next to the sofa, somewhere else in the apartment I can hear talking. From Amira's bedroom, I'm guessing.

I pick up her and Tony's plates and glasses, wander into the kitchen and try to think how I can avoid them. Clearly, he's put his travel plans on hold now they're back together. I make myself some toast, creep to my bedroom.

Grateful to be alone at last, I lie back on my bed and take out my iPad in the one small space that counts as mine. So much for the brief respite from Tony and Amira. Nate and Priya. Their names circle.

Absentmindedly I google them. Priya's recent announcement pops up first and I scan it. "There's such a big appetite among the reading public for eloquent books that investigate grief, and this one won't disappoint. I've known Nate for so many years, I'm thrilled to be working with him on his memoir," she announced to *The Bookseller* a month ago.

I google her again but nothing interesting surfaces. I try Eva and Priya instead. And up it comes. A much older entry of both of them at one of her sculpture shows. I pinch the screen to expand the image. They look young, barely in their twenties, presumably long before Nate and Eva were an item. Priya's hair is longer, wilder.

A shadow of a smile plays on Eva's lips. Their heads touch, arms around one another.

How much does she really know about what happened to Eva? Why hasn't she mentioned their connection to each other? I close my screen, shut my eyes, as their names swirl through my mind, Priya and Eva, Nate and Priya, a set of dots that refuse to connect.

# EVA'S SELF-REFLECTION JOURNAL

*5 March 2019*

*Me: "Do you ever talk about your anxiety with anyone?"*

*Patient X: "God no. Speaking to you like this, it feels like a huge step. Like nothing I've done before."*

*Patient X holds my gaze and I try to break eye contact but there is something in their expression that is so eager to engage, to acknowledge me, that I find it difficult to look away. In these early sessions I think it is crucial to build on that trust. I'm mindful of a new feeling right now, of wanting to really step into someone else's pain with them rather than experience it only within myself. Finally. I'm not as egocentric as I thought, ha. What a relief to help, to feel seen and appreciated for more than just my own condition.*

*Me: "That's so good to hear. I want you to know I'm here*

*for you, witnessing, hearing all these experiences you've been through."*

*We sit for a moment in quiet reflection, smiling at one another until Patient X breaks the thoughtful silence.*

*"I've been having nightmares. You see there's something that's been nagging at me lately, a sort of secret that's been weighing me down."*

*"That must be psychologically tough for you. The feeling of keeping a secret can often be so much worse than the content itself."*

*Patient X nods in recognition. "It's just I'm very afraid of the person who could expose it, expose me."*

*Me: "You mean they're using the secret to…blackmail, or control you in some way?"*

*Patient X hesitates: "I think that maybe it would be so helpful if I could talk to you more than once a week?"*

*I sense Patient X is on the verge of a breakthrough here. I know how significant it is to feel understood by a therapist, how transformational it can be, so of course I agree.*

# 14

A few days later, on the dot of 10:00 a.m., I hear two beeps outside my apartment. I hurry downstairs and out to the street, duck into the passenger seat of the sleek black 4x4. The harsh slam of the door jars with the lush silence inside. Nate's car purrs into motion as I wrestle off my jacket and throw it across the back seat.

"So, destination Dungeness it is," he says decisively, punching some digits into the satnav, and I watch the contours of the map swirl into life. "We should be at the coast in time for lunch."

Rain slakes the windows as the windshield wipers pound into action. He drives slowly, tailing the other cars in the rain and, as we head out across the river, the weather unexpectedly begins to lift. There is something strangely soporific about sitting here with him, watching the asphalt landscape flash past, empty office blocks and ghostly retail parks, flyovers, rows of pebbledash semis trapped on the edges of the divided highway.

"So how did your meeting with Priya go?"

"Kind of fine," I say, more as a question than a statement.

He glances across at me and we exchange a smile. "So she gave you the third degree?"

"Yep. You could say that. She suggested a change of scenery for a reason."

"Don't tell me, she thought it would be a good way to get me to open up about myself, let go a little?"

"You know her only too well."

"I know she likes to think she can read people better than they can read themselves."

"And can she?"

"She couldn't read you at all." He shakes his head. "You've probably worked out I was the one who wanted to hire you. She took some persuasion."

"She made that pretty clear in the interview."

"It wasn't really a personal thing, but she wanted someone older, preferably male," he says, throwing me a look.

"I gathered. Has she always been like that?"

"Kind of." He shrugs. "She and Eva met at college. They'd known each other for a while by the time I came along. She could be...possessive around Eva. But since she died, it's shifted." He shrugs. "Maybe it's grief; she's latching onto me to remember her. We talk about Eva a lot but sometimes, somehow—well. It's all complicated. I'm probably not explaining it very well. This is all new, talking about my life, my marriage, none of it is easy for someone like me."

"Well, we can take it slowly, don't worry," I say lightly, not wanting to frighten him off now that he's revealing a more vulnerable side.

We have exited the highway now and the narrow lanes are like lush corridors of green, a soft haze of sun filters through the clouds. Nate turns down a small lane with an expanse of horizon before us and I open my window, the saline tang of the sea drifting in. He parks on the roadside and we walk up the shingle toward the shoreline. I look up at the sky like a great glass dome and feel caught under its curves.

Sea kale, samphire and bramble bushes spread low along the ground and curl up between the rocks, giving it an edge-of-the-landscape feel. It's a wonder anything can grow at all but it does. Red poppies and yellow broom dot the shingle. I meander for a moment, enjoying the view. He strides ahead of me, past a scattering of beach houses, cubes of corrugated wood and mirrored windows. A derelict fishing boat lies stranded on the shingle near the tideline, its cabin windows smashed in.

Black telegraph poles line the path, outlined against a dust-colored sky. It's more arid desert than beach: a chunk of Arizona on the Kent coast.

Nate's figure shrinks to a black comma and, watching him from this distance, I'm aware how strange it feels being here with him in this setting, beyond the professional familiarity of his study. He turns and waits for me to catch up. Behind him the ocean is oily and muscular, shifting below the horizon. On the shoreline we stand a little apart, watch as the wind drops and a low watery sun turns the sea from dirt-brown to metallic-blue.

"When was the last time you came here?"

"A few weeks before she died." There is a stillness in the way he says it, a resigned emptiness. "In fact, the last weekend away we ever spent with each other was in a small cottage just down the coast. We meant to come back but I couldn't. I'd hurt my back quite badly, slipped disc," he says, grimacing at the memory.

"So that's where the fentanyl came from?" I say, thinking of my discovery that afternoon, the blister pack of pills in his glasses case.

"You did do your research that day, didn't you?" He looks at me wryly, smiling for the first time today. "Thank God for opioids—but don't quote me on that. Anyway, we never did come back here."

"If I'd known, I'm not sure I'd have suggested here." Though, I wondered, was this really true?

"Don't look so worried. I'm fine talking about it here. It seems different somehow." He covers his eyes from the bright sunlight, frowns into the wind. "It feels easier. At home, it's as if she's—"

"There—all around you?"

He turns to look at me.

"All the time. I mean not in a bad way, but she created that house and her studio; she's kind of everywhere. Sometimes I wonder if it would be healthier if I sold up, moved on." He bends down to pick up a stone, skims it across the waves.

"A break from the past?"

"It's not that easy, I know, but maybe I should give it a go. Somewhere different, a new start."

"Really? I can't imagine that somehow," I say, feeling a brief twinge of something I'm reluctant to define. It feels mainly like regret, that such a beautiful place will fall into a stranger's hands, that very soon it will no longer be mine to wander around; all those rooms, her studio, Eva's history still accessible to me— and still largely untapped.

He studies my expression. "It's something I've only really started thinking about recently. Maybe it's delving around in the past for this book. I can see how stuck I've got rattling around in that place. It's not as if she was that keen on it anyway."

"Wasn't she? I thought she adored it."

"She hated London by the end. She was desperate to get out. She tried to convince me that we should sell up and move here."

"Here? That doesn't seem very her at all."

He looks at me oddly, the veil returning.

"But you don't know what she was like. Not really. She

was restless, impatient, completely unsentimental. She loved designing the house and the studio but once it was done, that was it. She wanted to move on."

"And did you say yes to coming down here?"

"I didn't want to, we argued about it. A lot."

"Who won?"

"I'm sure she did, in the end, but I forget the exact details," he says, vaguely. "I forget a lot these days. But maybe that's for the best. What a curse to remember everything."

"Well, try not to forget too much." My hand closes around the recorder in my pocket. "We've got work to do."

"Okay, come on then." He turns abruptly toward the headland. "I'm ready for the full inquisition, but not on an empty stomach."

The Metropole is a faded movie star of a hotel that clings to the headland, staring dreamily out to sea. Rumor has it that a Hollywood gossip columnist fell in love with this part of the coast in the '30s, commissioning an architect to design it; a relic of American Art Deco washed up on a bleak English shore.

We sit in the curvilinear dining room, complete with wrap-around glass-and-mirror ball. I find myself loving the element of faded glamour to it all. As a milky light sparkles off the sea through the blistered Crittall windows, I can half imagine Fred and Ginger tap-dancing their way across the chipped parquet floor. I glance out the window and notice the tide edging its way up the shoreline, consuming the shingle as if we're out at sea.

"So," he says, after our drinks arrive. "I think I owe you an explanation."

"Really?" I say as he pours us each a glass of wine.

"Yes. For being a bit touchy when you were commenting on my notes. And for not being straight with you about a lot of things. I know it can't be easy for you...putting up with me and now Priya." He tapers off. "It's going to be different."

"Good." I take out my recorder, placing it between us. The waitress arrives with our food. My tagliatelle, swimming in a pool of buttery cream, seems absurdly oversized and I realize I've lost my appetite.

"Wait." His hand reaches across the table for the recorder at the same time as I do, his fingers grazing mine. He presses Pause, moves it to the edge of the table.

"Sorry, I didn't mean to... Come on, let's eat first."

"Anything to postpone the pain?"

Nate smiles, picking up his fork. "So what about you?"

"Er, what about me?"

He pushes his plate a little to one side, leans forward. "Come on. Regale me with a few details about the fascinating life of Anna, ruthless journalist-turned-legendary ghostwriter."

I say nothing and he tilts his head, expectant.

"C'mon. You never give anything away: who you live with, even how you spend your time outside work. You can't blame me for wondering?"

I sigh, put down my fork. "I thought you were desperate for lunch, no questions on an empty stomach?"

"I meant your questions, not mine." He smiles, picking up his wineglass and ignoring his unfinished chicken. "Besides, I'm easily distracted, you should know that by now."

"Well, I'm sorry to disappoint you. There's not much to say, really." My voice sounds hollow.

"I get it. You need to be neutral, unknowable, a blank can-vas. I respect that...but I haven't forgotten our first interview for the book, how you couldn't escape the conversation quickly enough when I tried to analyze you."

"I'm the interviewer. What sort of ghostwriter would I be if I started telling you everything about my awful childhood or my boring job."

"And why *was* it so awful?"

"Stop it."

"You see, there you go again. That hostile glare you throw out when I'm onto something."

"Something like that," I say. My fingertips grip my thigh, nails jab a little deeper, the shot of pain quickening my resolve. I catch the waitress's eye and ask for a black coffee.

"You know, I once did a peer-reviewed paper on the neuroscience of what we choose not to tell others, how our brain chemistry suffers when we hang on too long to our secrets, even the ones we deem most trivial. Which, I suspect by your behavior, yours are not. It's in the *Annual Review of Neuroscience*. You should look it up sometime."

"Oh, I'll definitely do that."

"Anna, it's not good for you. The stress of holding on to stuff completely rewires our minds, pushes our amygdala into overdrive, not to mention—"

"Rubbish," I say, more emphatically than I intended. "My amygdala is just fine."

"Okay. But would it hurt to open up a little?" he says. "How about you tell me something about yourself, and in exchange, I'll tell you something too?"

"The price I'll pay for getting back to work?" I quip.

"Sure." He smiles and I think briefly of my life beyond Algos House, a world that I can never truly share with anyone. Sometimes I picture my past, as a spiky fortress that I am forced to guard, forever wary. I have built my walls high, manning my borders and patrolling them well, and for good reason. Sometimes I yearn for the lightness that sharing would bring, that others take for granted; intimacy, connection. But I don't have that luxury. Disclosure can only ever be a game to me, and maybe Nate knows this too.

"Sure, why not? Ask me something."

He inclines his head, quizzical. "So who's the guy who keeps texting you all the time?"

I open my mouth in surprise.

"We sit next to each other every day. I'm not that unobservant."

"Fair enough. Well, he's my brother. Tony. He travels a lot and when he's back, he wants to see me. Hence the texting."

"Ah, *Tony*. Tony Tate?"

"That's his official name on his passport and stuff. But he prefers using his father's surname, Thorpe… He's my half brother."

He looks up from his plate. "Half brother," he repeats quietly, absorbing this for a moment, as if trying the word out for size.

"Anything the matter?"

"Nothing, nothing at all. I used to think he can't be a very nice boyfriend, judging by your reaction when he texted. You always looked…upset."

I manage a small laugh. "It's not so bad. I'm all Tony's got, really, in terms of family. He makes things difficult, I'll admit, especially financially. I'm helping him out a bit right now. To be honest, I'll be relieved when he goes away again."

"I kind of got the impression things weren't easy, whoever it was."

"I don't know, are things ever easy with family?"

"Quite. Thanks for sharing, Anna," he says and I smile, relieved that I got away relatively lightly. Is it purely coincidence that my professional life has been spent chasing other people's secrets while I'm always on the run from my own? In the end, you only come back to the beginning.

But no more. It's time for the real work to begin.

"Quid pro quo," I fire back. "Your turn now. That's the deal."

# 15

"Don't worry. Take your time."

I glance down at his hands interlaced on the table and the slim gold band gleaming on his wedding finger. As I look, he reflexively touches it with his other hand, his fingers sliding it up and down, an imperceptible shift in mood.

"Everything okay?"

He swallows hard, arms crossed tight around his chest. "Sure, I guess, but before we get into all this, I've been thinking."

He hesitates, pausing as a waitress approaches us. We sit in a moment or two of insufferable silence while she removes our unfinished plates, glacially circling our table. As she finally walks away, Nate starts again.

"I can see it's been a bit of a battle for you, trying to get to the bottom of the story. I know how I can come across. It seems to me we've probably got a bit more in common than we thought."

"I somehow doubt that," I say, dryly.

"I meant we're inquisitive but too good, perhaps, at deflecting personal questions. Both of us have different reasons. I have theories about yours—"

"I've just told you all there is to say," I cut through impatiently. "And what's *your* reason?"

Silence. He looks unconvinced, but then lets out a longer sigh. "It absolutely can't go in the book, or anywhere."

"Of course, I've signed the NDA form. Whatever you say is completely confidential."

"There's no way you can record any of this. For Eva's sake. You do understand, don't you?"

I pick up my recorder sitting between us, slide it across to him. He checks it's switched off and passes it back toward me.

"No one has to know about whatever you and Eva are hiding, but you *need* to tell me what really happened, even if it's only to know how we're going to conceal it." My voice has fallen to a whisper.

He glances down at his hands. "Our marriage was complicated."

"As most marriages are."

"Ours more than most, I think."

I look at him in silence, willing him to say more.

"Eva and I were so different. It was a case of opposites attract, you could say. She was open...to all sorts of things when we first met, sexually, recreationally. Drugs, well, cocaine. I'm not sure exactly how often she took it. It was a social thing, mainly, but it contributed to our growing arguments."

"You knew about it? At the inquest you denied you knew anything."

"I needed to protect her. I was her husband. Kath was convinced her sister wasn't a regular drug user and I wanted to support her. I'd told Eva many times she was mad to take it, that her mom had died of a heart attack in her fifties; there was a history of heart disease in her family. But she told me I was making a fuss. What's the harm in a line or two, she would say. What could I do?" He shrugs. "But it wasn't just drug-taking. The fact is...she was seeing someone else."

I blink, taking this in. *You little fool. Of course, it was an affair.*

"Nate, I'm so sorry. I had no idea."

"No? You, the journalist who can read everyone?"

"Well, perhaps not everything. Anyway, you can never really understand any marriage unless you're inside it and even then... But are you sure?"

"No doubt at all, I know she was." He lets out a short bitter laugh, gives me a shattered look. It's difficult not to feel sorry for him. His love for her etched in his crushed expression. My empathy lay with Eva for so long, but now I'm not so sure.

"It must have been hard for you to carry all that alone. Does Priya know?"

An uneasy silence falls between us.

"Priya," I repeat slowly, and as I do, I think of that picture, the rage that passed across his features when he caught me in Eva's study. "She took that photo, didn't she?"

He nods. "They were always close friends, and for a long time, I never suspected anything..."

"And she knows you knew about them?"

"No, she'd be horrified if I knew," he says quickly. "It's our secret, Anna, you understand that? It can never be part of the memoir we create."

*Create.* That word snags on me briefly, but I let it go, in favor of the other word: *we.* I nod, but I still feel there's something he isn't telling me.

"Of course. Can I ask, how did you find out?"

"How everyone finds out: by accident. If you believe in accidents."

"You think she wanted you to discover them?"

"At some level, yes. I believe anyone who has an affair always does. It's a catalyst. So they can be forgiven or punished or released, or whatever it is they're really searching for. But it wasn't the affair that upset me most. That was only one part of what I discovered that day," he says darkly, before we're interrupted by his phone. It vibrates, lights up with a message, and he glances at it. For a moment I'm afraid I'm losing him.

"You can tell me, Nate," I press. He looks at me uncertainly, lost for words.

"What happened?"

"One afternoon I came home without telling her. Never a good idea. I'd been preparing a lecture I was really excited about, the results of a breakthrough we'd made in identifying a particular gene, SCN9A. An hour or two before I was supposed to leave, I realized I had the wrong notes. Somehow, I'd printed out an old version and forgotten to pick up the new one stored on my home computer. I called Eva to email them to me but she didn't answer. So I rushed back."

"And found them together?"

"Worse than that. I think that would have been easier somehow. After I found my papers, I went to the bathroom before leaving the house. And that's when I saw it, on the surface next to the basin."

He pauses, takes another breath.

"I thought it was a thermometer at first, lying there on its side, until I turned it over. There it was. That miracle hormone HCG."

"HCG," I repeat. "Pregnant."

He nods, his features strained. "The thin blue line in all its glory. It was pretty miraculous, given that we barely had sex that year. By the end I felt as if we inhabited two separate islands with no way to row back. Instead, we left the gap open for someone else to walk in, another reason I can't help but blame myself for her affair with Priya." He shakes his head. "But then finding this…"

"The pregnancy test," I press on. "What was the problem, you didn't want to have a baby?"

"To the contrary. I was thrilled when I saw it. I was ready to be a father. I thought, here is this miracle that could bring us back together after years of drifting apart. Naively I assumed she might feel the same way. But as soon as I saw her expression later when I confronted her about it, I knew something was horribly wrong. She froze."

"And?"

"She told me, very calmly, that she didn't want to have this baby, that she didn't want to raise a child with CIP, for its sake as well as ours, knowing the mortality risks involved. We both knew the chance of inheriting her condition was fifty percent. I suggested genetic testing, reminded her that this was an opportunity, but she'd made up her mind.

"She had planned to keep the whole thing a secret from me. I tried to persuade her. I said I'd be willing to take a sabbatical, go part-time, whatever it would take to make it easier for her. She gave me this look, a sort of, 'you just don't get it, do you?' expression. I was upset, dumbfounded. Then she said there was something else she wanted to tell me."

"About Priya?" The photo of her flashes brightly in my mind, their arms sloped around each other.

He stares out across the dining room. "I was angry, of course, at the deception and infidelity. But then something else, something I didn't expect. Relief, maybe?"

"Why is that? Unless…you were having an affair too?"

"Honestly, I think it felt like something had lifted, that suddenly it wasn't my fault it had all gone so hopelessly wrong. Now I was absolved. In the end that's all that marriage boils down to, blame. What you can avoid, what you can stick on the other person. She blamed her affair on me. I remember her saying, 'Any wife would do the same. I sit in trainee sessions listening to client problems and I think, if only you knew. I'm the one who needs therapy. Someone to help me understand my fucked-up work-obsessed husband.'" Nate recoils, looking pale and weary in the gray light.

"As she tossed the pregnancy test in the kitchen bin, she told me her plan. She would have an early termination. She was on her way to qualifying as a psychotherapist and had a big sculpture show coming up. And here I was, on the verge of publishing my paper about the real possibility of a pain-free existence—ironic, given the circumstances." He lets out a hollow laugh. "And so many findings were based on her. I remember her shouting at me, 'The most interesting thing about you will always be me.' She was right. Without Eva, there was no pain research. No publicity, no world interest. We agreed to carry on, that I would support her decision to terminate her pregnancy, there would be no children."

"And none of this came out at the inquest?"

He scans my face, seeing the doubt reflected there. "I didn't say anything because I wanted to protect her. I didn't tell a soul about the affair or the pregnancy. If I'd said something, the press would have had a field day. I couldn't bear that."

"You didn't feel uneasy, holding back that information from the police?"

"There was no reason to tell them by then." His face is riven with fresh anxiety. "Perhaps I've told you too much. I should have—"

"No, I had to know. I won't tell anyone, and none of it needs to go in the book. But, Nate…do you ever talk about it with her? Priya?"

"Never. Priya adored her, she was devastated when Eva died. I think that's why she's so obsessed with this memoir, desperate to get it published. I guess it's her way of closure, to set the record straight."

"And what about you and Priya? You're not…"

"Never, no. I promise you it was only ever really about Eva. I was mad about her." He touches his hand to his chest, reminiscing. "But in the end, her compulsion to seek out new experiences made me feel I wasn't exactly the novelty she was looking for."

Not for the first time I wonder if there was a strange codependency at the heart of their marriage. Her self-destructive flaws were the key to him being the perfect scientist, to be seen to be caring for her while using her to find a cure for pain. I suspect that unconsciously he didn't want it any other way.

"So why did you do it?" I ask. "Why did you say yes to the book, why continue to work with your wife's ex-lover, knowing all this, that it's all so—complicated, such a mess?"

"I owe Grayson another book. And as I say, it was Priya's idea, not mine. But lately I'm not sure it's worth a book contract, or that I can preserve Eva's legacy." He gives me a wistful look. "What can be gained by constantly raking through the past? Who's it really serving?"

*You*, I want to say, but something holds me back. Maybe the nagging sense that what he's told me still doesn't make sense, it doesn't quite fit. Something about the time frame…

"Sorry, Nate, where did you say this lecture was?"

"At the Rosen."

"Okay, and when did it happen, I mean, how long before she died?"

Nate looks down, frowns with the effort of remembering. "I guess it must have been March. That's when I was working on that particular paper, so three months before she died."

"Three months," I echo. "You're sure?"

"Yes, completely sure."

"So, you're telling me that after the day you discovered she was pregnant, you made up and life returned to normal?"

He hesitates. "*Normal* isn't the word I'd use. True to her word, she had an early termination and I supported her through that. It wasn't easy but we made a go of it. We had always been a team of sorts, but maybe just not a very romantic one. We needed each other. Everyone loved her at the clinic fundraisers. My reputation as a neuroscientist would help her in the psychotherapy field. We worked as the golden career couple."

He sits back, folds his arms, waiting for my reaction.

"It sounds so cold, so transactional."

He shakes his head, looks down.

"Look, I realize I wasn't exactly a sympathetic ear for her. I was wrapped up in my research, not thinking about the emotional toll of her condition. It must have tortured her, feeling she couldn't have children because of the genetic risks. I was in my own denial." He shakes his head. "I'll always have to live with that."

I don't say anything for a moment, glance up at the couple sitting next to us who are about to leave. One of the waitresses is cleaning the glasses, there's the solid clunk of cutlery as she circles each table, laying them for supper.

Something dark flares inside me, a deep unease. Is this guilt all truly genuine? He's still evasive about Priya's affair with Eva, notably lacking in detail. There's something about it all that doesn't ring true, Priya's and Nate's body language when they interviewed me, the familiarity between the two of them. As if they're in this together. I also wonder how he could have forgiven Eva so easily. Although it could explain why he had been so upset when he saw me taking a picture on my phone.

I sigh. "You do know it's going to change everything, all the work we've done so far?"

"All I know is that I wanted to be honest with you. It's such a relief to talk like this." He sits up straighter, his eyes alight.

"Thanks, Anna, for listening. You don't know how good it feels to finally share all this with you."

As we walk back along the beach to head home, the curve of a new moon turns the shoreline to silver. We reach the car park, the woodland on one side now shrouded in darkness.

"Everything okay?" he asks, noticing my distracted expression.

"Sure," I reply, a wave of anxiety slides over me. My mind spins with the complexities of his story, their past. I want to believe there are no more secrets lurking.

We're in the car park and he reaches for the key; the electronic bleep of the car doors cuts the air like a final full stop. I slip into the passenger seat and he starts the engine.

"I guess every memoir creates a version of the truth, and that's what I'm asking you to do," he says. "You're so good at adopting her voice. For a narrative that suits all of us? Makes us all our best selves?"

"Sure. It's just—it's a lot to think about, a lot more work. We need a plan," I say, more decisively than I feel.

He peers through the windshield, a fine rain like needles streams into the beam of his headlights as he navigates the narrow lanes back to the highway. We say little on the ride until London draws nearer and our conversation lightens. I joke about the waitress who took a shine to him as we continued working on the book at the restaurant. At some point we fall into reflective silence instead. I think back to his confession, the shifting sands of truth in the Reid marriage, wondering how accurate his memories really are, what he's really hiding from me.

Either way, I tell myself, it's a better story, even if we have to edit and remold. The ultimate power couple, gilding each other's achievements, gilded on the surface, rotten underneath.

In the hypnotic glare of the highway signs that flash up before me, my mind fizzes with possibilities. There's a lot of stuff to reframe now, but also so much more material to work with. We'll definitely need to bury the infidelity, but we can allude to their smaller struggles and differences, how every marriage needs hard work to maintain it, the nature of forgiveness and growth. If I hit the right tone, it could be exactly the kind of "honest material" Priya's looking for after all.

Nate fixes his gaze on the road ahead as we draw closer to my apartment. I'm suddenly acutely aware of his presence beside me in the car. How funny that at first it was Eva that drew me, her voice inside my head calling me on; I had to follow her story to the source. Now, somehow…as Nate draws up to my street, it is his voice in my head, reciting the new opening chapter of his book, *our* book.

"So." I sit up straighter as he parks the car, turns to me. "I have a road map in my head. Changes, revisions, more interviews. We need to be way more focused in the short time we have. But I think we can do it."

"I know we can," he says. "Thank you for being such a good listener, Anna."

I click off my seat belt and his arm reaches over reflexively to say goodbye.

His lips graze my cheek, shrinking the distance between us. There is a beat of stillness when one of us could or should move away. But we don't.

My chest freezes. I tilt my face up to his, lips parting. His mouth moves over mine into a kiss, an exquisite second of free fall. I press against him in the darkness and he shifts his body, a statement of sorts, kissing me more urgently. He breathes hard, I find it difficult to breathe at all. For a few brief seconds there is nothing except us, but then, a sound. A car door slams nearby and we pull apart instinctively, the world outside the car slipping back in. In the dull trickle of streetlight, we study each other in silent bemusement.

"Ah. Anna, the last thing I want to do is make this difficult for you—for us. It's been a strange dynamic, over this past month of working together." He hesitates, fumblingly he reaches for my hand.

I nod. "I suppose this trip didn't make it any easier."

"It was a terrible idea," he says and we both laugh as he pulls me toward him again, his mouth on mine, longer and more intense. This time he pulls away first, looks at me intently, his demeanor shifting. "I should let you go. I'm so sorry." He shakes his head. "It's…bad timing, all wrong. I—"

"No, you're right. I should—"

"I want you to know I'm not normally like this," he interrupts. "You're the first person I've been remotely… Well, the first time since…" I can't bear his apologetic tone. Glancing out the window up at my empty apartment, I feel a sudden nausea, an overwhelming desire to be away from him.

"Really, it's nothing," I say, pointlessly.

He kisses me more chastely now on my cheek. I move away, stung by the formality of it, by his self-control, ashamed somehow that it is he who holds back, not me.

*He crossed a professional line for her, why won't he cross the line for me?*

I reach down to grab my handbag, scramble to release the door. The rush of raw air from outside wraps around me as I step out.

"Bye, Anna," he says. I smile, struggling to regain my senses, to appear unscathed.

"Nothing happened. Nothing at all," I repeat to myself, over and over, in the darkness.

# EVA'S SELF-REFLECTION JOURNAL

*12 March 2019*

*Me: "Can we talk a little more about your upbringing? Your parents?"*

*Patient X: "I don't really have much family to speak of. Most of my family is dead."*

*Me: "That must have been tough for you, and you're an only child?"*

*Patient X: "No, though sometimes I wish I were."*

*Patient X stifles a laugh at this point, which I read as a defense mechanism, a sign of more beneath it. I watch emotions struggle on their face, how their eyes darken with the anguish of remembering. For a moment I think they're about to cry and my instinct is to reach across to comfort them, but I hold back.*

Instead, as Janet has encouraged me to do, I reflect on the feelings they're provoking in me.

It's funny how the consulting room is our very own theater of emotions, separate from the outside world. Whatever feelings arise in this one-hour session are no more real than projections played upon a movie screen.

Patient X: "I guess there's a lot of baggage with my family. For a long time, I carried all of this guilt, but I'm not prepared to do that anymore."

Me: "Why not, what's happened?"

Patient X: Sighs heavily. "I can't say. Not now, not yet—"

Me: "What I'm sensing is a desire in you for change, for these feelings to break to the surface, but perhaps also a fear about the consequences that may bring?"

Patient X: "I feel I can tell you, but—"

Me: "I'm here for you. Seriously, trust me on this. I think we both know it's time to rip away the sticking Band-Aid, find out what's underneath?"

# 16

*All About You*

We are all alone in our pain because whatever we feel is notoriously difficult to share and communicate, and never more so than when we're actually in the throes of agony. In her essay *On Being Ill*, Virginia Woolf noted, "…There is the poverty of language. English, which can express the thoughts of Hamlet and the tragedy of Lear, has no words for the shiver and the headache… The merest schoolgirl, when she falls in love, has Shakespeare, Donne, Keats to speak her mind for her; but let a sufferer try to describe a pain in his head to a doctor and language at once runs dry." Over the centuries, medicine has compensated for this limitation, devising its own index to measure pain.

In the '70s, Dr. Ronald Melzack began to classify the words patients used most often, including *shooting, radiating, stabbing, sickening*, etc. This evolved to become the standard measure—The McGill Pain Questionnaire—still widely used in pain clinics around the world.

I keep my phone close in the days that follow our kiss, but Nate doesn't text me. I don't—won't—text him. As the time goes by, our trip to the coast takes on a surreal quality. Images ripple and flicker in my thoughts, leaving a dangerous afterglow, a slow burn of desire and despair. It should have been me that drew a line, acted like a grown-up, not him. I despise myself for wanting him more because of the restraint he displayed.

I distract myself as best I can, run to the river early each morning, watch as the sky ripens from peach pink to deep plum.

Stay in motion. My app tells me I'll burn 520 calories and cut my time by thirty seconds if I keep to my current pace. I focus on my breath. Inhale for five seconds, exhale for five seconds. Yet memory curls like smoke through the cracks. His fingertips on my hip bone, the melt of his mouth on mine. I blame him for this sabotage, that my mind is no longer my own, a rogue state I can no longer govern.

Last thing at night, first thing in the morning, he is there. Is it physical attraction, or something else too? The way we're both shackled to a past that we don't deserve, desperate to break away and start again. Or, if I'm honest, isn't it his unavailability that seduces me more?

I try to divert myself, plan out a new structure for the book. I set targets, deadlines, but my defenses are down. What did we agree on the journey back, that he'd text first on Friday or that I'd go straight to Algos House?

On my run, I speed past rows of gloomy redbrick mansion apartments, beyond the tennis courts and the overpriced garden center. Cutting through the tunnel under the railway arches, I feel the strain in my chest and sprint for the last two minutes, savoring the burn because I know I can stop it whenever I wish. That at least pain is within my control.

Tony is already there on the terrace outside the café, huddled under a blue umbrella and nursing a coffee. In the cold air, his watery eyes take in my jogging gear, narrowing into an expression of bemusement. For him, any form of exercise is a perverse affectation to be avoided at all costs.

"Hi, sis." He waves. "I could do with another, if you're buying." In the morning light I notice his skin looks papery and gray.

"Heavy night?"

"Part of the new regime, is it, jogging every day?" he bats back at me. "Must be getting in shape for someone?"

I avoid the insinuation in his stare. "How's Amira?"

"How's Nate? Long hours you've been working lately." He winks. I pick up his cup, turn sharply away and my trainers scrape abruptly on the gravel as I get him another coffee, and my own. When I come back out, he is hunched over the table, skimming his phone.

"So, come on. I asked first. You two seem pretty into each other."

"Oh, all fine." He shrugs lightly. "I finally got that travel commission I was after. Barcelona to Cádiz by train, eight-hundred miles across Spain starting next week, then down to Tarifa and a ferry trip to Tangier."

"Sounds like a long trip. Maybe a good time for a break from Amira, given you're going away for a while. It's probably for the best, don't you think?"

He squints at me, wounded, his chin juts out a little.

"Why are you so keen to split us up? I'm not going to hurt her. I'm actually hoping she'll join me on the final leg of my Spanish trip."

"Is that really a good idea?" I reason. "It's just that—"

"You think I'm being irresponsible? What about you, Anna?" He stares at me, his features slackening. "A whole day at the seaside with your work colleague?"

I laugh in disbelief. Did Amira tell him? Now I suppose I'll have to assume she tells him everything. Even more reason for them not to be together.

"It was my editor's idea. She suggested a change of scenery to mix things up a bit."

"And did you?" He wraps his hands around his cup. His knuckles look raw and chafed.

I look at him blankly.

"Did you mix things up a bit?" He blinks at me, and I notice the rims of his eyes, pink and watery. "No need to answer. Although I think you already have."

"So what if I did? What's it got to do with you anyway?"

"Anyone else I'd be fine about. You know that, Anna."

I sigh. "Thanks for the concern. I came here because you said you wanted to catch up. Come on, let's walk." I stand, eager to outpace my irritation, and he follows. Together we head toward a patch of woodland and the ornamental lake at the far end of the park.

"Not going to Nate's house this afternoon?"

I shake my head. "Transcribing and writing all day."

"So devoted to your work."

"That's me."

We stop for a moment by a small wooden gate and I step in front of him to open it, keen to keep walking, to move the spotlight elsewhere, but he continues to press in that playful way of his.

"You're not telling me something, A. What is it?"

I smile stiffly. Tony has been using my initial a lot lately—something our mother used to do—maybe to thaw the ice between us.

"I'm stressed, that's all. There's a lot of pressure at the moment to get this book done. The deadline is insane and I just want to get through it."

We chat some more about his upcoming assignments, circling the duck pond back into the neglected woodland where kids climb over the high Victorian walls to mess around at night. There's a patch of burnt grass in the center, the remnants of a recent fire. Graffiti covers the benches nearby.

Tony leans over the bridge, picks up a handful of pebbles, skims them one by one at a beer bottle floating in a tangle of weeds.

"Doesn't he give you the creeps?"

"Who?" I ask, still distracted.

"Nate."

"Not particularly, no."

"I can see what's happening, Anna," he says, giving me one of his sideways looks. "You know Dr. Reid is manipulating you, making you feel special in some way, so you write the book he wants you to write."

I feel my features harden once again. "You don't know him, and you don't need to stress about me. Focus on your travels, a new start, getting away from this place."

"But I'm leaving you all alone. I worry for you, that's all," he says, tilting his face toward me. I sigh. I know however obnoxious his execution can be, deep down he's just trying to help look after me. It's part of the deal.

"Tony, please—" I grip the slim metal rail of the bridge, stare into the brackish water below. I gulp, that familiar catch in my throat as I try to take a full breath. Maybe it's being back with Tony, in this spot, just a couple months past the anniversary of our mom's death, but I feel my childhood rushing up to meet me, my body keeping the score. That night comes back to me in shades of blue. French blue. The color of my father's Ventolin inhaler, his puffer. They were everywhere when I was growing up. In the kitchen drawer where my mom kept the freezer bags and the spare keys, the bathroom cabinet behind the acetaminophen, the glove compartment of his car, a subtle ever-present reminder of my father's asthma.

The scattered cries from children playing on the swings nearby pulls me back. Beside me, Tony's face flashes briefly into something that should be a smile but isn't.

"I guess it must be heaven for a journalist over there. All that nosing around. Have you been inside her room yet?"

"This isn't some silly game, Tony. I'm taking my work on this book seriously."

My phone vibrates and I hold it in my palm, angled away from Tony so he can't see.

"Anna?"

But I'm distracted by the text.

Sorry hvnt been in touch. Back from conference in Oxford. Are you free tomorrow to work on book? Let me know. N

My heart beats in double-time.

"I have to go." I am suddenly lightheaded, dizzy with childish elation as I slip my phone back in my pocket. "Work."

"Anna—" he repeats.

"What is it?" I laugh briskly, on edge, trying to keep the strain from my voice. "You know I love you but I've got to go."

"Funny, I've always wondered…" he muses, his tone contrived, too casual. "You meet Eva. Now here you are doing her memoir. Strange that order of things, don't you think?"

I look up at the sunless sky, register a reflexive shiver through the thin nylon fabric of my tracksuit.

"What the hell do you mean?" I snap, desperate to leave. "I chatted to Eva a couple of years ago for a short interview. That's it."

"Really? I seem to remember you said how inspiring you

found her. Didn't she even invite you into a therapy session? You sure you're not becoming a little too obsessed?"

I stare at him, bewildered.

"Please, Tony. I need to go," I repeat, watching his fingers tremble slightly as he rolls another cigarette paper. His tongue darts along its edge, the half-moons of his nails stained with nicotine. When he is finished, he raises the rolled cig to his mouth, lets it rest there.

"And I don't know what you're getting at, but this is bullshit. I get a chance to do this thing that could change my career and you want to ruin it for me."

Every time I try to claim a new world for myself, he somehow taints it. I glance down at my hands gripping the rail, pathetic and limp, and try to see myself through his eyes. As if I'm so eternally malleable, suggestible, someone whose life he thinks he can play with and demean.

"You really like him, don't you?"

"What?" I retort. "Actually, scratch that. I don't want—"

"It's sweet. Kissing in the car like teenagers?"

My jaw tightens and I start to shake, humiliated. "You were there."

I falter, the vision of Tony, my brother, watching from his car. Of course, the slam of that door breaking the moment, maybe when it got too much for him?

"Oh, c'mon, Anna." He lets out one of his little laughs, reaches out to touch my shoulder tenderly. I push his hand away. "If I am your keeper, you only have yourself to blame."

# 17

*All About You*

At first Eva's lack of pain was something she didn't notice at all and when she did, she thought about it as a liberation, released from the burden of her own biology. Childbirth, period pain, endometriosis. She would never have to suffer those conditions. Yet something changed as soon as she was diagnosed. She felt diminished, pitied rather than envied by those who read about her. And that didn't suit her. She began to crave what was denied to her, the body's siren when we're drawn too close to the flame. But I wasn't really paying attention as her craving grew. Burning, throbbing, aching. All she wanted was the gift of pain.

The next morning, in Nate's house, we face each other across the kitchen island, the distance between us as solid as the cool flecked marble beneath my fingertips. I scan his face but it only mirrors the uncertainty he must see in mine. If I am a little distracted, it's not for the reason he suspects. I try to tell myself it was coincidence Tony happened to slam his car door at the moment we kissed. Was he sitting there waiting for us to return?

As I lay in bed last night, Tony's intimations and the sad reality of his words spun around me in the darkness. After my father died, it's true that we became each other's keepers, grief and guilt binding us more tightly than I ever would have wished.

Our past was shaped by one soundtrack. It's there when I run, my body replays it in the tightening of my chest, the fire in my lungs, the struggle to inhale. I know it's there for Tony too. That sound. The rasp of my father's breath, followed by the compressed hiss of his inhaler opening up his swollen airways. Tony and I grew up witnessing the power of this small miraculous invention. Yet the night my father suffered his final fatal attack, when his last barely audible words were, "Help me," we couldn't find a fresh one. Waiting for the paramedics to arrive, we searched through the house high and low but there wasn't one to be found, anywhere.

I catch Nate's quizzical stare, haul my mind, like a dead weight, back to the moment.

"Anna, I—" he starts, his face looks strained, even a little gaunt. "We should talk."

"No, really," I say, flatly. "There's nothing more to say."

There is everything to say. My life is more complicated than he can ever imagine. Nate assumes he took control that evening, cutting short our kiss when we were interrupted, but the exact timing was down to Tony.

I find it hard to meet his eye, follow my finger instead as it traces a faint silver-gray vein on the marble countertop. His hand moves across the stone surface, the edge of his fingertips graze mine. "I should apologize. I feel it's my fault. I had no right to put you in that position and I promise you whatever did or—didn't happen," he falters. "I won't tell anyone and I assume you won't either."

"Absolutely not, no. Forget about it. I have. It's gone." I brush my hand in the air as if to flick it away. "We're working together, let's leave it at that."

"Really?" He searches my expression and I reflect back at him what he most likely wants to see. Relief, indifference.

"Yup, really." I smile, breaking eye contact to rummage through my bag for my notebook. "So. I've been planning a new way into the material and here's how I think it'll work." He takes a moment to recalibrate as I flip through the many pages of dense notes. I stand up and so does he.

"Right," he says crisply. "Shall we make a start?"

Initially, it takes an iron will to concentrate, sitting side by side. I hunch over the desk, legs folded to one side. He leans back, hands clasped behind his neck, our eyes steadfastly fixed on the screen.

"Something like this?" I say, as we scrutinize an unfinished chapter on-screen.

### Chapter 3—Meeting You

That first day you came into my office, I heard you before I saw you. Your voice quiet yet forceful, pointed and assured. Delicate, fine-featured, your sea green coat matched the color of your eyes. Long raven black hair skirted your shoulders, kinking up at the ends. You had sloping bangs that fell across your eyes. I remember you would tuck a loose strand of hair behind your ear any time you struggled to find exactly the right word to describe your symptoms.

We were used to working with people who were suffering acute pain, where even a featherlight touch to their

skin would cause intense agony. You were the polar opposite, your features perfect, your complexion flawless.
I couldn't help thinking you were a glowing testament
to the potential of a pain-free existence.

"Long raven black hair and her complexion flawless? A little over the top?"

"I don't think it's that bad," I counter. "You've said yourself that she looked absurdly youthful, unblemished by anxiety or pain."

"You know you make her sound a lot more glamorous than
she was."

"Wasn't she?" I ask. You only have to look at images of
her online, every inch the old-school film noir siren, liber-
ated, desirable and desiring. Why does he want to play that
down? When I think I've got closer to her essence, it's as if
he's trying to lead me away. But I say nothing. I compromise
and slowly we become experts in deciphering one another's
micro-responses; a tut, a raised brow or even a cough is a cue
for one of us to rephrase or re-angle.

But still, I can't help myself. I am irresistibly drawn to
guessing her likes, her tics and preferences. I have a Pinter-
est board in my mind devoted solely to her tastes: vintage
turquoise necklaces, Zelda Fitzgerald, Talitha Getty in Marrakech, Smythson stationery, every dress by The Vampire's
Wife. "Eva wouldn't like that," I sometimes blurt out, as if
the character I've conjured up on the page is an old friend.

"How would you know?" He throws me increasingly
strange looks. "Surely you can't intuit all that from just a
fifteen-minute phone interview?"

"I'm a journalist. I can find out a lot in fifteen minutes."
I shrug.

When we wired you up with sensors in the Pain Laboratory, your lack of response to pain was strangely mesmerizing. My team fell silent as we observed you chatting, asking questions, oblivious to the burns and pinpricks marking the delicate skin inside your arm.

"Feel anything now?" I asked you, knowing already what the answer would be. In that moment, I realized it was nature's cruelest trick to deny you the privilege of pain.

Nate reads the last line out loud twice, emphasizing the final three words.

"I like that." He leans back. "Was that me?"

"Nope, afraid not. One of mine."

"Really?"

I look up and check the time but Nate's in the zone.

"Come on," he urges. "Next chapter."

That day rapidly becomes a blueprint for the rest and a shorthand evolves. As Eva takes center stage, it is easier for us to bury any messier feelings we may have had, and the more I am able to enjoy this strange little universe we've carved out in the seclusion of his study, intimate but respectful. We inch forward, like a forensic team on its knees picking through the debris, sculpting a version of his past and hers.

It seems to be working. For the first time Priya is content with the updates, and we're hitting our deadlines.

*Chapter 13—In Your Thoughts*

My love for you began with your brain. I thought about what was inside your head a lot, exactly what made your billion or so neurons so different to the rest. I wanted to see your mind unfold in real time. Not just the mechanics of it all but the originality of your expression, your artistic playfulness constantly mining new ideas, new perspectives.

Of course, beyond your imagination, you fascinated me clinically. That may sound cold but scientists like me are eternally searching for that one medical anomaly who can shed light on their particular area of expertise. And that medical anomaly happened to be you.

Nate tilts his head doubtfully.
"Getting into her brain? Sounds a bit mad scientist."
"Wasn't it?"
"Not in the way you describe here."
"It's staying. It gives you an edge, makes you sound intriguing. The sexual attraction bit comes later."

*Chapter 14—Feeling Your Pain*

I wonder what would have happened if my research hadn't drawn media interest from around the world. Overnight you were photographed and interviewed by newspapers and TV channels.

The extraordinary attention your story received meant that there was a reason to keep in touch—the media often wanted to interview both of us. I was the one who offered scientific insight but it was you they found compelling.

When you asked to meet me one evening, I knew it wasn't strictly professional, given we'd only just finished our research project. I convinced myself I'd only hook up for a short drink...but four hours later we were still talking.

"And you kissed her that evening?" I ask, aware that I'm more interested than I should be.

Nate leans back, exhales.

"I know it's a delicate subject but I think we really need to include it in this section." I glance at him, offer a reassuring smile.

"Ah, you mean the oh-so-significant first kiss."

"Well, readers will want to know. So what really happened?"

We met in a featureless pub at the end of my road. You told me how you'd always come across as different to people, all your life. How you had struggled to feel the same as everyone else, to *feel* anything at all.

As I looked at you, the way your eyes glittered, how animated you seemed, I wanted to help. I began to realize the bitter irony of it, that I'd set out to find a cure for pain but now I felt you deserved the very opposite, the chance to feel it. I sometimes wonder what would have happened if I hadn't met you for that drink. Would we have drifted apart once the media interest ended? A blank moon hung low in the sky as I walked you to the subway and we shared our first kiss.

"Well?" I said, leaning back, pleased with myself.

"It's good." He deliberates, head tilted. "But not remotely true?"

"Most of it is. You *did* kiss her."

"We didn't kiss at that point. It was the next time we met, at her apartment."

"But it lends something to the moment. It's still being true to the spirit of it, the significance of every first kiss."

He looks at me. "Every?"

"I meant, mean, your and Eva's kiss," I stumble, sensing his presence next to me, his energy intensifying. Is he about to say something, name what's in the room? For a brief moment I am held by that look in his eyes. His hand, next to the keyboard, almost touches mine and, in a second, I could break the silence, call this out for what it is. He could too. All of a sudden it hits me, that this is how it will be between us, our first kiss, not theirs, burning away, unresolved. I move my hand away, primly, glance at him in profile, jaw clenched, inscrutable. Why would I risk being hurt again?

"Nate—" I sigh, shake my head "—don't let us go there."

"Go where exactly?"

His semi-playful tone irks me, particularly when we're writing about the first time he met his wife. Is it all a game to him? He has so much less to lose than me.

Nate catches my pained expression and lets it go. With concerted effort we focus our gaze on Eva.

# 18

Nate invites me back the next morning to work on some of the final chapters. By now they are almost complete but his attention to detail is obsessional, and he doesn't like me working on the memoir alone.

"You know ghostwriters don't usually hang out this much with their interviewee, don't you?" said Amira as we passed each other in the hall this morning. "You're going way beyond the call of duty."

It seems I don't have much choice. When I arrive at Algos House that morning, Jade stands in the doorway, giving me a baleful stare as if I'm an unwelcome inconvenience.

"Oh, didn't Nate let you know? He rushed out to a meeting and won't be back till after lunch, I'm afraid."

"Really?" I ask. "How odd. But we arranged it yesterday."

I check my phone and, sure enough, a text from him flashes up.

Sorry I'm not at home. Unexpected meeting, but you can work at the house and I'll be back by 2. Nate

"It hardly seems worth going back," I say. "He's suggested

I stay here and work in his study. That wouldn't be a problem, would it?"

"I guess it's fine," she says a little doubtfully. "If he says so, come in. I'm making soup, if you'd like some?"

Her tone is slightly less arctic, and I follow her into the kitchen area where there's a sweet, savory aroma of butternut squash and shallots. She places an extra bowl on the marble island between us. There is a plate of crusty white bread, iced water poured into pale blue stemless glasses. She sits down opposite me, waiting for her bowl to cool down.

"So. How's the book coming along?"

"All good. Nate's really enjoying it, I think."

"He's really okay about it all?" She tilts her head.

"It all?" I repeat.

"I know there have been some…reservations."

I dip my bread into the soup, let it coat the crust. When I look up again, she is watching me.

"I think he's enjoying the whole process actually. He's letting go a bit and it's all been quite…therapeutic." I smile at her, and she looks puzzled rather than pleased. "Sometimes it helps to talk about the past, don't you think?"

"Maybe to an actual therapist, but—"

"But not a journalist," I complete her reply, watch as she lifts the soup to her mouth, sipping in quick birdlike movements. She puts down her spoon.

"It's a whole different thing, isn't it? One is designed to be helpful, and the other, I guess…"

"You have a problem with journalism," I say, as kindly as I can. "I can understand that. All those reporters hanging around here after Eva died, the stuff they wrote. Insensitive, untrue. It must have been so difficult for all of you. It's just we're not all, I'm not—"

"It's not the journalism, it's the memoir that some of us have trouble dealing with."

"Us? Who else?"

She sighs, smooths her hair behind her ears. "It's not a personal thing. I guess I'm just allergic to this current obsession. Confessional journalism, memoir, whatever you want to call it. Putting it all out there on display, self-cannibalizing." She almost spits the word out.

"I think Nate is a very willing self-cannibalizer. It's exactly what he's signed up to."

It must be a superpower, I think, Nate's ability to inspire devotion like this. Priya is another disciple too, those glances during the interview, a chemistry that hums below the surface. Priya and Jade alter imperceptibly when he's around, something stirs in them. I recognize it in them, a hunger for his approval.

Yet, I realize in that moment, sitting at the table across from her daughter, that it's Kath I really admire. She exerts her own power. But Priya told me soon after I got the job that talking to Kath for the memoir was off-limits. Why?

Nate has told me how close Eva and her sister were; only seventeen months between the two of them and Kath had always looked out for her. Kath's home was apparently covered in her art. Eva had also been Jade's much-adored godmother as well as her aunt. I think of her often, the newspaper picture of her after the inquest, looking haunted but grimly determined. Fighting for her little sister with a burning passion that someone should pay the price for her untimely death. I'm no stranger to that. Siblings who've become so fiercely loyal and protective that it can be a little extreme at times.

"So what worries you about the memoir?" I ask. "The fact that Nate's doing one at all or that I'm ghostwriting it?"

"It's one thing," she says carefully, "to write about yourself, reveal your private life to strangers, share personal details, whatever. But when it's scavenging Eva's life too..."

Heat rises up my neck.

"Hardly scavenging, is it?" I retort. "It's biography, a reflection on his own loss too. It's a way of remembering her, of being true to her life."

"If it is true. We'll never know."

"It's as good a chance as any for Eva's voice to be heard, don't you think? Now because of Nate and this book, her work, her art, can be appreciated by a whole new audience," I say with passion.

After all, Jade and Kath would surely be grateful we're not telling the whole truth in the memoir, doing our best to protect Eva's reputation. If they really knew everything Nate had confessed to me, they'd be grateful that this memoir was preserving the best of their marriage.

"I don't think her artistic achievement is really what this book is all about, do you?" She gives me a broad smile, her tone still withering.

"Well, I think you should wait to read it."

"My mom would like to, but Priya has never offered and neither has Nate."

"Well, I'm sure they will at some point before it's published. I can see why your mom might feel concerned but tell her she really shouldn't be."

Without answering, Jade picks up our empty bowls and carries them to the sink. There is something balletic about the way she holds herself, in the starched line of her back, the sharpness of her shoulder blades. She takes out fresh mint from the fridge, snips it over two cups of boiling water in small precise cuts. Even her posture is somehow a rebuke to me, virtuous, upright. Nate has told me how helpful she is at the Rosen, yet I can't help wondering again what she's really doing here, beyond hanging around the kitchen looking glum and vaguely judgmental. Tending to Nate whenever she gets a chance.

"I should be going. I'm meeting my mom for the afternoon at the bookshop."

"Sure. I've got loads to do. I'll get going too," I say, picking up my bag. I hadn't planned for this. Algos House all to myself. My heart beats a little faster and I can't deny I am strangely thrilled by the idea. It's only when I hear the click of the door as it shuts that I realize I have been holding my breath.

I exhale, flop onto one of the sofas. How differently a house breathes when there's no one else here but me. I angle my face into a shaft of light that beams through the high glass above me, feel the prickle of velvet upholstery on the nape of my neck. Lying back, I close my eyes, put myself in Eva's place for a moment. Imagine how she spent her days when Nate was at work; absorbing this same view, savoring this particular texture of silence, rich and dense and soporific.

I get up and go back to his study, opening my laptop at his desk. For a moment I stare back at my empty silhouette reflected in the black screen, uneasy, until curiosity gets the upper hand. I text Nate to see how long I've got.

Got your message. All good. I'll catch up on rewriting chapter 25. When are you back?

Around an hour. Hope Jade gave you some lunch

I put a thumbs-up emoji by his message. Finishing off a chapter now, hopefully we can run through when you're here. No rush.

Out the window, I can make out the angles of her studio through the trees, a strip of river beyond. It's a tantalizing thought, Eva's studio, where she died, but it's out of bounds. No doubt it's locked anyway. Safer to stick closer to home.

Instead, I'm drawn to the floor above: her bedroom. I glance over at the sofa where the cat is asleep, remembering Jade's warning about how she must never go upstairs. I scoop her up in my arms. She wriggles, indignant at being woken, and I grip her harder. I had to go upstairs to find Nico, I could say. As alibis go, it's not bad. My steps on the staircase are light and urgent, taking me up to the only part of the house I haven't yet seen. I pause for a moment, motionless, the silence thrums in my ears like a radio frequency turned to high.

Ahead are a set of double doors, one left slightly ajar. I step in and deposit her on the bed, making sure she's settled. At the far end of the room, venetian blinds are drawn up to reveal a large picture window. Weak sun slants inside, turning the floorboards caramel and the silk rug next to the bed iridescent. The walls, the scallop velvet headboard and the bedding are shades of iced teal.

I inhale: an aroma of sandalwood and paper, dry and musky, fills the air, the kind that nestles in the back of wardrobes. The potent smell of absence. It is everywhere, a tangible weight in the room, air deadened by the past.

There in the corner is one of her textured glass sculptures, a female torso on a plinth. Hung above it is a silkscreen image; Eva and Nate, her head resting on his shoulder, replicated across an acid tangerine and yellow canvas.

I move through the space, my fingers brushing the thick satin throw on the bed, into her en suite bathroom. An open door at the other end reveals another bedroom almost identical to this one, and I find myself peering as if through the looking glass. His and hers. I take it all in: his ruffled bedding, yesterday's discarded clothes. Something stops me from stepping in there. A transgression too far, even though I'm tempted.

I can't help registering a discreet buzz of satisfaction at the geography. Nate wasn't exaggerating on that score. Adjoining rooms, separate beds, the froideur he mournfully described to me. Were they delineated when their marriage got rocky? Did Priya ever stay in this room with Eva? Or could it be yet another privilege of the wealthy to double up on everything, including their sleeping arrangements?

I glance at the silkscreen of them and my eye travels down to a small polished walnut bureau beneath it, its curved drawers edged with gilt. I can't resist. I wrestle with the top drawer first. There are boxes of old makeup mixed up with vintage jewelery. Gold necklaces, paste earrings, a pretty cushion-cut emerald cocktail ring catches my eye.

I try the second drawer, equally chaotic. Nate told me how disorganized she could be, never throwing anything away. There are hair clips and old paintbrushes mixed with receipts and invoices. A vintage brooch, a pot of varnish, postcards. As I comb through the rubble of her life, I register this as another fact about Eva, her desire to collect, a magpie drawn to the next shiny thing that came her way. Other people's stories, their emotions, above all their pain, trying it all on for size.

I try to push the drawer back in but there are dislodged papers at the back, which are jamming it. I need to clear the gap behind. Carefully, I edge my fingers around the side of the drawer and feel my way around the corner of…a pad, or a book of some sort. Slowly, I slide it back and sit back on my haunches, take a second to catch my breath.

The cover is glossy, with an intricate design of flowers and leaves. In black italics across the front is printed *Self-Reflection Journal*.

I have around half an hour left before he gets back. I picture his expression if he could see me here, furtive, deceitful. The threat of getting kicked off the book project, of

Nate's disapproval—his anger, even—unmoors me, but not sufficiently enough to stop myself from opening the journal.

The first page has several suggested areas for self-reflection from her supervisor. *How do you feel about your current client? Have you picked up on any transference today? If so, what feelings came up?* The spaces left for written notes are blank. I flip through all of them. Inside are a few receipts along with several pages filled with writing. I take them out. My stomach lurches.

Her entries.

I stand up too quickly, feel the ground give way and the room spin.

*28 March 2019*

*It hasn't gone away, this sense of being overwhelmed by emotion, drowning in it since I've met Patient X. I'm out of my depth. It's something I've never experienced, not even in marriage. The power of it, the raw emotion. Their pain makes me feel alive. I can't imagine a better feeling.*

My hands shake as I turn to another page. I begin reading her entries about a patient she starts seeing regularly, Patient X. Their complex, emotional sessions, how they slowly open up to her, first about surface-level anxieties and then deeper histories. Family trauma. My stomach spikes with adrenaline, her words in that perfectly neat handwriting begin to blur.

*Me: "I know this is difficult for you but I wonder if we could return to that night you mentioned early on. Can you unpack that a bit more?"*

*Patient X inhales sharply. Their tone shifts, features soften.*

*It feels like a privilege to create this atmosphere of trust that I hope I've helped to nurture. To finally, finally share their pain.*

*Patient X: "I guess it's the smell I remember first. The kitchen was filthy, flies at the bottom of the fridge, rotten food. We were all there together."*

*Me: "But this evening was different from the rest?"*

*Patient X: "We'd started eating and the windows were open wide, it had been a hot day, kind of close and airless too. The weather affected his mood. He'd been furiously impatient all day. His outburst was vicious but right in the middle of it, the weather broke. Sheet lightning, thunder. Somehow it triggered the smoke alarm, there was this unbearable high-pitched sound and maybe it was the shock of it. He collapsed with chest pain, struggling to breathe. He usually keeps an inhaler close to him, or another couple in the bathroom but—" Patient X falters "—we couldn't find them. We searched and searched…by the time the paramedics arrived it was all too late."*

*Me: "I'm sure there was nothing you could do."*

*Patient X looks down, chews their lip.*

*Me: "You know it's universal, this feeling when you witness a loved one dying in a situation like yours. We would do anything to save them but it's all beyond our control so we punish ourselves, continually ask what if?"*

*Patient X doesn't reply.*

*Me: "So what happened next?"*

Patient X: *"I stayed with him, watched him struggle for his last breath until the paramedics arrived. By then, of course, it was too late. Only...there's something else, too..."*

*Tears well up in my eyes, my throat burns. I try at first to conceal my response, to think of Janet. Stay focused, objective, use what you're feeling, don't get absorbed by it.*

*Patient X glances at me, puzzled, confused. "What's the matter?"*

Me: *"Give me a moment, I'll be fine." I wipe my cheek with the heel of my hand.*

*Patient X moves forward in their seat, offers me the box of tissues. "You're upset?" They lean forward and gently place their hand over mine.*

I only have time to read a couple more pages, an intense, overwhelming dread overtaking me as I read about the night of my father's death. It's all in here, all my secrets spilled in these lines. To anyone reading this, the identity of Patient X would be unmistakable. Nate obviously doesn't know it even exists, or he'd never have hired me.

I freeze. A shiver of movement outside the door. I quickly close the journal and shove it under my jumper, gripping it close to me with my arm across my waist. Quickly, I glance at the bureau to make sure everything's in place, no sign of intrusion.

"Nico," I call, in a singsong tone. "Ah, there you are."

I pick her up from the bed where she's still curled up, as if I've just found her. Just in time.

"What the hell do you think you're doing in here?" I turn

to see Jade standing in the doorway, the cat draped over my shoulder.

"I'm so sorry. I was going to the washroom and saw her dart upstairs. I followed her up. I remembered what you said about the bedrooms, how much Nate hates her escaping upstairs?" My face snaps into a smile. She doesn't return it. "What happened to the lunch?"

"Mom had to leave early so I thought I'd come back and catch Nate. Maybe it's lucky I did," she says, archly, walking over and sweeping Nico from me. She motions me to leave. "Go on, Nate's just got back. I'll tidy this up," she says, sweeping nonexistent cat hair off the bed with her free hand.

As I leave, I catch sight of myself in Eva's ornate full-length mirror by the door, my face flushed, my pupils dilated. I look exposed, different somehow. Is this the real me? Scurrilous and guileful, stealing from Eva and lying to Jade. I walk away, haunted by what I've read, haunted too by my own reflection, as if I've unexpectedly met a ghost, someone I used to know.

# 19

*All About You*

Women have never fared well when it comes to pain. Centuries ago, priests believed no relief should be offered to women during childbirth because the suffering helped to reinforce the maternal bond. A necessary self-sacrifice.

Nowadays, paternal views of female pain persist in a different fashion. These days it is more likely to be the medical profession, not priests, who can make the suffering worse. Known as the gender pain gap, research shows that a woman's experience of chronic pain is treated less seriously than a man's. A study from 2003 showed that men suffering pain following an operation were significantly more likely to be prescribed pain relief.

In contrast, women are far less likely to be believed, and even if they request a painkiller, they're more likely to get a sedative. Eva, actually, is the one who taught me this.

I make it to the study door before he does, sit down and fire up my computer.

"All good?"

"Sure." I smile up at him, touch my face, smooth away loose strands of hair behind my ears. I gulp hard. "Although I do have a couple of questions about that last chapter I've been working on."

"Fine, let's get started."

For the next couple of hours, we plow on as usual and if I am a little more silent than normal, he doesn't seem to notice. Several times I change my mind, concoct weak excuses so I can escape back upstairs to replace the journal. But it's too late. I made my decision as soon as Jade left the house and now I'll live with it. Tucked away in my bag, it is shameful evidence, pages that reveal so much more than anyone could really imagine.

I'm a fraud, an imposter, sitting here politely asking him to confess more about his dead wife after snooping in her bedroom, stealing her possessions. The burden of what's in those entries weigh me down, even more so the knowledge of what I now have to hide from Nate. About Eva, about myself...

"Anna?" Nate prompts me and I turn my attention to the screen, nudge the bag with one foot a little farther under my chair.

"Ah yes, right, is there anything else we can add here, perhaps?"

I force myself to focus, fashion my features into a studious smile. "Maybe more of a sense that understanding pain was an emotional journey for Eva? What do you think?"

He makes a face, leans toward the screen as he absorbs my words.

*Chapter 15—Life After You*

It was only when you died, in the midst of overwhelming grief, I realized how one-dimensional my work had been, how I had turned away from the holistic experience of pain. Thanks to my recent research, we know that someone who suffers from depression and anxiety is more likely to have a lower threshold—mind and body are inextricably linked. An inability to feel pain will impact you conversely on an emotional plane.

No one was more aware of this than you. I was proud of your decision to become a psychotherapist. You told me you wanted to immerse yourself in emotional pain, that you could be truly objective and impartial, to offer counseling and advice from a unique perspective.

Nate lets out a short dry laugh. "I was proud?"

"Why wouldn't you be?"

"How little you know," he muses. "She wasn't interested in people in that way."

"What do you mean?"

"I wasn't surprised when Eva decided to train as a therapist. She was greedy for experience. It's not true of all cases, but for her, not being able to feel any physical hurt was linked to her emotions too, or lack of them. She could experience some negative sensations like fever and nausea, but most repercussions of pain, like fear, trepidation, anxiety, were alien to her. I'm not sure I ever once saw her cry." He reflects a moment. "So much human emotion is connected, physically and emotionally. They're intertwined. Eva could understand all that, but not on a cellular level. No single emotion ever consumed her."

"So being a therapist must have been a real struggle for her?"

I play along, but of course I know this not to be true. The words in that journal scream louder, knowing now where that struggle was leading.

"At first, yes. I think understanding emotion, watching someone burst into tears, say, was like learning a new language from scratch and I don't think it ever came naturally. The truth is that a lot of the time I was much more lonely in her company than when I was truly alone." It's as if his whole body wilts under the sadness of this memory.

"That's the worst type of loneliness, isn't it?" I agree.

"I mean, obviously, I'm fine about it staying in, but the truth is I was worried, not proud."

"Really? How can you be so sure? Arguably at least she was trying. Maybe it was a genuine attempt to learn empathy. Is that so unhealthy?"

"Honestly? I believe Eva was incapable of empathy, of ever stepping out of herself," he says, his tone low and quiet. "Her desire to immerse herself in emotional pain, as you describe it, was voyeuristic, not remotely therapeutic for her patients or herself. It was darker than that. Don't put this in, obviously. But it was more about a fascination with what she couldn't have or know for herself. Some sort of thrill even. Even so, in her supervised sessions as a trainee, patients seemed to love her."

"What could be so bad about that?"

"She was very flattered, she lapped it all up, which is never a good sign for therapists," he says, gloomily. "She wanted to be popular. It was always about her. I was fearful for her patients. But there was nothing I could do."

"Why fearful for them?"

"She had no boundaries and that worried me. How would that play out in the consulting room? I wasn't sure how professional she was. Everything was a game to her."

His expression changes quite suddenly and he shoots up from his chair.

"Shit," he mumbles. "I'm meant to be back at the Rosen for an interview." He strides to his desk, distracted. "We're almost finished here, aren't we? I'll text you about times I can make in the next fortnight."

"We're almost there, Nate. A couple more days and it's done."

"Really?" He stops for a moment by the door. "How did that happen?"

We both look at each other, his expression reflects back my own bemusement that soon it will all be over. I follow him upstairs and Jade is there too. It's only as we're about to leave that I realize. As her slim pale hand brushes his shoulder to say goodbye, I see it.

On her little finger, the gleam of Eva's cushion-cut emerald cocktail ring. I glance again and her hand has slipped into her pocket, concealing the narrow band of gold.

But I know I saw it there, she knows it too. She catches my eye, the shadow of her smile meets mine.

Back in my apartment, I go straight to my bedroom and lock the door. Amira is here. Tony's footsteps are in the hall. I can hear the clatter of the kitchen coming to life. I'm not sure they've guessed I'm here yet. I take the journal out and open it again. Nausea spirals in my stomach. It's all there, the details of that night, the way that my father died; these memories finally catching up with me, condemning me too.

# 20

Two days later, Amira texts with an unexpected press invite. A fundraiser at the Rosen for Nate's latest high-profile project, identifying brain signals linked to chronic pain in young children. I am torn about whether or not to go. If Nate hadn't invited me himself, then surely it's better to stay away. We haven't spoken since our last meeting.

But then again, isn't it a good opportunity for the book, to observe the subject in their own domain? Besides I should probably keep an eye on him, given that he probably knows more than he's letting on. I can always lurk in the shadows and disappear early.

I hesitate, then pick up my phone to text Amira.

I find myself taking extra care over my appearance, opting for a dark velvet dress, darker lipstick the color of blood. It seems I don't want to melt away after all. Not dressed like this, a vampire's wife.

The Rosen's library is all solemn mahogany grandeur. Oil paintings of Victorian scientists glower down from the claret walls as the clamor of voices rise upward. The room is soaked in a rich amber light with marbled pillars and deep leather sofas, and the faintest scent of old books and cigar smoke.

I sweep the room looking for Amira, but with a jolt of surprise I immediately spot Nate and Priya instead, deep in conversation in one corner. He is talking into her ear and her hands rests on his elbow. A look passes between them. My phone vibrates and I see a message from Amira.

Sorry, Anna. Can't make tonight. Something's come up.

You're joking. Like what? Here on my own. Save me!!!

I'm SO sorry. It's serious. Tony's upset. Says we need to talk. More later. How can you be lonely when Dr. Pain is there to look after you?? You'll thank me—have a fab time. Xxxx

I shiver, annoyed at how easily she yields to Tony's whims over mine, how much she's changed in these few short weeks.

"Anna, you're here." Nate's voice, suddenly at my shoulder, startles me. He looks caught out somehow and I struggle to tell if my presence is welcome or not. Judging by his expression, I assume the latter.

"I should have let you know. Amira invited me."

"No, it's great you're here," he says, awkwardly. He stares at me as if he wants to say something more but stops himself, diverted by someone calling his name.

"I'm sorry, bad timing…"

"Of course, I should let you mingle. Go for it." I turn to walk away and he reaches out, his hand touching my shoulder.

"Wait," he says, quietly, urgently. "Can we talk…later? If you give me ten minutes. That's all I'll need."

"There's no rush, I—"

"Just ten minutes," he interrupts, then disappears as someone calls his name. I watch as he circulates, animated, engaged, a mirror of his guests who light up as they pass by. Why does it still surprise me, his fame, the ease at which he slips back into all this? The high-powered academic courting his followers.

I busy myself chatting with another reporter I recognize standing near the wall, and we swap pleasantries until I feel my phone vibrate again.

I'm two floors up on the terrace. It's no entry at the top of the stairs but ignore that and take a right through the double doors.

I smile in spite of myself, breath catching in my throat. I don't rush, take pleasure in letting him wait for a bit while I finish my champagne, observe the scene. Then, heading for the stairs, I duck under the red rope barrier at the top and turn right as he directs. I open the doors into an empty banqueting space that has yet to be cleared up, with the melancholy feel of a celebration abandoned too early.

I weave my way around tables littered with empty wineglasses, bottles and dirty plates, napkins are strewn on the floor, a dinner jacket hangs on the back of a chair. At the far end, Nate is outside, leaning over a small balcony, watching his guests milling around below. In the distance a tawny strip of the Thames glints through a line of silver birch trees.

He turns around when I reach him and we face each other for a moment. "I wanted to get away for a moment," he says. "Talk to you without being distracted by a lot of boring guests."

"Boring?" I smile. "Your valued fundraisers?"

He shrugs, moves closer. "Deadly boring," he murmurs. His hand grazes my shoulder, his other arm curves around my back. Back in his study with the book to focus on, I was full of resolve. A voice in my head screams at me to make my excuses and leave. But my body won't obey. I lean back against the wall, out of view, and Nate moves closer.

He pulls me to him and we kiss. For a moment or two I am lost in the emotion of it all. But then I freeze, scorched by the memory of Eva's journal. All those insights and reflections flash up before my eyes. What a terrible fraud I am.

Does he know what she's written about me? My head spins. Nate's arms loosen around me, as if he intuits something off, and then a sharp peal of laughter rises up from one of the guests on the terrace below.

I turn and he follows my gaze. Priya is standing down below, her face tilted up toward us, an indecipherable expression I can't make out from here. We duck farther into the shadow.

"Shit," Nate says.

"She can't have seen us, can she?" There's a ripple of alarm in my tone. "I shouldn't have come up. This was a bad idea."

I think of my job, all I could lose so close to the finish line. I wait for Nate to reassure me, but he doesn't. He's distracted. How quickly his body language shifts. He rakes his fingers through his hair, adjusting his shirt. Guilty, furtive.

"You're right. I...I should really get back down there," he says, turning abruptly toward the door. Retreating, as always. I stand for a moment, aching with the inevitability of it all. How did I allow this to play out? Following him up here, compromising myself, everything I've worked for, everything he thinks he knows about me.

"Ah, so you're here," Priya greets me as I step out onto the terrace about five minutes after Nate's exit. Fairy lights twinkle on the balustrade and guests shiver, valiantly pretending it's summer in the stony April chill. "I've just been looking for you."

"I'm all yours," I say, dryly.

She looks at me, strangely jubilant. "I was just saying to Nate earlier how brilliantly you've done—we both want to thank you really—for being such a star with this punishing deadline. I know it was a rough start. None of it has been easy, but it's all come together. The timing is going to be perfect for America." She arches her eyebrows.

"America?" I echo.

"I know, exciting, right? Your sample pages you shared were so great, an American publisher wants to pick it up. He's been hoping to do research in New York for ages, applying for fellowships and funding, and this gave him a way in. We can release the book over there just before he moves to New York."

"A way in." I barely register my parroting. My mind starts spinning.

"Columbia University. Nate's starting there next month. Didn't he mention it?" I catch an unmistakable glow of satisfaction in her eyes, her lips twitch with triumph.

"It's an amazing opportunity for him. You probably read that *New York Times* piece last month about the new neuroscience center, the largest of its kind in the world?"

"Yes, I think I did," I manage. I nod and smile, each muscle in my face aches with the effort.

"They're keen to work with him on a new laboratory there, similar to the one here but much bigger, newer. His new baby. And, it'll all be thanks to you."

My body reacts before my brain, a thud of despair in the pit of my stomach, heavy like stones. It really is a game to him. Why can't he ever be honest?

As I watch Priya float toward Nate, I'm struck with a new idea. There's one person out there who may hold some answers, the only woman who appears to be stubbornly resistant to his charms, who doesn't seem to like him at all. She could at least shine a light on the real Dr. Nate Reid, what he really wants, who he really is.

# 21

Kath's bookshop on Brick Lane is easy enough to spot with its bright green paintwork and white mullioned windows.

*Books—the original handheld device!* is chalked in jaunty pink-and-yellow bubble writing on the blackboard outside. Priya had forbidden me to make contact but it was too late now; I needed to talk to her. It was surprisingly easy. I emailed her via the shop website on the pretext of asking her to verify certain dates from Nate's memoir, and she replied almost immediately.

Anna, at last someone has got in touch with me. I've read bits and pieces and I'm extremely concerned, so much so I'm consulting my lawyers. I tried to contact Nate and Priya, but no response. Really useful if we could meet at the shop later today. Kath

If Nate and Priya weren't in contact, how had she managed to see some of the material in the book? I think of Nate's study, his printer, various edited chapters lying around on his desk—

Jade.

Of course, who else would have such easy access? She's been a source of intelligence for her mother all this time. I hesitate for a moment, distracted by the pretty window display of recent baking books, carefully arranged around a vintage cake stand scattered with silver almonds. The work of a frustrated set designer, perhaps.

I remember Nate telling me that Kath had shared the same creative flair as her younger sister, but she liked to claim there was room for only one artistic ego in the family. Eva made up for the two of them, she said. At university she studied classics rather than fine art, spending a year in Greece where she met Jade's father, Michel, a lawyer from Athens. After Kath's and Eva's mother died, Kath used her share of the inheritance to buy an old betting shop, transforming it into Emerald Books, the name above the paneled door in swirling gold italics.

I finally step inside, wandering from one table to another until I spot her, perched on a small book ladder. Kath reaches to the top shelf in a balletic posture. I can see the shadow of Eva in her profile; the delicate curve of her cheekbones, the straight-edged nose and heart-shaped chin. There the similarity ends. Images from my lost hours in Eva's wardrobe flash back to me, the giddy extravagance of all those outfits. Where Eva was exceptional, Kath is more conventional in her Breton top, ballet flats and white jeans.

I head for Biography while she finishes chatting to a customer, study the rows of bestselling memoirs from Michelle Obama to Elton John, Tara Westover to Deborah Orr. As I take down Henry Marsh's *Do No Harm*, a voice behind me breaks the silence. A voice that sounds eerily familiar to her younger sister's.

"Aiming high. I'm not sure Henry Marsh needed a ghost-writer either. He could manage pretty well on his own."

I twist around and meet Kath's stare, clear and shrewd and searching. Before I can think of a suitable reply she extends her hand, as cool and dry as parchment.

"Anna? I recognize you from your byline pic," she says, half smiling. I follow her to the back of the shop where there is a cluster of tables, the smell of roasting coffee and fresh pastries. She brings over two mugs and sits down opposite me.

"Thank you for coming this morning. I appreciate you seeing me at such short notice. None of this is easy, especially since Nate and Priya seem so unwilling to talk to me."

"I understand you hadn't been offered a chance to read it, but I'm sure once the draft is finished you can—"

Her sleek eyebrows ruffle, her eyes a hard arctic blue. "I'm her sister, and no one has even asked my opinion about it or offered to involve me at any level."

I hold her gaze for a moment as we assess one another. I guess she is closer to fifty than forty. Her complexion is line-free, her skin glowing from a recent trip that Jade told me about, visiting relatives outside Athens. I imagine a strict regime of Pilates and raw vegetables, elemental coastal walks and restorative spa breaks on Aegean Islands.

It dawns on me that perhaps Eva's death is the first time wealth and privilege has failed to protect Kath. I had read in the news about her quiet, articulate anger when she told reporters the police had been neglectful in their duty, that she wouldn't rest until a second inquest was opened.

"I'm sorry to hear that. But you say you have read bits of it?"

"It became obvious to me I wasn't going to get a chance to see the book until it was too late, so I asked Jade to intervene. What?" she asks, catching my anxious expression.

"Nothing. It's just, well, maybe there was an easier way for you to read it. I'm sure Nate would have let you—"

"Really? I very much doubt it. You two have been locked away, according to Jade, in your bunker creating this thing that has no bearing on Eva's life. None of what I've read is true to who she really was or, I believe, to what really happened between them. You made her up. There's nothing of the sister I knew in there at all."

"My job was to write down Nate's memories of her and that's all I've done. I haven't made anything up," I say steadily, catching her eye, hoping I'm not betraying the guilt I feel inside. Although maybe it's a case of touché—Eva recorded, unwittingly, a version of my life in her journal, now I'm fashioning a version of hers. "Believe me," I add, "I want to get to the truth of Eva too."

"I can see you're in a difficult situation and none of this is really your fault. I understand that. You've been drawn in by Nate, manipulated even."

"I don't think that's—"

"You really don't know who you're dealing with, Anna. You have no idea what he's capable of, how persuasive he can be." She shakes her head. "But I need him and Priya to know that I will take legal advice over this. I don't want it going ahead, if what I've read already is anything like the rest of the book."

I inhale sharply. "Look, I'm sorry you're so upset by it but maybe you've taken it out of context. Reading the odd chapter here and there can be misleading."

She gives a small dismissive laugh, makes a vague gesture with her hand. "I doubt that. I got a pretty good impression of how you're painting her. As some fucked-up hedonist, a beautiful victim defined by a powerful man. I mean, couldn't you or he be a little more original at least? If you are going to do a memoir, surely it should have some integrity? You can tell Nate from me, Eva would have been furious."

She steeples her hands on the table in an effort to regain her composure, a large opal stone glitters on her wedding finger.

"Look, I know how crucial it is to get this right for Eva," I say. "If I talk to Priya, there may be stuff I can add in. I'd need to run it by Nate obviously."

"Obviously," she says and I ignore her pointed look.

"What sort of stuff would you want included?"

"I have plenty of anecdotes, if anyone had bothered to ask. I know my sister wouldn't have wanted a sanitized version of herself in print. Anna, I can help you make it truer to Eva, give you a bit more background, convince you that what I'm saying is true. Especially if your subject seems so...hard to fathom?"

"Why do you say that?"

She sighs. "Obviously, Nate has a lot to hide. He has kept secrets and built a wall around them. I can see it on your face, you know this too, deep down. But you're trying to convince yourself otherwise, that he's a good guy worth believing in."

She looks at me kindly and I can't help recoiling. In her eyes I am a naive fool to be pitied, another female acolyte.

"You know, when I first met Nate, I was so hopeful," she says. "So relieved for Eva's sake. At last, someone who truly understood her! He genuinely wanted to help her and his diagnosis was huge for us. Looking back, it was obvious something was seriously wrong but we didn't know what help or resources to seek. Nate helped us understand why Eva was different, how to support her. At first all he cared about was her, until his career really took off. Somehow everything changed, something was lost."

"In what way?"

"The whole race to find a cure for pain, he got swallowed up by it, obsessed with his ambitions."

"Wanting to help rid the world of pain is hardly such a selfish ambition, is it?"

"Without Eva there would have been no more research. No profile. No recognition. She gave all that to him. But he took so much from her. She felt used, at times." She shakes her head quickly, her eyes shining. "I can't help thinking he's created a lot more pain than he claimed to cure. Now he's taking from her again, profiting with this memoir."

I shift uneasily. "That's not the whole story. It can't be. He genuinely wants everyone to benefit from his work, it's his vocation."

"Come on, Anna. What was the real reason you came to see me?" Her gaze is expectant, unblinking.

"I wanted more background, I guess…"

"Sure you did."

"Nate told me Eva was having an affair," I blurted, waiting to see how it lands. She doesn't seem to register any surprise. Did Eva confide in her? "Obviously we're not putting any of it in the book but…did you know?"

She presses her lips closed in a slim firm line, as if she's torn between speaking or keeping her counsel. She finally lets out a small sigh. "Yes, that's what she had alluded to with me too."

I can hear the relief of disclosure. She wants to let me know. She wants to tell someone. I can see it in her eyes, hooking into mine, direct and clear.

"Did Eva say any more about it?"

"A few months before she died, she told me she'd met someone. Nothing had happened but…the word she used was *unprofessional*. I assume it was via her or Nate's work. I mean, the way she got together with Nate himself wasn't exactly professional, given that she was the focus of his research paper. She said they waited until his PhD was finished but I'm not convinced. Waiting wasn't exactly her strong point."

More or less professional, I wonder, than his advances toward me? Nate and Eva shared that in common, I realize, happily crashing their way through professional boundaries. Maybe both Eva and I are Nate's victims; he's toyed with both of us in different ways, manipulating the power imbalance to please himself. What a rich seam of discussion that could have been between the two of us, I can't help musing.

"What did she actually tell you?"

"She wouldn't go into detail, but I could see that it troubled her. She knew that it was wrong. Something about it worried her deeply…"

"And you believed her?"

"Yes, I really did. Eva could never really see the point of lying, partly because she never felt guilty enough to cover anything up." She allows herself a brief smile. "She lived by different rules to most of us. But she could be pragmatic too. Eva knew transgressions could be hugely destructive. Anyway, she only ever talked about it once and it was never clear to me how far it had really progressed. I think, if anything, she tiptoed to the edge with him."

"With *him*? Are you sure it wasn't *her*?"

"Her?"

"Priya."

"Whatever makes you say that?"

"Something Nate told me, that Eva and Priya were a thing?" She looks at me blankly, shakes her head.

"Absolutely not. She would have told me."

"But their trip across Morocco, their…friendship…?" I trail off, knowing how I must sound.

"And that constitutes an affair?" She gives me a withering look. "Really, Nate is spinning you another line, surely you can see that?"

I feel myself redden, stare down at the crumbs on my plate, press the pad of my index finger to each one and watch as the tip slowly turns white under pressure.

"Either way, Eva's infidelity would have made him furious. She told me that his anger could be scary, unpredictable. As I've said, none of this is for publication, but I've had a private forensic toxicologist reevaluate the findings, and there is some speculation that the cocaine wasn't lethal because of its purity. It was cut with something else."

My skin prickles , something bitter rises in my throat, déjà vu. I already know exactly what she's about to tell me. I look down so my hair falls across my face, hoping to conceal the heat rising in my face.

"Fentanyl."

"Fentanyl," I echo, weakly.

"That's what the lab came back with, the results are with the coroner ahead of the second inquest."

"I'm not sure I understand the implication," I stammer. Nate had told me when we visited the coast that day about his slipped disc, the acute pain he suffered. Later, he admitted how easy it was to get hold of it in his Pain Laboratory. The date on it was May 2019, prescribed the month before she died.

Kath watches doubt creep across my face.

"Oh, Anna," she says, again as if chiding a small child. "I'm sure you can make the connection. Fentanyl is often used as an adulterant in street cocaine because of its high potency, a little goes a long way. Florida has been awash with coke contaminated with opioids. They call it blue cocaine, apparently. Even just a trace of it can prove fatal. And that's what showed up. Who else has that guaranteed access except for our King of Pain? Nate has a temper. If he found out about the affair, all he needed was a quick, traceless way to retaliate. You'd have to agree it makes Nate a number one suspect in all this?"

"But you've said yourself, it's a thing. That doesn't point to Nate. There's even a street name for it."

She shrugs. "Well, the police are due to search Algos House again by the end of the month and hopefully we can find answers to a few more questions. I think the clues were there all along. In fact, Eva had mentioned she kept a journal, so I had asked Jade to look for it in case it divulged any details about Nate's behavior around her death. She never could locate it, but the authorities certainly will."

My stomach drops at the mention of the journal. Trying to keep my composure, I say, "If you're that sure about his involvement, how can you carry on letting Jade stay there in the house with him?"

"I've never been happy about her being there. But she loved her aunt, wanted to be closer to her."

*So close, she liked to nose around her bedroom and take her things.* Maybe we shared more in common than we thought.

"Anyway," continues Kath. "She managed to persuade me it made sense to stay, that it was advantageous to us. Which it was. But she's been there too long, and I don't want her anywhere near him. She packed up and left yesterday morning, told him there was an illness in the family and she needed to be with me. I'm relieved to get her home."

I think about those small blue pills, casually left in his bathroom cabinet. If he'd really cut the cocaine with fentanyl, wouldn't he have covered his tracks and disposed of the evidence? Even if it wasn't those pills, the name itself in his home would surely be damning?

Kath's eyes are on me, scrutinizing: "Does Nate appear to be worried about any of this? I mean, don't you ever wonder about the timings? Why he was so keen to do his memoir now?"

I think back to that first interview with him and Priya and how I had posed the same question.

"He told me before we started that he wanted the book to help others out there in a similar situation. People like him, devastated by sudden loss. And he wanted to do Eva's legacy justice. I believed him."

"You believed. Is that past tense?" Her expression hardens.

"No, I believe him now," I insist, and my jaw tightens. "I

mean, if anyone is manipulative here, isn't it Priya? Why is she so keen to get him to America?"

"Ah, yes, Columbia University. Jade told me last week. She wasn't very happy about that either." She shakes her head lightly, regretfully. "You see he's just doing what he always does. Seducing people, ruining their lives, and leaving other people to pick up the pieces." She smiles teasingly except her eyes are hard and sharp, needled by pain.

"I'm sorry. I mean about Eva," I say, pointlessly.

"I'm sorry too. For you as well, that no one is immune to him. You shouldn't be caught up in it all, not like this," she says, with a piercing look, as if she can see straight into me, a ringside seat to the dark dilemma blazing inside.

# 22

*All About You*

In the past, individuals with CIP (congenital insensitivity to pain) were treated no better than people at circus freak shows. One of the best-documented cases was Czech immigrant Edward H. Gibson, a vaudeville performer known as the Human Pincushion. In 1932, the *Journal of Nervous and Mental Disease* recorded his pain-defying stunts where he would invite audience members on stage to skewer him with fifty to sixty pins "anywhere but the abdomen and groin."

Sometimes Eva could relate to poor old Edward H. Gibson, a mutant on show. Soon after her diagnosis, she was a global news story too. The *New Yorker* profiled her, speculating that cases similar to hers had died in terrible circumstances, of frostbite and heat stroke, hemorrhages and heart attacks without feeling a single thing. One TV channel asked if Eva would like to appear on their show so the audience could watch as she placed her hand in a flame or, failing that, consume a bowl of Scottish bonnet chilis live. This was a different sort of freak show, but it was made clear to her that, for the sake of her art career, she'd be foolish to refuse.

The night before I see Nate again, I sleep fitfully, my dreams spiked with nameless demons. I walk on eggshells at home, the atmosphere curdled because Amira and Tony are getting on badly, shouting at one another or grimly silent. Reluctant to take sides, I stay out of it, inwardly tormented about where my loyalty should lie. I wake too early, brittle and frayed. As I walk along the avenue to his house, the river glistens in the spring sunlight. There's a charge in the air, the energy of one season erasing another.

"Hey," says Nate, answering the door. He is unshaven, relaxed, in a T-shirt and jogging pants. His tone is neutral, neither warm nor distant, impossible to read. It's as if the other evening has never happened. He's clearly unphased by it. Was he ever going to mention Columbia?

Inside his study, the air is dark and cool and airless. I sit at his desk, glance up at the whiteboard that hangs above it, the row of handwritten chapter summaries on there. Our scrawled notes still colonize one wall, his cursive black loops and mine, neat block letters in red:

More of E's experience of pain here? Footnote to pain research? N's childhood? E & N meet here or further on?

Yet they seem like relics from another age; everything has changed. Now doubt splinters my mind, longing on one side, mistrust on the other.

Kath's expression had said it all as she confirmed his move to Columbia, launching himself in New York with Priya on hand to support him. Maybe Nate did lie about Priya's affair with Eva to cover up for their own. I glance back up at our notes, shake my head in quiet disbelief. How easily I had been won over by him, his puppet, reducing his marriage to a fiction spread over thirty index cards. How inexorably his secrets, and now mine too, are pushing us apart, the accumulation of all the unsaids ruling out the potential for there to have ever been anything genuine.

Yet here we still are, back down the rabbit hole instead, where it is easier to self-deceive. I cling to these final hours of the memoir because they've become something else for me. A place to retreat and hide, from myself as well as him.

Nate reads and I try to edit, my mind skittering from one barbed anxiety to another. It's getting crowded, all these unspoken words piling up, threatening to erupt. I've avoided everyone's calls since I met Kath, including Tony's. He texts instead, always when I'm at Algos House, as if he has a sixth sense I'm here. His messages are increasingly urgent, paranoid. He despises Nate, wants me out of Algos House for good.

Don't hang out there. Seriously, Anna. The guy's dangerous. Finish up and get out. He's a fucking NARCISSIST!!!

I manage to reply something while Nate makes coffee, but he won't be appeased.

Everyone's a narcissist. LOL

Why don't you ever listen to me, A. Do you want this to play out like last time?

Like last time.

I stare at the screen, my lungs freeze, air sucked from the room. Nothing could play out that badly again. Surely.

"Are you okay, Anna?" Nate's voice springs from the silence. He stands behind me, hands me a mug over my shoulder. There's clear concern in his gaze.

"Sure. Just work hassling me."

I drop my phone in my bag. Eyes back to the screen. Engage. Somehow the day takes shape. I push the outside world away, delete and rewrite, discuss and confer and, by late afternoon, we're almost done. He reads and I watch the knot of muscle work in his jaw as he chews the end of his pen, his eyes critical, reproving.

If the two types of loss are expected and traumatic, mine was undoubtedly the latter. Exactly a year ago my grief was all-consuming, but in writing this book something has shifted.

I see clearly now that I can never step back to how I used to be, only walk a different path. Finally, I have embraced that simple truth, as the ancient Greek philosopher Heraclitus put it: "All is flux, nothing stays still." I have finally processed that everything shall pass, the pain and the pleasure.

One of the many gifts of writing has been to find meaning in the unbearable; to contain it in words has been a huge comfort.

Spring has arrived a little late this year. I can taste it, elemental and fresh. The cherry trees are already shedding, turning the pavements into carpets of confetti, sun piercing the branches and, for the first time in months, I no longer see only darkness ahead. I cannot forget Eva. She is part of me. She'll be with me, somewhere, somehow, in the next chapter of my life. But there's no turning back, I'm ready to step into the light.

"A little bit florid?" he says, finally. "Too—"

"Emotional, corny?"

I scan the words, assume his voice, his dispassionate tone, in my head as I read them silently.

"I see what you mean, but I still think it's good to be reflective, offer that sense of emotional growth, light at the end of the tunnel."

He leans back, arms crossed, staring the screen down. "Okay, well, I can always have a final reread tomorrow."

"No more rereads. I need to send this to Priya in two weeks. Any amendments have to happen now if we want to wrap it up."

"You're right. Let's do it. I'm going with your instinct. It's not exactly me, but I'm happy if you are."

"Sure? I can always change—"

"No. All good." He leaps up, strides to the wall of index cards and scores through the final one. I get up too and we stand back to admire our work. "We're there, Anna."

"Well, not quite," I remind him. "We still have to work together on the final edit."

"Sure, but we've crossed the finishing line." He looks at me and I can't help breaking into a smile. Should we shake hands, embrace? Knowing what has come before, of course we do neither.

Quickly I sit back down again, save it onto a new Google document so we can both work on it remotely over the next two weeks. I copy it to my own email address, just in case, and press Send while Nate checks his phone. He glances across at me, his expression lightens. There's a brightness in his eyes and somehow he looks years younger.

"Come on," he says. "I reckon this deserves a celebration, don't you?"

# 23

The riverside pub at the end of the road is dark, low-beamed, the print-lined walls are mottled brown with age. I choose a corner table and Nate comes back with a bottle of red. He smiles as he sits down opposite me, sloshing the wine into two oversized glasses and handing one to me. "To the book," he says and we clink glasses.

"Look, Nate, I—" I stall, watch him distracted by his own thoughts.

"I need to say something first." He leans forward, palms outstretched on the small table. "I'm sorry about last week, the way it all happened. Sending you the text, everything, it wasn't fair on you. You were absolutely right to walk away. I was an idiot." He shakes his head, falls silent. Always on cue with an apology.

"So you're going to New York next month, aren't you?" I ask, neutrally. He opens his mouth but I carry on. "Nate, it's fine. It's an amazing opportunity. You said you needed a change in your life and this is—"

"Wait, Anna, stop. Whatever Priya probably said, it's not what you think. I haven't made up my mind yet. Not completely. There's a book tour opportunity and a three-month tenure at Columbia. Nothing is finalized." He looks at me, frowning in concentration. "Seriously, I wanted to talk to you about all this first. It's not fine. It all depends on—"

"Priya?" I suggest.

"Priya? What makes you say that?"

"You're really asking?"

He sighs. "Anna, she's my editor."

"Well, you should know something else," I say, and he looks back at me warily. "I visited Kath last week, after that evening at the Rosen. She wanted to see me and...I agreed."

"I see. And?"

"She wasn't happy. In fact, she's furious with you. She said Jade had shown her parts of the book. I think she took some chapters from the printer."

I watch his face cloud over and decide to mention nothing I learned of the affair, Nate's lies about Priya and Eva. "Kath's in touch with her lawyer about it. Reckons it's a fabrication, that she doesn't recognize her sister at all."

"I'm not sure she ever did." He lets out a small dismissive laugh. "She's just throwing her weight around because she feels ignored. There's no legal issue, I've spoken to Priya about it."

"I wouldn't be so quick to dismiss her, Nate. You should know something else."

"Really?"

"The cocaine they found, the toxicology report on it. She had it reevaluated. They think it may have been cut with another substance."

"That doesn't surprise me. Street cocaine is cut with all sorts of stuff, talcum powder, laxatives, caffeine, you name it."

"Fentanyl," I say slowly, holding his gaze, my heart pounds in my ears. I can't help myself. Every cell in me needs to know, to witness his reaction, to make up my own mind. His eyes darken but he doesn't blink, doesn't miss a beat.

"You know about my prescription you saw in the bathroom

that day. It's not as if I tried to dispose of them. I told you about my slipped disc, excruciating pain for six weeks. What? You think I tampered with some cocaine, who do you take me for?" He looks at me, indignant, defiant. "It would be an insane move, especially if I casually left my medication lying around for anyone nosy enough to look."

I nod, the inner critic silenced, for now.

"I'd be better at covering my tracks, believe me." Nate moves his hand toward mine across the table. His defensiveness has thawed slightly, and now his eyes are almost pleading. "Anna, whatever Kath told you, remember she has an agenda too. I know what she's like, it's in her interest to turn you against me."

"But why?" I say. "Why would she do that?"

"Because she needs someone to blame it all on, to point her finger at, to *other*. And that person is me. I understand that, I get it."

"She's convinced, Nate, that's why Jade left—she wanted her out of there, away from *you*."

He laughs, incredulous.

"I pushed for a second inquest to support Kath, I still do. Why would I do that if I was hiding something?"

"Do you ever talk about any of this with Kath? Knowing she's like that, shouldn't you have involved her a bit more in the book? Given her even an illusion of being involved?"

"Probably you're right. But it would have been painful, for both of us and after all, it is *my* grief memoir."

I say nothing and he studies my expression.

"She told you more about her theories of me? That's what you're still thinking about." He exhales, pressing his fingertips into his temples. "Kath really did get to you, didn't she?"

"I hate all this, Nate."

"Don't say that," he says, gently. "Whatever doubts you have, ask me."

My head spins, torn between all their conflicting stories. Priya, Kath, Nate, each so plausible in their own way, winning me over whenever I'm in their presence. I despise myself, needling, insecure, on the attack, his answers to my questions only creating more subterfuge, not less.

I take another sip of wine, feel the alcohol slip through my system, blurring the edges.

"Look, I really don't know what to think, who to believe. Except, you know, who cares, really?" I throw my hands up. "What's it got to do with me? Seriously. I'm only your fucking ghostwriter."

He opens his mouth to object but starts to laugh instead and so do I, at the absurdity of it all. A waiter hovers next to us with plates of food. Nate leans back, folds his arms, as he arranges the small dishes of tapas between us. There is salt cod in crispy batter, deep-fried cheese laced with honey and buttery prawns, but neither of us are interested. Nate leans in, speaks softly, urgently, into the distance between us.

"Seriously though, you're not only my ghostwriter. You know that." He doesn't laugh this time and I look down, break his stare. When I look up, a self-conscious grin flickers across his face.

"Have you ever thought about working in America, Anna?" he asks, his tone quiet. "I think it could be perfect for you. The next step up for your work. Another book we could work on, but this time in your name?"

I say nothing for a moment, struggle to conceal the slow fuse of my smile reflected in his. He refills my glass and I take a long sip, allow myself briefly to luxuriate in the possibilities. New York. Away from my worst fears, my past, the ultimate reinvention. Nate's profile igniting mine. I could sell up my apartment, pay back Tony's share with interest, even have a little extra to support him if he needs it. Escape all the secrets, live in the future and kill the past.

Doubts still needle, but I try to bat them away. Nate's response about Columbia was pretty flawless. Emotionally genuine, logical. Maybe I am too cynical. We both have pasts that are flawed, twisty and messy. I think once more of those diary entries and wonder what right I have to judge anyone, least of all him? And he wants me to come. Isn't this what I wanted?

I swirl my glass, watch the wine undulate like a crimson wave, silk and oil at its edges. I register how featherlight I feel, soaring outside myself, existing only in the moment.

That way he checks his watch, his sleeves rolled up, the glint of steel bracelet on his wrist, the tendons working beneath. Even though I despise myself for abandoning my resolve so quickly, something inside me contracts, quickens with anticipation.

The waiter clears our plates and late afternoon presses in on us as we exit the pub. Outside it begins to pour and I make a show of scrolling through my phone to order an Uber home. Nate shakes his head, flicks his hand in the air. I feel a twist inside, watching him walk ahead of me, bristling with innate conviction, no faltering, no flip-flopping.

"Come on, you'll get soaked," he calls back to me, his voice raised above the sound of the downpour. "Book a cab from my house."

Algos feels empty and cavernous, the rain beats on the glass above us, casting liquid shadows on the walls. He opens the glass door and we stand next to each other under a strip of awning. The air is humming, charged.

"Cigarette?" he says, shaking his jacket pocket absentmindedly, searching for a lighter. I take one and we smoke in reflective silence for a moment.

"I've been thinking of that brother of yours," Nate says thoughtfully. "How are things between you two?"

"Oh, same old. I'm not sure if anything will ever really change."

"You know, your insights when we were editing together got me thinking. You were so perceptive about loss and pain. It was the kind of perception one could only really know if they went through something themselves. Perhaps…with their own family?"

"I guess I do have experience of it too. I lost my parents when I was relatively young. So, I did know what you were talking about, what you went through, to an extent."

"Anna, that's terrible. How? I mean both at the same time or—"

"No. Mom died of cancer when I was young and my dad from an asthma attack when I was around nineteen. Tony was there too. We tried so hard to save him…"

"I'm sure there was nothing you or your brother could have done. Had he had attacks like that before?"

"Yes, it was a pattern," I say. His attention is like a balm, an invitation I so desperately want to take. When you experience any sort of shocking death, it creates these strange points of connection with other people's shocking losses. You search them out for comparison, reassurance too.

Of course, I can't tell him everything about that night. I still struggle to fit the pieces together myself, a night measured out in chaotic sensations and snatched images, nothing close to coherent memory. I remember how much I was looking forward to a night out at my best friend's house party. How long I had spent getting ready. The red ankle boots, the midriff top, my pale bare legs. My dad took one look at me and started yelling. Why would I go out looking like a slut? That word, burnt into my memory, was the catalyst for me. At this point in the evening, Tony was only the passive observer, while I was a whirling dervish of white heat. "I'm nineteen years old. I'm an adult. Fuck off!" I screamed back at him, failing to register the rage etched on my father's face. The rigid fury in his angled features. The scrape of my heels on the hall tiles.

The rest I remember in slow motion. The feel of my father's hands like iron circling my ankles, dragging me down the stairs step by step. The way I struggled for breath. A taste of what was to come. His arm on me, twisting mine. The rip of pain, the pitch of my howl. It had all happened before, to me and to Tony. By then we knew my father's temper was unpredictable and extreme. If I hadn't riled him that evening, how differently things could have turned out, as Tony often used to remind me.

Nate is looking at me intently, waiting for answers.

"There's not that much to tell really. I was meant to be going out that evening but in the end I didn't. I went upstairs to change and when I came down, all I remember is that he'd collapsed. His inhaler ran out. We called an ambulance but it was too late. It was tough. Really tough," I manage.

"God, I'm sorry, Anna. You let me talk so much about my loss and all the time—" He shakes his head, features creasing in sympathy.

"Well, ghostwriters aren't hired to talk about themselves, are they?" I say, crisply. "Anyway, my parents died a long time ago. Before I knew it, I was at uni... Now I'm more or less fine about it all. I feel sorry for my friends when I know what they'll have to go through. I can see the fear in their eyes and I know it's behind me. People assume it's been so terrible for me but really it hasn't."

Nate looks at me doubtfully, clearly not buying my plucky

survivor performance. "I perfected a similar speech about Eva too. You probably remember. Most people swallowed it and moved on, except you. You were the first one to ask how I'd really felt when we first sat down to write the book. You told me that rehearsing a speech about how well I was managing was a sign that possibly I wasn't doing that well, and you were right."

"It's a coping mechanism, isn't it? I guess it's that thing of people feeling sorry for you, seeing you as this tragic figure to tiptoe around. Don't you hate that look in their eyes?"

He nods. "When they tell you you're brave."

"Brave's a killer," I agree and we grimace. "I know, pity is the worst, isn't it? I can remember bumping into a neighbor in the park after my dad died, asking all about me and saying something like, *you poor, poor children*, with this strange little smile on her face. I hated her. She made me feel like a Victorian orphan."

We both fall silent for a moment, hurled into our separate wounds. I tilt my head back and shoot a trail of blue smoke into the air. I thought I'd drunk myself sober over lunch but now I realize I'm struggling to hold myself straight. I glance around mournfully at the garden. Somehow it has never looked lusher or greener. I inhale the earthy tang that comes with heavy rain, aware that it looks all the more perfect because it's about to end.

"You know it would be such a shame to lose this place." My tone is a little more wistful than I intended.

"Selling up Algos House? I'm not sure I have any choice."

"I understand. You said yourself it feels wrong being here for so long, that it's like a mausoleum." The word makes me shudder and I can't help picturing Eva's bedroom, all that teal, frosted and frozen, a boudoir fit for an ice queen.

He sighs and lights another cigarette and I watch the amber

singe glow as he inhales. "You know there's so much I hadn't really realized about myself until this book, talking it through with you day after day. I guess I realize how much I've struggled bearing it all alone."

"I think the memoir has been cathartic for you."

"Not just the memoir," he muses. A gust of wind sweeps leaves up into the air and it starts to pour again.

"We should go." I turn away sharply and an acute wave of pain shoots across one eye, a piece of grit must have slipped behind my contact lens. I rub it reflexively, which only exacerbates it. "Bloody contact lens," I gasp, cupping my eye. "Excuse me, I'll just be a moment."

Nate waves me in and I dart straight into the downstairs cloakroom. Pinching the lens off my pupil, I study the tiny dark speck at its edge, marvel how something so infinitesimally small can create such obliterating agony. I'm still tending to my inflamed eye when I see him behind me, leaning in the doorway.

"Your eyes, they're different colors," he says as I hold up my fingertip, one lens balanced on it, catching eyes with him in the mirror, as if I've been caught in a weirdly intimate act.

"Green contacts, yes. They're my spares, a freebie I was sent at work. Not my first choice but I lost my glasses recently." I overexplain but he's not really listening. I thought maybe they made me look more attractive, perhaps even a bit inspired by Eva, with her gray-green eyes.

"Sometimes I wonder if there's anything real about you at all," he says. His words land as an accusation, but he is smiling, as if he's seduced by his own idea of me.

We've shared our vulnerabilities, but in the grander picture, it's as if the less he knows, the more he desires me. I think of everything I've learned about Nate, and wonder if maybe it's the same for me too. He watches me adjust my lens, blinking to regain my vision.

"I could ask the same thing," I reply. "What is remotely real about you?"

He catches my reflection in the mirror and we lock eyes.

"What is remotely real at this moment is how I *feel*—" he smiles, lingering on that word "—about you. That's what's real."

I say nothing, turn around to face him, watch the outline of his collarbone under his open shirt, the curve of his skin there. My eyes travel up to meet his, and we look at one another for a brief moment, holding our breath. "You know that, Anna, don't you?" he whispers and I nod.

I don't say a thing and he reaches out, gently, lifts my hair from my neck and kisses me there. I tilt back my head, close my eyes as his mouth moves over mine. His hands move up my back as he presses me against the wall, lifting my legs around his waist. I register this from a distance until I register nothing at all, dissolving into the moment, all sensible thought melting away.

# EVA'S SELF-REFLECTION JOURNAL

*Patient X: "Eva?"*

*I hear them ask during our session, more insistent than before.*

*Me: "It's nothing," I hear myself stammer. "I admit this is new to me, this feeling of shared grief. I wish I could make it better for you, with everything that happened to you and your younger sister—"*

*Patient X leans forward, offers me a box of tissues. "I didn't want to upset you."*

*Me: "You haven't at all. You expressed yourself and I was simply responding. It's so moving to witness someone's resilience, reliving such a traumatic memory... For a moment I felt as if I shared your pain, which is truly something I never thought I'd be able to do."*

*Patient X: "You're the first person I've told these things to. I wanted to say how much happier I've been feeling over the last few weeks, how different it is really talking to someone. You have no idea. I hope I haven't made you uncomfortable?"*

*Me: "No. No, I was wondering if you felt it too."*

*Patient X: "You know I do."*

*I pause for a long moment. "You've heard of Freud's work on transference. Love, yearning, anger, contempt. All these can come up in the safety of the consulting room, projected onto the therapist. Then, of course, there's countertransference when the therapist has to work through difficult feelings too."*

*Patient X: "So?"*

*Me: "Well, I worry what we're feeling here is a form of emotional transference, which can be utterly destructive for both patient and therapist. There is no good outcome. I need to explain that. You have to know."*

*Patient X isn't really listening, their gray eyes fixed on mine. "Stop reciting from the textbooks. You know this is different, right?"*

*I try my best not to smile. Everything I've explained is erased, meaningless. Nothing else matters except being right here, our little theater of projections, safe from the outside world.*

# 24

Him and her.

In the end, it made all the sense in the world that Tony was Patient X. Naively I had told him about my interview with Eva, and her offer of a free therapy session. But I never told him I had agreed to it, even though our chat barely constituted a session, at least not one she'd bother writing up. I was too reserved to tell her anything of interest and after forty minutes, I thanked her and left. That was the last time we ever spoke. The mystery is how he knew where I'd been that day—what led my brother to Eva?

I had examined those pages so carefully when I found her journal, the sacred line between patient and therapist disintegrating. It was all there, simmering in the spaces between the words, boundaries yielding, the potent sense that it was only a matter of time before their relationship would break out of the consulting room and into real life. And my secrets too revealed along with it.

I wake to daylight seeping through my eyelids. Replay, recalibrate, rewind. Cushions are scattered on the floor, his clothes and mine in a twisted trail, forming strange shapes in the morning light. I can still feel him, on top of me, inside me, the scent of us heavy in the room.

Up it floats, the hazy chronology of last night, the bathroom and, at some point, one of us had signaled a move elsewhere. How willingly I had followed him up here, walking ahead of him into his room. Lying on his bed, I remember how I had turned my head toward the soft beam of light from the bathroom, saw a glimpse of an open door that led to Eva's bedroom. Somehow it unnerved me, and I got up from his bed to close it.

"I feel as if I'm being watched," I had said and he'd laughed at the melodrama of it.

"It's a little late for worrying about that," he had quipped, lightly kissing my stomach, lowering me back down onto the bed.

Now I watch him ocean deep in sleep, his arms curled around a pillow. Sleep suits him, I decide, melting away the frown lines and the creases around his eyes, a smile teasing at the edge of his lips. Part of me knows I should get up and leave, creep away before it's sabotaged. But I can't bear to quite yet and I shift positions instead, feel his arm move across me, the exhale of his breath on the nape of my neck. I drift off.

When I wake again, the bed is empty. I hear him moving around in the bathroom, the thrum of the shower, the whirr of a shaver. I luxuriate in these sounds, the clicks and creaks of the heating coming on, a cleaner tidying up somewhere downstairs.

He walks back in, gets dressed. "I'll be back in two hours, we'll do something," he says. "You always make a habit of running away, don't do that again."

"Sounds good," I say, sleepily. I smile up at him and then he is gone.

The cushioned silence of the room presses in. I get up, nose around the bathroom, stare at my reflection. My body feels tender, aching. My hair is a mess, frizzy from the downpour last night, traces of last night's makeup smeared beneath my eyes, my lips stained red. I am undone, but something radiates through me, a rawness, a hunger of a different kind.

I study myself for a moment. I seem as opaque to myself as I am to him. I turn to the bathroom door—her connecting door. Once again, I'm driven by the siren call of what lies behind.

My feet lead me through before my mind can object, drawn inexorably by her life and how it is melting into mine. I step into the walk-in closet; the mad extravagance of it, a glittering dressing-up box for grown-ups, for women who surely can't exist beyond films or fantasy. Each section is meticulously arranged by color, print, dress type, even hem length. There is night and day wear; Grecian metallic dresses; velvet jackets, satin jumpsuits, sections for denim, sections for leopard print. There's a lingerie drawer too, which I begin to slide open but something stops me and instead I pick up a black scarf with golden embroidered stars. Running the velvet fabric across the back of my neck, I inhale the scent of it, vanilla and old cigarettes still cling to its fibers.

My eye is caught by one of the silk slip dresses in eau de Nil and I pull it from its hanger, a slash of black lace at its edges. I feel giddy with the illicit thrill of it, caught between desire and fear he may return. I unwrap my towel and shimmy the dress over my head. Stepping into a pair of patent nude shoes with their trademark flash of scarlet sole, I sway down the short aisle between the rails.

The dress clings to my body, brushes my legs. I twirl and sashay, seduced by the film playing in my head. Except when I check myself out in the mirror, it's not like that at all. The delicate silk that should fall into loose Grecian folds stretches cheaply across my breasts, its seams gape at my hips. I notice my pale skin pressing through the stitching and a wave of re-vulsion sweeps over me. Her superiority on so many levels, losing at a game I realize now I've been playing all along.

I slip the dress off awkwardly, my elbow knocks a row of handbags on the shelf above me. One of them falls to the floor and, as I stretch up to replace it, I see a bulky plastic Superdrug bag that looks out of place, take it out and look inside. There are Duracell batteries, Nurofen, emery boards and an almost-full bottle of sparkling water that long ago lost its fizz. Like a small time capsule. I wonder how long they've been lying here.

I'm about to replace them when I spot something else, a slim blue-and-white cardboard packet ripped open in a crevice of the bag that I missed, and behind it a receipt. I take them both out, turn it over in my hands.

Ninety-nine percent accurate, it says along the top in yel-low. I glance at the itemized list and there it is right at the top:

*Clear Blue Early detection test—£21.99.*
*Superdrug King Street. 24 June 2019*

The date jumps out at me and I freeze.

The day Eva died. Nausea seeps through me like a poison, black dots prickle the edges of my vision. Eva would have taken this test two years ago. She would have felt sick too perhaps, her hand shaking as she crouched over the toilet, peeing on the stick, willing that second blue line not to come into being.

An icy certainty sweeps up my spine. The stark reality of that date hits me. He told me he had discovered the pregnancy test many months before Eva died.

*Three months. You're sure about that?*

*Yes, completely sure.*

I check again, the numbers blur before my eyes. I struggle to think of a reasonable explanation.

*Fuck, Nate. You lied.*

I cry out loud, on my knees now, in Eva's wardrobe, the smell of her clothes, the satin slip dress like a discarded second skin beside me. The receipt is crystal clear. I scan it once more, nausea rising all over again. Then I catch the payment details below it.

*MASTERCARD* \*\*\*\* \*\*\*\* \*\*\*\* *4617*

The last four digits of a credit card, one that's all too familiar to me. These are the numbers I have tapped into my online banking app countless times to transfer rental income or the odd sum to cover a flight.

Tony's card. He paid for Eva's pregnancy test.

Did this mean that Tony was the father? Did Nate know?

Worse, had he really found out about Eva's affair right before her death?

*You lied. You're a seasoned professional after all, poisoned by more secrets than I am.*

These omissions flay me. He had known this whole time, that his wife's lover was my brother, that's why he questioned me about Tony's surname back in Dungeness. He was piecing it together right then, in that moment. He lied about Priya to distract me from the real affair. I knew it didn't add up and that's why.

He told the inquest that he left early in the morning for his university conference, that he was away for the whole of that day, returning the next morning to find her body. This test could be different to the one he found, but that seems highly unlikely.

What was he so desperate to conceal? Kath's theory about the fentanyl flashes in my mind. So does the image of her sculptures, the female statues scored through over and over.

Right across their bellies. Who would have done that and why? Eva, in an act of defiance, a final work of art: expressing her fury at the way men chose to control her body, her condition.

I wrap the towel tight around myself, replace everything except the receipt. I grip it in my palm, close Eva's door and I'm back in Nate's room. Swiftly I get dressed, turn my back to the bed, the coil of sheets where we lay last night. Another country now.

Anger burns in my throat, spiking my veins. I'm struck for a moment by how novel it is to feel self-righteous. My secrets amount to nothing compared to his. His fake compassion, the interest in my past. Our future that he dangled before me. The possibility of a new start in New York. A brilliant strategy to divert me from the real story, the one he was never going to tell me with a second inquest looming.

And what's more: if he did find the pregnancy test on the day she died, it means he still had the chance—and the drugs—to react accordingly. When I get home, I lie on my bed, try to cry but I am beyond tears. Carefully, I unfold the receipt, look at it again until the numbers and letters blur. Outside there is the steady metronomic thud of a child kicking a ball against the garden fence. Over and over, two questions circle and land.

*Who was Eva most undone by? Who did she fear more—Tony or Nate?*

# 25

Late in the afternoon I take another shower, turn the water up to scalding. On a cellular level he remains, last night shimmering through me, despite my best efforts to despise him. I wanted so badly to believe everything he said was true, how he felt about me, what was really happening between us.

I'm barely dressed when I hear the buzzer and run to the hall. One more buzz, a moment of silence followed by the mechanical click of a key in the door.

"Hey."

I freeze. "Tony? How come you've got a key?"

He steps in and closes the door.

"It's Amira's." He dangles it in front of me. "Nice welcome."

I notice how large his pupils are, black orbs blotting out the iris. I wonder what he really knows, what he's really divulged? My mind flashes to him sitting opposite Eva, sharing all our family secrets. I try to join the dots of their relationship, the arc that began in her consulting room, led to the purchase of that pregnancy test, and all that followed.

"Come in," I manage curtly. His lips brush my cheek and I grimace inwardly, turn away.

"You look as if you've seen a ghost." He steps back to appraise me. "What's up with you?"

He follows me into the sitting room, glancing at the mess that I haven't had a chance to tidy up, an old pizza box on the sofa, an empty wine bottle, a glass tipped on its side on the rug. Amira has left for a fortnight visiting her mother in Paris and her absence compounds the air of neglect.

"So where have you been?"

I slip a scrunchie off my wrist, twist my hair up into a ponytail, avoid his stare by turning to scoop up some debris from the floor and taking it into the kitchen. "I haven't been anywhere," I say. "Just working here mainly."

"Come on. Don't be coy."

"Are you checking up on me? Did you let yourself in while I wasn't here?"

His face stretches into an amused smile. "I do own half the apartment, you know. Why are you upset?"

"I'm just tired. Working hard on the book; it's finished now. All over, you'll be happy to hear. Coffee?" I open the fridge door, smell the curdled milk in the carton and pour it down the sink. "Forget that."

"Anything stronger?" he asks, and spots my iPhone on the side, removes the charger from mine to attach his own. One simple act that says so much. I say nothing but my insides broil as I replace it back in my phone.

"Anna, come on." He laughs teasingly, as if I am the child, not him. "I'm down to zero. You're on forty percent."

He picks up the last apple from the fruit bowl, bites into it. His mouth is slightly open and wet. Flecks of apple skin catch in the corners of his mouth. I shake my head, my stomach churns.

"What's up with you? It's only a phone charger. Anyway, tell me, how's lover boy?" Tony squints at the bottom shelf where there's a couple of lemons and a carton of unopened tomato juice. "How about a cheeky Bloody Mary?" He pulls

out a bottle of Grey Goose vodka in the freezer compartment. "You don't mind if I fix myself one of these," he says,
distracted, plonking the bottle on the counter.

"Not for me, thanks, but help yourself."

"Something really must be up."

Instead I make myself a cup of green tea, try to swallow
down nausea as I watch him slosh vodka over bloodred juice.
He clinks my mug.

"Well done and cheers. So you did stay over with him?"
He winks, lingers indecently on the word *stay*.

I open my mouth and shut it again. I know I'm giving myself away.

"Ah, the celebratory fuck."

The words hang for a moment, sharp and ugly and true.
He's right, of course. I hate myself because, somehow, he can
still read the temperature of my mood so well, he still sees me
after all these years.

It was a transaction after all, a means to an end. Nate got
what he wanted, his memoir all wrapped up, a gullible ghostwriter who was a good sport.

Nate studies me, softening.

"Are you okay? Seriously. I mean you look like shit. I know
it's none of my business but I worry for you." He drains the
vodka, eyes still on me, before his gaze turns gentle, familiar.
"Whatever you've got drawn into, whatever you feel about
him, you should know he's bad news. You can tell me," he
says, his voice barely more than a whisper.

"I found something," I say, a crack of emotion in my voice.
*Tell him. Don't tell him.*
*Patient X…*
I blink hard, fall back through the years, to a time when
we were coconspirators, having fun even when the grown-ups
weren't. Six years old and playing slapsies in the back of the

car, the ennui of a French campsite where he taught me how to kill wasps in tumblers slathered in jam and honey, sneaking my food onto his plate when my father's back was turned so he wouldn't lose his temper. We took care of one another. It's what siblings do. But now I'm not so sure who I can trust anymore, least of all Tony.

"What did you find?" he asks more gently and I look away. I can't confront him quite yet about Patient X.

Instead, I tell him a warped story about the receipt because somehow I need to tell him something. It's clear he knows I've discovered information, but not what. Perhaps this will be enough to give him a little bait, let me bide my time.

I don't tell him exactly how I discovered it, or that I was in Eva's bedroom, or any of my questions about Tony's involvement. I stick instead to the incriminating dates, the fact that Nate lied. "So he must have been with Eva on the day she died, not at a conference all day, as he told everyone. And Eva was pregnant with his baby," I finish, testing Tony for a reaction.

"He's lying to protect himself," he says, his tone firm. I notice if anything, he looks strangely more calm than usual. "So we know he was at Algos House much closer to the time of her death than he admitted either to you or the inquest. Just be careful, don't tell anyone. Remember how Dad could be? How quickly he could turn? We've seen this before. We know where it leads."

"You really think I should be scared of him?"

"Of course, he's a classic manipulator. Charming one moment but always covering his tracks. You've said yourself, whatever he tells you never quite adds up. You were right all along, Anna."

I try to move away from him but his arm grips mine.

"Can't you see it? Eva would still be alive if it weren't for him. He's responsible. I hope it was worth it, spending that time all alone in that basement study with his piles of books and his creepy cat portraits." That calm demeanor melts away and his mouth twists as if he has ingested poison. "Don't you see what you've done? You've written the perfect alibi. He killed her, Anna, and you've helped him get away with it."

I feel his words like a punch to the gut, not only because of the weight of his accusation, which is bad enough, but what he lets slip out. How would he know about the newly hung pictures in Nate's study?

## 26

Nate keeps texting me. I don't reply, press Delete. I can't face either of them anymore, these two men in my life who I should be able to trust, to love, yet now each of them begins to scare me. Who is really lying? Which one of them was there when she died? My mind spins with the scenarios, the endless lies and subterfuge.

The receipt sits on my desk, daring me to act, but I do nothing. A day or so later Priya emails to let me know we have nothing to worry about as far as Kath's threats are concerned. Nate is cc'd in and they exchange barbed comments about Kath, how unreasonable she is being. Factually, the memoir is watertight, she can't sue on the basis that Nate's recollections of Eva sound nothing like the sister she knew.

The subjectivity of memory works in our favor. Don't we remember everyone differently? And, she says, you can't libel a dead person. I stay out of it, leave well alone.

It is the following evening when I'm a little over halfway through editing the final manuscript. There's a ripple of knuckle on the door. My heart plummets. I assume it's Tony until I remember he has Amira's key.

I peer through the spy hole and a convex reflection of Nate's face peers back. My hand springs to my mouth. I dart back into the sitting room, quickly rip down the photos pinned to my board, of Algos House, of Nate and Eva, aware that my professional research could be mistaken for prurience, obsession even. I stash them in the back of my desk drawer, along with Eva's receipt, and fly back to the hall door.

He raps again, with full-fisted urgency.

"Nate?"

I open the door and he pushes past me into the narrow hallway, a wild look in his eyes, as if he hasn't really planned beyond this point.

"We need to talk," he mumbles as I let him walk ahead of me toward the half-light of the sitting room. His eyes dart to the corners. I take Nate in for a moment before the accusations fly.

He briefly scans the books on my shelves, the stacks of memoirs and biographies on the floor. Medics and scientists from the frontline of grief. He stares sourly at two photographs above my desk, Tony and I as children, my mother and father. I watch him absorbing all this, the dimensions of my life that have always been so mysterious to him, trying to work out the shape of me, exactly who I am when I'm not with him. We are strangers to each other now. He could be capable of anything, a ruthless killer standing in my front room.

I inch toward the hallway, wondering if I could make a run for the front door if necessary. I can't help noticing how out of place he seems, away from the opulence of Algos House, pacing up and down the short length of my sitting room. I realize, watching him, how much I rely on degrees of separation to give me an illusion of control, how anxious it makes me when the boundaries dissolve between his life and mine.

"Nate?"

"Please, I have to ask you first." He stops pacing and turns to me. "Why the hell did you do it?"

"Do what?" I struggle to steady my voice, indignant that he's got there first. I should be the one accusing him of dishonesty and deception, worse.

"You went into her room after I left you alone." His tone brims with rage. "You *took* something of hers, didn't you? Her journal is missing."

I bite my lip, playing for time.

"You waited until I left the house and then you went through her things. How far does this go back? Your obsession with Eva. I thought about that night, how preoccupied you'd been with her room. Your intense interest, I couldn't help noticing, when I joked about showing you around. After you left, I went in to check. I wanted to think I'd misread you." He shakes his head, his eyes ablaze. "Jade told me about your last little visit, making some excuse about finding the cat."

"I guess she told you about how she took one of Eva's rings too?"

"You're accusing Jade of stealing from my wife's bedroom too? A new low, even by your standards."

"Nate, she was wearing—"

"Eva's ring? You think you're some sort of detective and I didn't know that?" His muscles stiffen with anger. "I let Jade have some of Eva's jewelery. Eva gave her gifts all the time. *Let someone enjoy it* is exactly what she would have said. Jade isn't a thief. You on the other hand—"

"Stop it." I twist away from him. He could be testing me, but he sounds as if he definitely knows this isn't true. His eyes burn into me and I feel as if I've reached the end of the line, all out of options.

"Alright, yes. It was her self-reflection journal, the one she used for work," I say, so quietly I can barely hear myself. "I found it jammed in a space behind one of the drawers."

"You really were thorough, weren't you, turning over my wife's bedroom?" He lets out a bitter laugh. "Fucking hell, Anna, you're a piece of work."

"I'm—"

He holds his arm up. "I don't want to hear it. Just tell me where her journal is." There's a tremor in his voice, a wariness that is new to me.

"So you've read it then? I need to tell you something before I do. About my brother, Tony."

There's a pause as I let his name permeate.

"My half brother. You know exactly who I'm talking about. I know you know about the affair...their affair."

His features harden, his mannerisms brittle as glass. He has reason to be explosive but how much will he take it out on me?

The moment stretches. Outside there is the familiar London sound of suitcase wheels on pavement, the flinty sound of transience and escape. I wish I could be anywhere but here. Nate taps his foot on the floorboards.

"Eva was also Tony's psychotherapist," I say, emotionless. There's no way to soften those words and so I don't bother trying. "That's it. That's all I know. After my telephone interview with her, I remember I enthused about her to Tony, and I suppose it was enough to make him think of her when he wanted to see a therapist."

"Your brother," he echoes, incredulous, more to himself than to me. His voice falls to a low snarl. "Go and get it. Now."

He stands up, moves toward the desk, squints at the photos there of Tony and myself that hang above it. Black dots pepper my vision as I walk across the room and open the drawer.

Nate strides toward me, rips it from my hand, leafs through her entries and reads one. I imagine Eva's smoky tones resonating, curling closer around us as he scans her words with new eyes. He needles his temples with his fingers, looks up at me with a granite stare devoid of emotion.

"My brother was Patient X, not me," I say, evenly. "But, Nate. I didn't know. I only discovered it myself when I read the journal. We got on well and she offered me one session with her. That's all it was. I agreed I could write an interesting piece on it."

"Of course you did," he sneers.

"Listen, I went along and…it didn't work out. As you can imagine, I hated talking about myself, digging up the past. I was there for around forty minutes and I left, never saw her again. I swear it's the truth."

Nate ignores my protestations, begins to read.

"*Patient X: I wasn't very—I mean, I struggle to be open, to talk about myself, what I've really been through. That's what people tell me.*" He lets out a deep sigh. "It just sounds an awful lot like you, Anna. Almost as if that first therapy session she offered you may have led to many others?"

"If you keep reading that journal, it's obvious. She even writes that Patient X had a younger sister."

"Is it?" he cuts in. "If it's Tony, have you told him about it?"

"God, no. I was too scared to tell him." I laugh, a little unhinged, as the words hang between us. "I swear it's not me in that journal. I was never Eva's patient, and I didn't go into her room looking for it. It's unforgivable that I went behind your back. I wanted to find out more about her, to get closer to you, find out if I stood a chance, I suppose. If I could ever measure up."

"Working with me gave you the perfect opportunity to dig around for any dirty secrets you could find to sell to the papers, didn't it? The way you lit up that day when I said you'd have the afternoon to yourself," he muses. "You probably cased her bedroom then, didn't you? That night, everything before that, was a means to an end."

"You're not listening, Nate. What do you want me to say? You meant nothing to me?"

"At least it would be more honest."

"You really think I could have spent all this time with you as part of some bizarre plan to expose your past for the sake of my career? The evening you drove me home, at the Rosen? The other night?" I glare at him, blood rushes in my ears. "You think I'm that person?"

He shrugs. "Nothing would surprise me. You've spent the last few weeks insisting that honesty is everything, no more self-deception, open up on the page. All the time you've been a liar."

"It was so wrong of me, I'm sorry. Really I am. But I couldn't help feeling there were answers in her room, answers you weren't telling me. I think Tony went to see Eva after I did because maybe he was worried about something I'd tell her. If he started seeing her himself, there was a chance he could find her notes from my session, or rewrite the narrative to protect himself? I don't know, Nate. It's a theory but—"

"A theory," he mimics. "And what terrible thing could you have told Eva about that he'd fear so much?"

"It's beside the point. You're such a hypocrite. While we're talking about lies, what about you? If you're so innocent, why didn't you tell me you were with Eva on the day she died? Why didn't you tell the inquest?"

I watch as confusion clouds his expression. "You know I wasn't with her that day—I was in Manchester."

"Were you? Look at me and tell me honestly that the day you came home to find the pregnancy test wasn't the day she died?"

Something in his expression crumbles, hollows out. In the

sunlight slanting through the blinds, his complexion looks ashy, strands of his hair stick up at right angles. He looks vulnerable in a way I hadn't allowed myself to notice before, shattered, utterly alone.

"I have the receipt for it," I say levelly. "That was in Eva's bedroom too. It's how I know you know about her and Tony. You came back, found the pregnancy test and you fought about it. You left her in a terrible state, vulnerable to using again and lied about it afterward. That's the truth, isn't it? And the fentanyl—"

"I was there that lunchtime," he cuts me off, voice cracking. "I didn't tamper with the drugs she took that evening, if that's what you're insinuating. She confessed her affair with an *Anthony Thorpe*. We rowed and screamed at each other. She ran at me, swore in my face. I know there's no excuse but—" He inhales to steady himself. "I guess I gripped her too tightly, the fingermark bruising on her arm was me. I felt terrible but we talked afterward, I apologized over and over. By the time I left, we'd made up and then I drove up to Manchester."

"But somehow you forgot to tell the inquest about it. You've lied all along, left stuff out when it suits you. You've known since Dungeness that she was having an affair with my brother."

"Look, I should have told you when you mentioned Tony at the lunch. It was only then the name fell into place, the surname that was different to yours."

"I could tell you were thrown but you improvised pretty quickly and lied yet again, making up that affair between Priya and Eva to distract me."

"I was weak, I realize. I liked you. If you'd discovered the truth about Tony at that point, it would have thrown the whole project into jeopardy. There was no way we could have carried on… I didn't want that to happen."

"Agreed. Very weak," I say, bitterly.

"I was scared too. I knew how damning it would look for me: the vengeful scorned husband, discovering his wife is pregnant with another man's child the exact same day she dies? I didn't plan to lie to you, but I had to cover my tracks to look as if it happened three months earlier. I knew it was too early in her pregnancy for it to show up in the autopsy, and there was no reason for them to do a pregnancy test. Surely the important thing is I had an alibi that evening. Plenty of people saw me at the conference in Manchester around the time she died. There's no way I could have been with her."

He sits back down at the table facing me, the journal gripped in his hand.

"But we can't really *know* that you didn't lace the drugs. On the scale of deceit, yours is way worse than mine," I say, realizing how suddenly frightened I am that it could be true. "I think the police would agree with me."

He shifts in his seat, looks at me. We are so close, his hand an inch away from mine. A sense of self-preservation takes over me, my survival instinct. I know how quickly his temper can turn. I could call the police.

"You must know I'm innocent. Look at me, Anna." His voice drops to a soft murmur. "I've devoted my life to trying to help others, trying to cure their pain. I'm a good guy. I'm not guilty of anything."

"Aren't you?"

"Well, aren't you?" he echoes back at me.

"I've never harmed anyone," I say, emphasizing each word.

"Really? I wonder." A savage glint shines in his eyes. "The harm you've both done. You and Tony. The pair of you. Destroying my marriage, tainting our lives. You're both... damaged. How could you think we had a future together? You and I never stood a chance."

The contempt in his tone is a final twist of the knife.

"Please, just go," I almost whisper, turning away. A moment later the door slams.

It's only when he is gone, I realize he took the journal with him.

# 27

My eyes snap open to the drab symphony of gray morning light seeping through my window. When I get up, my body aches. Behind my eyes. In my heart, my guts. I find myself googling symptoms. Pain: acute, chronic, persistent.

Images of last night flicker up, the final realization that so much has ended, all choices extinguished. A future with Nate, an escape from Tony. These two men helped to destroy Eva's life and now they're closing in on mine. I can't help thinking, how can I escape her fate?

Outside my window life carries on the same, shrill and ceaseless, in the excitable chatter of children on their way to school, the metallic clang from a building site opposite. The hours stretch, all the more elastic and endless since Amira is away. I miss her, and yet even if she were here, I'm not sure I'd want to confide in her. Where would I begin without alarming her unduly? What could I tell her that I know for sure to be the truth?

Priya emails, brisk and businesslike, oblivious, I assume, to all that has happened. She's expecting a completed manuscript by the end of next week and wants to know how it's going. All good, I reply.

I wake up at 7:00 a.m. the next day feeling different somehow. Clear-headed, single-minded. I tidy up the apartment, clean out the fridge, order in healthy food, give up alcohol. When I'm not proofreading, I go for long runs. Without music. Unexpectedly I find myself engaging with the outside world. In the snap of twigs on the muddy path, the way my exhalations and inhalations hang like misty clouds in the morning air. But still the rhythmic slap of my soles on the path sounds out two names: Tony, Nate. Nate, Tony. The faster I run, the more the consonants blur.

What a fool I was. Indignation fires me up, deepens to molten rage. They are the arch manipulators and yet now they accuse me of being the villain. A thief and a liar. Stealing from Eva's bedroom, creating a memoir to gain access to his house, cover for my own crimes. Each claims I've betrayed them to protect the other. Such a difference a fortnight can make.

My dreams shift up a gear. They are no longer bland but replete with revenge, ice-cold, bloody and exacting. For myself as well as Eva. How dare they? Tony always taking what doesn't belong to him. Taking. Taking. Taking. Shackling me to our shared past to keep me weak. Nate blaming and belittling me when his crimes are potentially so much worse.

I was sleepwalking into our affair, and now in the gray dawn of each day, I start to wonder how much he used his knowledge of neuroscience to seduce me. He spent his life absorbed by the brain, in particular our unconscious and the power it exerts over us. Didn't he tell me one afternoon, alight with its potential, how it's entirely possible to provoke a response, a set of behaviors even, without the victim realizing, simply by knowing the right way to play them?

*The nonconscious you is the powerhouse of every interaction, every reflex and desire, even sexual attraction. Crack that and you can control any aspect of human behavior.*

On my morning runs, I find myself jogging back towards

the river, drawn to somewhere my mind won't acknowledge quite yet. The sky is a seamless blue, my breath cold enough to snap. In my head, I run a defense trial where I am exonerated and Nate is guilty as charged.

I should turn back and head for home but instead I've slipped down the underpass, below the rumble of the Great West Road. I emerge at Furnival Gardens and, a few minutes later, I find myself at the Upper Mall close to Algos House.

Outside I allow myself a sideways glance up at the Georgian windows, the tendrils of lilac wisteria creeping through the black railings. I think of the last time I was here. Nate's voice above the hiss of rain, urging me to call a cab from his house.

I turn on my heels. I think I've seen enough. But something catches my eye. The flash of white board, an estate agent's sign. Sold.

He must have been much further ahead with the sale than he'd implied that night, his plans way more mapped out than he let on. Another deception to add to the pile.

As soon as I'm home, I scan Rightmove, greedy for details of Algos House. "Immaculate and stunning architectural home close to the park with easy access to central London. Generous garden and studio with glorious views across the river."

I flash through interior after interior, the double-height atrium, the glass gallery, gleaming kitchen island and walk-in wardrobe. The overall impression is vaguely disappointing. Even through the estate agent's wide-angled lens, the rooms appear smaller, less opulent and characterful than I imagined, like a series of sterile stage sets.

I run back home, carry on editing the book except that every word I read feels inauthentic. Kath's words ring in my ears. *You made her up. There's nothing of the sister I knew in there at all.*

As all these fragments merge to form a bigger picture, deep unease seeps into my bones. Nate despises me now, he made that much clear. I'm also the only person who shares his secret: that he hurt Eva and lied to the inquest about his whereabouts. Anger turns to anxiety and finally fear.

Late one afternoon, when I am in the Google doc I used to share with Nate, I see his cursor hovering on the page. I scroll down swiftly to another section of the manuscript until I see it follow me there too. He hangs back and tweaks a paragraph I've been working on. I wonder if I am the first female to feel harassed in the context of a shared document.

It happens again the next day, his digital presence looming there like a veiled threat, name bolded up in blue. He is watching each word I write.

*STALKER.*

*STALKER.*

*STALKER.*

I copy and paste the word over and over, only to watch each one being deleted.

*YOU'RE SO VAIN, YOU PROBABLY THINK THIS BOOK IS ABOUT YOU.*

His cursor twitches there, before eating up the words.

I copy what I'm working on into a separate document to avoid his scrutiny. As I scroll through the chapters, it is like wandering into once-familiar rooms yet all the furniture has moved around, the decor is different. My phrases are vanishing, they've been ghosted away. It occurs to me that, finally, he has erased my voice—and Eva's.

★ ★ ★

Early on Wednesday morning it happens. I am tinkering on the final chapter when I realize I'm there. I've touched the finish line. I write a short covering letter to Priya and there's nothing else to do but press Send.

I have read about this euphoric milestone many times, the authors who celebrate with a glass of champagne or a cigarette. I have yearned for it, the giddy euphoria of the final period. Yet now I'm finally here, the moment seems tainted.

I declutter my workspace, bag up the notepads and the transcript and dump it all in the bottom drawer, stare transfixed at the space above my desk. One more thing on my list. I call a locksmith to change the locks. No more surprise visits from Tony.

Later, I am on the sofa watching TV when there's a buzz at the communal door. I don't move but someone on the ground floor lets them in. Steps echo from the stairs and my heart flip-flops. A knock now, more urgent this time, on my front door. I run to the hallway and press the intercom.

"Anna? It's me, Amira," comes a voice, out of breath, the south London vowels warm and familiar. "Sorry, I haven't got my key."

I exhale, relieved, and help to carry her bags in from the landing. We hug briefly, the scent of travel clings to her; of international departure lounges and fast food and taxicabs.

"I thought you weren't back until Friday," I say as she sinks onto the sofa, kicks off her trainers and rubs her toes.

"I thought so too, but surely you've heard about Jess?" She looks astounded, as if it's global breaking news I somehow failed to pick up on.

I shake my head, confused.

"Where have you been?"

"Here. Chained to my desk, out of the office loop. Something called finishing a book?"

"Ah, the great masterpiece." She rolls her eyes and I realize how much I have missed her.

"Anyway, tell me about Jess," I say, pleased by the distraction.

"Skiing accident. It was only a green slope but she managed to smash her knee in two places, and she's done her back in. They're operating on Monday. Reckons she'll be laid out for at least two months. On top of dealing with my parents for two weeks, I now have to look after the magazine." She exhales, leans her head back on the sofa, rakes a hand through her hair and groans. "No more lunches with you. There goes my social life."

I throw her a look of disbelief.

"What?" She frowns, barely able to conceal a smile twitching at the corners of her mouth. I hear myself laugh for the first time in days, at her lame attempts to disguise her delight at this unexpected promotion, her ineluctable ambition that's impossible to conceal.

"Jess out of the way. Amira, editor of her own magazine? It's a dream come true for you. Come on. You're thrilled. You must be. It's all you ever wanted."

"It's not like that though. She'll be all over me, micromanaging remotely, pulling features at the last minute." She shakes her head lightly, grimacing, and I frown in disbelief.

"Spare me the humblebrags. It's brilliant news. You know it is. Possibly three months as editor and you can get a job anywhere."

"Well, maybe you're right." She softens, gives me a reluctant smile. I ask her about Paris and staying with her parents. She tells me about her father who is growing more forgetful, confusing her twice with her younger sister, her frustrated mother, and how guilty she feels living so far away.

"Sometimes I envy you, Anna. That you no longer have to worry about your parents. I mean, I'm sorry. That's an insensitive thing to say," she says quickly, scanning my expression.

I shake my head, accustomed to small comments like this from Amira over the years. "No, I think I know what you mean," I say. "My biggest childhood fear, of being orphaned, is behind me. I'm an adult and I'm free." I'm giving her the reassurance I know she craves. I can't tell her that it's more complex, that how you lose a parent is the real measure of the freedom you may feel, depending on how guilty or responsible you may have been. Nor can I explain all the complications with it, like how often it feels like the world divides into orphans, those who no longer have parents and those who do. But that's one piece of wisdom she'll have to discover for herself.

She stops herself and I know Tony is about to come up in the conversation. I'm struck with guilt, not sure what to share. How do I begin to tell Amira any of this, the subterfuge, the threats, Tony and Eva's history?

She looks down, chews her bottom lip. "Anna, I'm not even sure how to tell you." Tears fill her eyes and her shoulders slump. "We broke up, Tony and I."

Alarmed, I sit down next to her. She breathes sharply as if to brace herself for what she's about to share.

"He called me in Paris a few days ago unannounced, ranting and raging. About you mainly. About Nate and Eva. How we were all against him and that Nate was an evil bastard manipulating you. None of it made much sense. We fought again when I returned home, and I tried to calm him down but... he got so angry."

She looks at me for a moment as if in two minds, almost as if she's ashamed in some way.

She pushes her ringlets off her face to show me a livid purple and yellow bruise blooming at her temple.

I say nothing for a moment, a wave of emotion breaks inside me, fury that my brother would do this to my best friend, but something else too. Guilt. Why did I not act sooner, intervene in some way? I was too self-absorbed by my own dramas.

"Amira," I gasp. "That's awful. I'm so, so sorry. There's so much I should have told you. He came round here too, a few days ago. We had a big argument. I was going to call you. I can't believe I let this happen."

She considers me for a moment. "You couldn't have stopped this, Anna. I should have listened to you more. He always seemed so plausible when he talked about you relying on him—"

"What the hell happened? What did he do?"

"It was just an accident. We were arguing and I tried to leave. He pushed me, I must have tripped and hit one of the coat hooks."

I watch her making excuses to protect his actions, a dark unfathomable rage rising up in me. "You should report this, Amira. I'll support you if you do, whatever you need."

We hug, briefly. Her fingers reflexively touch her temple. "I'll think about it but the main thing is it's over. He's out of our lives now and that's all that matters," she says, firmly. If only I could believe her.

I cook supper for her. Glancing around the room, she notices the blank space above my desk.

"What happened?" she says. "Where's it all gone?"

"Big cleanup. All done, over," I say, brightly, rubbing my

hands. "I sent the edited manuscript to Priya and we're meeting tomorrow."

"That's amazing, Anna, you got there. I hope you give us first go on serializing it. And Priya likes it?"

"So far, yes."

I sit down opposite her at the small kitchen counter and it strikes me how relaxed I feel when it's just Amira and me. Without Tony polluting our friendship, everything feels complete.

"So what next? Your own book?" She catches my expression. "I thought that's what you wanted most of all, so why do you look so horrified at the idea?"

"Right now, I can't imagine ever writing again."

"Really, that bad. I thought it was going well with Nate." Her eyes search mine. "You did, didn't you?"

I look away, my face burning.

"Oh, Anna," she says, putting down her wine.

I can't hold it in any longer, any of it, the secrets I'm carrying. And so I begin to tell her only what I can bear: about Nate and me, the day at the coast, Nate's confession about Eva, our kiss. How hard I fell for him, how stupid I was to be taken in. Then the doubts, small but sharper by the day. I blink back hot tears. She nods, quietly absorbs my explanation.

I don't tell her about Eva's journal. I can't go there yet, can't risk Tony getting to Amira. Instead, I tell her about nosing around Eva's bedroom and finding the pregnancy test receipt.

It is her turn to put an arm around me and I can't hold my tears back anymore. They slide down my cheek, my mouth twists.

"Anna, you poor thing. Thankfully you found out when you did, before it got more serious."

She leans forward, her expression grave as the implications of my discoveries sink in.

"But honestly. You could have been in danger. You still could be. Do you think he actually could have killed Eva?"

Even though I've tiptoed around that question, it's the first time I've heard it articulated before. Spoken by someone else, it carries extra weight. I struggle to digest the possibility it could be true.

"It sounds fantastical, doesn't it? I can't believe we're even having this conversation." I roll my eyes at the absurdity of it but notice she's frowning.

"Why is it so far-fetched, Anna? I'm not sure you're taking this seriously enough. The guy lied about his timings. He was there the day she died. If that's the case, you have to tell the police."

I nod slowly. "You're right, I probably should."

"Does anyone else know you have that receipt?" she asks, sternly.

I hesitate. "Only Tony. And Nate."

"Only?" Her tone is alarmed. "Anna, why did you tell Nate?"

"I wanted to find out if he was really lying, I guess. Part of me wanted to come up with a plausible explanation."

"And?"

"I just don't know anymore. He was adamant that he wasn't there when she died and, honestly, I felt he was telling me the truth. But now I feel cheated, that he's not who I thought he was. He admitted to hurting Eva, gripping her so tightly that he bruised her, lying to the inquest."

"What sort of person does that?" she says quietly, and then her fingertips reflexively touch her temple. I wince once more at what I see there, unable to catch her eye.

# 28

I take the subway into town, weave my way toward a small Italian bar in Covent Garden where Priya has asked to meet me. Film stills of Italian film stars and opera singers fill the whitewashed walls. She tells me she has another appointment in forty minutes and doesn't remove her coat or scarf. We perch stiffly on stools at the counter. Clearly, she is dreading this as much as I am. She glances down to check her watch, thinking I don't notice.

"A little something to celebrate?" She eyes up the bar menu.

"Celebrate?"

"You've finished, Anna. Come on, you deserve it."

"Not for me. Water's fine."

"Good for you." Her eyes slip over me, trying to work out what's changed. "You're looking...well. Your skin or maybe your hair? You've had something done, haven't you?"

"It's called exercise, and no booze. Not working on the memoir probably helps." I let out a small hollow laugh. Something has changed in her too, as if she's lit from within and I think I can guess why. Everything's worked out well for her. I'm off the scene and Brand Nate is about to launch in New York.

She tells me her plans for the memoir in America, a gleam

of febrile excitement in her eyes. "They're mad for anything to do with the brain, look at David Eagleman. Just mention neurotransmitters and synapses and watch it rocket up the *New York Times* bestseller lists."

"He's off soon?"

"There already." She smiles but her lips stay sealed. "Starting at Columbia next week. He's flying here for the launch and after that he'll live mainly in the US, until he ties up the house sale in a few weeks."

"Ah, the house sale."

She nods.

"He was in two minds about whether he could get a good price for it, given what had happened there. I told him to get on with it. It's a great market and maybe, weirdly," she says, failing to suppress a smile, "it's even a USP."

"Eva's death a USP. That's a classy way of looking at it."

She ignores my barb, carries on regardless, keen to keep up the chatter before she can dump me for good. "Anyway, a French banker saw it and instantly fell in love. She bid way over the asking price in the end."

"How brilliant for both of you. I guess he got everything he wanted."

She considers me for a moment. "Wanted is a strange way to frame it. He's moving on from a terrible personal tragedy. What he really wanted was Eva to still be around, to have a wife and kids, a shot at family life. That was his dream."

"Really?" I say, keeping my voice steady and recalling Nate's words—he *had* wanted to be a father. He was ready.

My fingers interlace under the table, my nails cut into my palms, and I feel increasingly unsettled as my mind jumps a step further.

If Nate really wanted to be a father himself so badly, how furious would he have been to discover that Eva's baby wasn't his? That she didn't want to keep it? The very narrative he said he wanted to protect himself from—what if it was simply the truth?

"Look, I know how hard it's been for you. I think even an experienced ghostwriter would have struggled with some of the...personal challenges that you've faced while you were writing it."

"Personal challenges?" My face prickles with heat. What the hell had he been telling her?

"We don't need to say anything more, Anna." She holds up one of her manicured hands, gives a brief dainty shake of her head. "Rest assured Nate didn't go into detail but I completely understand. I was at that fundraiser. Anyway, it's not my business. Are you sure you don't want a glass of something?"

I shake my head, firmly. Inside I'm screaming, questions roar in my brain. "No, please tell me. What does he mean by personal challenges?"

"Well, he's really worried about you. Your family situation. He didn't give me too much detail but he mentioned a brother?" She makes a face. As much as Priya adores publishing the sordid details of people's lives, she is clearly repelled by any proximity to the real thing. "He says the book threw up some painful issues and it got in the way of you two, and he really hopes you can work them out now the book is finished."

"You must be so pleased how it's all worked out," I say, unable to resist, my tone suitably stony.

"Seriously, Anna, I didn't want this meeting to be difficult."

"Well, I should go anyway," I say. It's important I remain neutral, I'm pretty sure that every word of what we say will be relayed back to him. "It's been a pleasure."

"You know lots of ghostwriters go through this. They can feel disillusioned, rejected. It's a thing, Anna. You carry them around in your mind for weeks like a method actor. Then it's just you again. It'll pass. Give it a month or two and you'll be proud of your work."

"How could I write something I was proud of when there were so many secrets, so many no-go areas?" I say, anger bubbling to the surface. "All such a compromise."

"Well, it was your job to get past that. I was paying you to get to the bottom of it, that's what we discussed when you came to my office?" Her gentle tone enrages me.

"Or were you paying me to keep quiet? Perhaps you didn't want all of it out there in print? I mean, what I can't work out," I say, "is why he wanted to hire me in the first place. Surely it would have been easier if you'd both worked on it from the start, not bothered to involve someone like me?"

"Anna, he didn't want you to be his ghostwriter and tried to convince me not to take you on. It was me that made the decision." Priya's eyes glitter dangerously. "I knew it made sense, you were an unknown, not worried about the money."

"Malleable, eager to please?"

"Something like that."

"But given these…circumstances…with your family, Nate is keen to get you off the project. The truth is, he's asked for some editorial changes and he wants me to finish it."

I think about that Google doc, watching my text disappear. He must have told her to meet me to get me off the final rewrite, wrest it under their control. The truth of it hits hard. He doesn't want me because he fears what I know, and this alone points to his guilt. I'm struck with a deep regret that I hadn't been able to finish Eva's journal entries. What if Kath was right, what if there was incriminating information about Nate's behavior the day she died?

"Don't look like that. You got too involved. Remember, when you're a ghostwriter, you're only ever the midwife, never the mother," she says, standing up to leave, a lightness in her step now it's all over. "There is one more thing I need to tell you," she says. "It's about the book launch. I probably should have said this earlier but—"

"You don't want me to be there?"

"It's not me actually, it's—"

"Sure, of course. I get the message."

"Nate asked me to ask you. I think after everything that's happened it's for the best, don't you?" She watches me steadily. "We're both counting on you."

"Count away," I say, childishly defiant. "You can rely on me." Her features tighten, two tiny indents form between her perfect eyebrows. "For your own sake, Anna, you should stay away."

# 29

I am a ghost in the room tonight. A shadow no one will notice, exactly as it should be. Guests arrive, flowing toward the heat and hum of the glass atrium at the back of the bookshop and I slip in unobserved.

It is easy enough to lose myself here, hovering at the back behind a pillar. I've been paid to melt away into the ether but I doubt they'll be looking out for me.

So why risk coming along at all, what will it solve? I realize I need closure, to make my peace with the memoir, with Eva. I couldn't keep away.

I watch Nate climb the stairs to the balcony for his speech, now a mere stranger. He draws his fingertips through the back of his hair.

My mind spools back to the last time we met here, under very different circumstances. It was just before we began the book, a reconnaissance mission, he called it, to see what was already out there. What to avoid, what to magpie.

"Here you go. My gift to you," he said as we browsed the shelves of Memoir & Autobiography. *The Art of Ghostwriting* by Alan D. Mackintosh.

"Riveting," I said, opening the first page and reading aloud:

*"Ghosts can start out as a friend, muse and therapist, but you need to adhere to strict rules if you want it to stay that way. By the end of the contract, they can be pushed to arm's length, ranking no higher than a nanny or a secretary, or worse."*

The quote's earnest tone had made us both laugh. He bought me a copy but I never did bother to finish it. I was irked by Mackintosh's outdated voice, the author's presumption that a female ghostwriter is subordinate, likely to be exploited, then dumped.

His book—our book—is displayed on a table next to me. I leaf through a copy, turning to a random page. Those familiar words and phrases take me back to the endless hours we spent, the perfect collaboration, transmuting his raw experience into gold.

What would Eva think of her life packaged up for public consumption like this? Her true story, her authentic voice extinguished. Nate has made ghosts of us both.

Something in me deflates. I know that it's all over. I walk to the end of the aisle and stop in my tracks. There are Nate and Priya standing just yards away. As I walk briskly past them toward the door, he looks up and our eyes lock. Priya reaches for his arm. He pushes her away, follows me outside.

"Wait, Anna," he shouts after me. I won't wait a second longer. I have spent too long under Nate's skin and now it's time to burrow out.

I take off my heels, stuff them deep into my bag and start to run. Away from him. Still I hear his voice, urgent and cracked, calling my name. I turn a corner and break into a sprint, my bare soles slap the cold wet pavement. *Keep going*, I tell myself, my breath ragged, my lungs burning.

I turn off Marylebone High Street and weave my way through the smaller streets, each turn taking me farther away from him.

When I reach a small garden square, I lean against the wrought iron railings surrounding it to catch my breath. The sky is inky and starless. A light flashes on in the townhouse opposite and I find myself looking into its kitchen. An elderly woman opens her fridge, starts to wash up, stares blankly back at me.

I wipe the back of my neck, slicked in sweat, turn toward the sound of footsteps somewhere at the end of the street. I could, I should, run but my energy deserts me. I am strangely rooted to the spot. Nate stops until we are facing each other, he's more out of breath than me.

"Anna?"

The woman in the window draws down her blind sharply and Nate's face falls into shadow as he steps closer.

"I know I asked you not to come tonight. I've been furious about what happened, I know you have too. But I've been thinking, we both deserve the truth, one more chance to talk. I'm flying to New York tomorrow and I won't be coming back."

I close my eyes, shake my head. *He knows you have the receipt. Don't place yourself in yet more danger. Don't be taken in, not again.*

"I can't talk anymore, Nate. It's too late. But not to worry, I won't be going to the police, so your precious career is safe."

"The thing is I'm pretty sure I believe you, everything you told me about your brother. I don't think you were trying to protect him, I think you were genuinely scared. I found something clearing out her stuff just before I sold the house. I need to show you. If it's true, you need to take care..." Cast in shadow, his features look angular, etched with anxiety. About me.

The beat of my heart rings in my ears.

"Nate..."

"We both know Eva was having an affair with Tony. He was with her that night. I know it all, Anna. And I think you know that too." His phone rings. "It's Priya. I have to get back. But can you meet me afterward?"

I hesitate. "Where?" I hear myself saying in spite of myself, lulled by his low insistent murmur. I hadn't realized quite how much I missed that voice. Maybe he's right after all. In the end it is our unconscious that gets to make the most important decisions.

"Back at mine in an hour?" he whispers. "You know the code for the keypad to get in, don't you?"

"Yes, I think so," I say vaguely, even though there's no doubt in my mind. It's 220484. Eva's birthday.

I steady myself, inhale the chill air and watch him disappear, beyond the garden square, back toward the bookshop to meet Priya. I call an Uber and wait. My phone buzzes. Two texts. One from Nate. One from Tony. He's been away traveling for the last few months after breaking up with Amira but now he's back, circling, prying, up to his old tricks.

Nate: There's vodka in the fridge and cigarettes in the usual place. I'm leaving shortly.

I smile into the darkness in spite of myself.

Tony: I know where you snuck off to, Anna. Watch out. It's not safe.

My hand shakes as I press the keypad. I tap in the code, open the door and light sensors illuminate the dark paneled hallway in a sulfurous glow. I realize how much I've missed this house, like a theater set coming alive, purring its way to a final denouement. I'm not sure how safe I feel being alone with him, knowing what he could be capable of, but I'm willing to take that risk, to hear what he has to tell me. To finally find out the truth.

# 30

A sliver of new moon filters through the sweep of glass above me as I wander through the house. I walk into the kitchen, the last area to be packed away. Someone has started emptying the drawers, a disarray of plates, mugs and cutlery spill out across the surfaces.

I light a couple of tea lights out on the table and slip into the garden, my mind drifting back to the two memorable occasions I stood at precisely this spot with Nate. After he lost his temper during our interview and again on the night we slept with each other for the first and last time. Our sordid affair began and ended right here, both occasions sealed by the ritual of a final cigarette.

I gaze at the brooding outline of Eva's studio, a shadow through the trees, the dark shimmer of the river beyond. The one space that eluded me in Algos House, that I never got to explore. Forbidden, desirable, risky. I know it will be locked... but still. I follow the gravel path to the bottom of the garden until I make it to the door.

Just as I reach for the door handle, two high-pitched electronic beeps split the silence. I freeze, disconcerted. The alarm is coming from the main house.

I run back up the path. Maybe I disabled the lock when I entered the code.

The sliding doors are still open and I walk in, my eyes adjusting to the darkness inside.

"Nate?" I call.

"Anna."

The ceiling down-lights switch on automatically and suddenly I see him.

"Tony?" My voice rises in shock.

"Surprise," he says from the doorway, swaying slightly. "Aren't you pleased to see me?"

"You shouldn't be here now. You have to go," I say roughly and he makes an exaggerated frown.

"I've only come to say goodbye."

"How did you know I—?"

"Amira," he says, pushing me aside. His eyes have a bright, febrile quality as he glances around the hallway. "I called her, told her I needed to see you before I left. She told me about the book launch, where you'd be. I guessed the rest. It's pretty obvious where you two would meet for your final farewell."

We hover in the kitchen area, facing each other across the marble island. He stares indifferently at the rubble of mess on the surface, contents from the kitchen drawers waiting to be packed up. He sees the glass doors open into the garden, Eva's studio illuminated by the outdoor lights I've left on. He catches my eye.

"You want to go inside, don't you?" His voice is husky, insinuating. "Course you do. Come on."

He grabs my arm roughly and I let him guide me outside, back again down the path. I think of the last time I saw Amira, the state she was in thanks to my brother. It's safer to conserve my energy, pick my battle carefully. He punches Eva's date of birth into the keypad, the same one as the front door, the depth of his familiarity with Algos House slowly dawning on me.

Inside, the air is cold and musty. Floor-to-ceiling windows stare out across the river. Dusty ghost lines frame the walls where pictures hung and there are dents in the floor where a sofa used to be.

I think of Nate discovering her body here. Was it near the sofa, perhaps, or the kitchen area in the far corner? The only reminders of Eva are a few of her last remaining sculptures in the center of the room, bathed in a silvery glow.

"They're part of her final series," I say out loud to Tony, desperately trying to stall until Nate gets here. "Eva's alter ego cast in glass, personifying the goddess Hedone, who embodied pleasure and delight," I muse to myself more than him. Clearly he's in no mood for an art lesson. I slide my fingers over the curves, imagine her hands molding the hips, the sinuous edge of the thighs.

He looks at me for a moment, his features tense, volatile. Disconcertingly I can still see my mother's expressions play across his face, in the way he frowns, the faint raise at one edge of his mouth, his weak chin when he smiles. You can never quite predict how your parents will come back to haunt you.

Tony's eyes cast around the empty space, a lost look in his gaze. For a moment I sense his weakness. "You know this place, don't you, Tony? You've been here before? You were her patient. More than her patient by the end."

Moments pass before he finally nods, his eyes faraway. I open my mouth to tell him about Eva's journal but decide against it. Knowing I have that evidence to hold against him will only make him more dangerous.

He pulls out his phone. "That iPhone I gave you, the one I bought you from New York?" He flashes his screen up at me. "It's on my iCloud, linked to my account. I can read every text, every WhatsApp. The locator app was inspired." He grins at me, head tilted. My stomach twists, incandescent with rage but I don't react. I can't afford to, not yet.

"I'm sorry, Tony. I'm listening now. Tell me. What happened?"

"I loved her," he says, simply. "I really did."

A sentimental lilt creeps into his voice. His eyes soften and he looks at me like a small boy seeking absolution.

"At first, she told me there were rules. Transference. Countertransference. Meaningless terms really. She was desperate to leave Nate but when she found out she was pregnant, everything changed. She wanted to cool the whole thing down... get rid of it, keep it all a secret. She was really scared of how Nate would react if he found out, how furious he'd be that she didn't want to have it."

And then I see it, the blade of a knife in his hand, his knuckles white as he grips it. With a sickening lurch I realize he must have spotted it waiting to be packed away.

"We need to show him, Anna. Treating you like trash, Eva too. If it weren't for him, if it weren't for how badly he treated her, Eva would still be alive. We'd be together."

I have to let Nate know he's here, I need to warn him, tell him to call the police.

"Tony, please. We'll both leave now. I'll come with you. I'll do anything—" Slowly I reach for my phone in my jacket pocket. There's a thrum of alarm in my chest. Too late. Everything happens so quickly. He's behind me and I register a bolt of white-hot pain as he twists my arm up and behind my back.

My phone skitters to the floor. I shriek and his grip tightens. I twist my head to one side, see the gleam of metal still there. My body slackens in pain. He pushes me hard against the wall as I gasp for breath. I feel him stroke the knife down the side of my neck.

"How do you always manage to do this?" He sighs theatrically. "I'm not sure you really fully appreciate what I've done for you down the years. Keeping your secret for so long. Cleaning up your messes for you."

"No, Tony. Please," I stammer through tears. He leans in closer to me, resting the blade on my cheek.

"You think I wasn't good enough for Eva, don't you?"

"Tony, that's not what I think. You two were in love. I believe you."

I glance toward the open door, the path back to the house. But Tony stands in front of me, blocking any hope of escape.

"You still think he's coming! One fuck and it's true love," he sneers into my ear. I watch him, trying to gauge the volatile cocktail of emotions passing across his face—anger, jealousy, desperation—to protect himself. To survive at all costs. That's all he cares about right now.

He catches me glance at the phone on the floor and as he does, swipes the knife at my cheek. I wince, feel a wetness on my skin.

"You're right," I pant. "I was gullible, stupid, arrogant, probably, to assume it would work out. I wish I'd listened to you. I'm on your side, Tony. We can show him. You and me together?"

For the longest moment he looks at me, wavering. A muscle in his eye flickers like a small bug trapped under his skin.

"Tell me more about you and Eva," I say, softly, hoping to stall him. "Why was she so special?"

He reflects for a moment. "She was the only person who never judged me. She was genuinely moved by my pain, my story. Maybe it took someone as amoral as Eva to understand me. In the end I told her everything about my life, about what really happened that night."

I look away.

"She was scared of him, Anna, that's why she ended it with me. She told me he was capable of anything. You know why he wanted a baby, don't you?"

A slow malevolent smile creeps across his face.

"He longed to be a father?" I falter.

"Yeah, right. The perfect daddy." He looks at me, lets out a thin high laugh that jolts me. "It was all about his work. That's all he cared about. A chance to study Eva's baby, the genetic effects of her condition, all wired up in his pain lab. A rare opportunity to test whether the CIP gene is hereditary, another major breakthrough in his research. Gold dust for him." Before I have time to process this, there is a shiver of movement behind us.

"You're a terrible liar, Tony."

I jump at his voice—Nate, here at last.

Tony swivels round to face him. "I wondered when you'd drop by."

I try to walk toward Nate but Tony stops me. For the briefest moment, it is only the three of us, a dark triad facing each other down. I am frozen, my mind fixed on the blade concealed in Tony's hand behind his back.

"You were with her when she died, weren't you?" He glares at Tony. "It was your cocaine, you brought it round with you. Maybe it was already cut with fentanyl or more likely you—"

"Shut the fuck up, Nate," Tony spits.

"Nate, be careful. He has—"

Tony turns from Nate toward me, eyes glazed, and I fall silent, terrified. I've never seen him in a state like this before.

"Anna, I need you to know, that's not what happened. I swear the cocaine was hers, not mine. She was high when I got there, in one of her moods."

For so long Tony has been an unreliable witness, a keeper of memories that I never really recognized, yet there is something in his tone that rings true, an urgency. Something family just knows.

"Tony. I believe you. Tell me…"

"I was furious with her. She told me she was pregnant and yet, there she was, using in front of me. Watching her do that, ruining this chance we had of a new life…it destroyed me."

I watch him closely, something in his features looks bone-weary, broken. "She racked out another two lines and I couldn't stop myself. I screamed at her, couldn't she see she was destroying everything? Then she broke it to me, she didn't want the baby anyway, and the relationship was over. It was time to move on. It was the right decision—to stay with Nate. Just like that she decided, after everything she told me about him."

I make a sympathetic noise and throw Nate a desperate look, silently pleading with him to stay out of it, knowing that one word from him will break this moment.

"I could feel this pressure building in me, like an iron fist in my gut, watching her head tipped back, laughing, high. It's as if that whole therapy thing was an act, a persona. This was the real Eva, selfish, off her head. I couldn't bear it, being there, her humiliating me."

"So what happened?" I push.

"I watched her, seething. *Poor Tony*, she kept saying, over and over." His voice cracks. "That was the worst. Her pity. I thought she was laughing, this weird way she kept repeating my name, her voice catching. Then I realized she was gasping for breath, choking. Her head was still tipped back, she seemed scared…confused. I knew she couldn't be in pain but she was holding her chest. She reached out for her phone, told me she had to call 999—"

"And you were really scared, weren't you?" I say, softly,

reasonably. "You wouldn't have wanted her to call 999, that would have been too dangerous."

"There was no other option, nothing they could do by then anyway. She was too far gone."

"So you took her phone and…you left her?"

Tony closes his eyes.

There's a glint in his hand as he turns. It's only then I see the blade isn't one he picked up in the kitchen earlier.

It's smaller, almost like a glass cutter.

The one that went missing from Eva's studio.

It was Tony. Before he bolted, he defiled Eva's sculptures in one final vile act, anger, vengeance, grief. Maybe even to make it look like Eva's doing?

"You're a monster," interjects Nate, unable to control himself any longer.

"Fuck you, Nate," Tony says. His tone flips from vulnerable to vicious in a beat.

Nate's eyes are ablaze as he turns toward me. "Anna. I've read and reread Eva's journal, all of it now. In the flap at the back, she'd kept all the old invoices from an *A.T.* At first, I thought it was you, Anna Tate, until I saw the signature. Anthony Thorpe. Your stepbrother's full name. I wanted to believe you, but until I saw that, I couldn't trust you."

"You're a fine one to talk about trust. You lied about everything in the end. Eva and Priya's affair. Being with Eva on the day she died, that she was pregnant by you. You didn't even want me to be your ghostwriter, it was Priya all along. You both manipulated me."

"When's it going to stop, Nate?" says Tony. "First Eva and then my sister?"

Nate flinches but keeps his eyes on me, his voice urgent and resolute.

"Anna, I was torn. I liked you right from the start."

"Please, spare me," Tony interjects but Nate carries on.

"It was a minefield. This mystery *Anthony Thorpe* that Eva confessed she had an affair with, then you drop the bomb. Your brother. I couldn't get my head around it." He shakes his head at the memory. "I was horrified but intrigued too. I could have been repelled, I wanted to be. Somehow that would have been easier. But then I fell for you," he reflects, giving me a strange, lost smile.

"Please tell me you're not going to buy this? Nate could never love you, Anna," Tony's acerbic drawl cuts in. "And I'd never let my sister be with you. Eva told me what you were really like. How cold you were. You're incapable of loving anyone. She couldn't bear you anywhere near her."

Still Nate focuses only on me. "I know what happened to your father too. It's all in that journal, once I went back and reread it. Tony told Eva everything and she was seduced by the idea that she could be his salvation. I know what you did that night, Anna, the price you paid, how Tony has held it over you ever since."

Tony opens his mouth but then stops himself. A white-hot energy burns through me as the truth of Nate's words takes hold.

"You're right. I did it for both of us, for me and Tony. I took his inhalers that night knowing there were no spare ones in the house. Tony, you remember the row, I know you do, before his asthma attack. How he dragged me down the stairs, slapping and punching me, turning on you too while I lay on the floor…"

Tony nods, lost in the memory of that night. "I never told a soul, Anna."

"Except Eva," says Nate.

My brain fizzes, folds over for a moment. I'm back there now in my father's house. My head spinning after my fall, stumbling upstairs to the bathroom. I sat on the floor, my cheek against the cool tiles. That's when I saw both of them, on their sides on the glass shelf above the sink. In a dazed state, angry, I grabbed them. I walked downstairs, found the last one I knew he kept in the kitchen drawer too, and stuffed them all deep into the refuse sacks that the garbagemen would take away the next morning.

"You took his inhalers. I took her phone. I guess we're not so different after all. Doesn't that make us level, sis?"

"I never wanted my father to die, I just wasn't thinking clearly," I say to Nate, ignoring Tony's mocking tone. "My greatest mistake was confessing to Tony a few days later because I couldn't bear the guilt. I wanted to go to the police but *he* wouldn't let me."

*It looks premeditated*, he'd said. *They'd lock you up. I can't let that happen to you.*

So I became a prisoner of a different sort. Owned by my brother, the worst sentence of all. Unable to confide in anyone else, I could never move on, ruined by my own actions.

"Tony punished you, held you to ransom, instead of getting you the help and support you needed," says Nate, softly.

"I can see what you're doing," Tony says to Nate. "You lost Eva to me and now you're trying to win over Anna. It's pathetic. Separate beds. How humiliating," he hisses, triumphant, and the ghost of a smile flits across his face. Tony turns. "I swear, Anna, if you forgive him, if you buy this bullshit and go back to him…if you go to the police about me and Eva… I'll tell the police about your father. I won't keep your secret anymore."

"I doubt it," says Nate. "It's only your word against Anna's and who'd believe you?"

"The police. You know I found the inhalers. I guessed what had happened, the state you were in after Dad attacked you.

I took them to protect you, Anna. If anyone found out, it's a scandal that could destroy everything you've worked for, your journalism, your promising career."

"Please, no more, shut up," I scream, bursting. Nate swallows hard, features tightening.

"You destroyed Eva, Tony, and I won't let you do the same to Anna."

Tony stares at him, begins inching forward.

"Nate, he's got a knife," I shriek. Too late. Tony leaps toward Nate, the blade cuts through the air. Nate runs at Tony, who trips and falls, taking Nate down with him, and the knife drops to the floor. They struggle, both on the ground, tangled and enmeshed. Tony has split his knuckle open; there's a deep gash on Nate's forehead.

I am briefly immobilized. I hear a crack as Tony's fist connects with Nate's cheekbone. Nate falls back and Tony straddles him, slams his head on the marble tiles. "Do something!" Nate's voice is a strangled growl. The words are like a touch paper, galvanizing me.

I won't let Tony control me anymore.

Nate shrieks, twists his head in my direction, spitting blood on the floor. I run toward the knife and pick it up. Something else catches my eye.

Hedone. There she is, leaning against the wall as if she's been waiting all along. I grab the sculpture.

Her weight is reassuring in my hands, the power and heft of her. Tony howls as he heaves himself up, smacking Nate to the ground. They twist and writhe, Nate caught under Tony. He bends over him, one foot on his stomach, his hands tightening around Nate's neck. I shove the knife into Nate's hands behind Tony's back, but he can't manoeuvre properly.

The veins pulse in Nate's neck, his eyes glistening and rolling back. Tony screeches, provoked even more, and tightens his grip around Nate's neck.

"Anna," rasps Nate. Everything speeds up. I dart behind Tony, swing the statue unsteadily, striking his shoulder at an awkward angle. There's a muted thud of glass against flesh and bone.

"You bitch! You fucking bitch!" he yells, incredulous.

*You bitch. You fucking bitch.*

I won't hear those words anymore. Not from my father, not from him. The coercion, the lies, it all stops here. I am strong, I can do this. Once more I raise Hedone. For Eva as well as me. High, higher, I swing her above my head, my fingers tight around her, bring her down in one swift and fatal blow. I am lost to the moment, my one chance to vanquish my past. She lands, glass shattering into a million little pieces, glittering in a scarlet sea.

# 31

I took one last lingering look at Algos House as we left; its perfect Georgian windows glittered back at me in the moonlight, icily indifferent.

"We have to call the police," I had told Nate, hunched over Tony's lifeless body, checking for a nonexistent pulse.

"They'll understand," I said. "It was self-defense. He was going to kill me, or you. He was insane, we both know that. We have the evidence. Our witness statements, the therapy invoice and Eva's journal."

"Eva's journal," he had echoed.

I could see his hands trembling, his fingers raking his hair. When I picked up my phone from the floor, Nate's arm shot out.

"We have to think first about what this looks like, what you and I have done." He had stared at me, his pupils iridescent, his temple meshed in blood and hair. In the past, I would have believed him, done as I was told. But not now. Not after Tony.

Nate took time to convince. Implicating ourselves in another death just as the second inquest was looming and the book was about to be launched in America.

"We have no choice," I said. "It's the right thing to do. He wanted to kill us. He let Eva die too."

He closed his eyes, sunk to the floor, head in hands. "You're right," he said, finally.

It was almost morning by the time the police released us. There would be more questions, an inquest, but for the time being we were free to leave. Nate drove me home. I stared out at the empty London streets flashing past, my mind alive with demons, the stuff of horror floating up before my eyes. The whoosh of the sculpture as it tore the air. The sickening crunch of glass and chrome meeting flesh.

When I saw Tony's hands around Nate's neck, his life seeping away in front of me, I had to act and I needed Nate to help me. I couldn't live in fear that Tony would tell anyone else about that night, why and how my father really died. I was pretty sure that those old inhalers wouldn't count as proof of anything but somehow just the thought of them in his possession haunted me. And anyway it went beyond that. He'd attacked my best friend, I couldn't bear to see that abuse play out again, with Amira or any other woman he met. And there would have been more.

I've been reflecting lately about how anger is an ugly emotion, but in the right circumstances it feels like buried treasure, deep inside me, an energy flowing free, illuminating who I really am. Someone who will go to any lengths to get exactly what I want. Is that such a bad thing? No one truly knows how they'll act until the chips are down, until pure adrenaline and fear exposes our real nature. I've been there and back. Now I know who I really am.

I knew how dangerous Tony could be once he was out of control and that Nate would have lost his life. Tony would have carried on, holding that secret over me if Nate and I ever got together. I couldn't let that happen. I always admired Eva for her strength and spirit. But in the end, she was the victim I refused to be.

We both realized there would be consequences. Another death at Algos House. The publicity. The aftermath. The four of us entangled like knotweed, never able to break free. There are two survivors to this story, two victims we left behind.

I didn't want to go home right away and so Nate kept on driving instead. At one point he turned to me. We could always reframe this, tell another story, he said. I couldn't help smiling into the darkness. The way the words flowed out of him. That clever brain of his, never without a plan.

We began to share our thoughts, words spilling out of us as darkness turned to dawn. It felt like the early days. Side by side. The art of alchemy, when my fingers seemed to fly across the keys, divining memories he never knew he had. Really, it's what we do best, projections on a movie screen.

"You've always underestimated your own potential," he said. "Let's face it, Anna, writing in someone else's voice is your superpower. All those hours in the study. Apart from some very bad thoughts about exactly what I wanted to do to you, most of the time I was in awe. It's a gift, don't you see?"

And, yes, I did see. Eva's self-reflection diary that I had given back to Nate, that we planned to hand over to the police. Wouldn't it be such an easy addition, he suggested, to craft a final damning entry about Tony and erase the fight we had? For the first time all evening, his patrician features had relaxed into a sort of smile.

"I don't really believe in bad publicity, do you?" he said, accelerating hard across Albert Bridge, lights strung across it like milky pearls. A marbled light seeped across the horizon and the sky was stippled pink like the faintest streaks of blood. Nothing stays still. Nothing is quite what it seems.

"So we know what we're doing?" I nodded and glanced in his direction. We didn't kiss, didn't even say goodbye. He surveyed me for a moment, his expression no longer inscrutable or remote. I got out of the car, watched him drive away.

As I walked up my street, let myself into my apartment, my brain was already alight. Thanks to him. Always thanks to him. In my mind, words spun and circled, like lottery balls colliding in the air. All I had to do was write it up just as Eva remembered it; her small neat lettering was easy enough to emulate.

# EVA'S SELF-REFLECTION JOURNAL

*24 June 2019*

*1:00 p.m.*

*Nate has just left to go to his conference and I'm writing this alone in my studio. It's funny how the worst things can turn out to be the best. For a while I suspected I may be pregnant. It was unlike me to be a week late and I began to feel vaguely nauseous. I didn't want to tell Nate, I thought I'd wait until he left the house.*

*But then he came back unexpectedly, went to the bathroom to get his glasses…and that's when he spotted it. My pregnancy test out on the side. I knew he'd be so disappointed I didn't intend to keep it.*

*Poor Nate. All he really wanted was to be a father. He came down and confronted me. For a moment he looked devastated, broken. I told him the whole truth, about the affair, how deeply I regretted it all, how much pain I had caused to everyone around* me, how irresponsible I had been as a therapist. I began to cry and was so relieved to see that Nate seemed more conciliatory.

"Let's put it behind us," he said. "I love you, Eva."

"I love you too," I whispered, touching his shoulder before he left.

2:00 p.m.

I've just texted Tony. He's on his way round for the very last time. I owe him an explanation and I hope he understands. I know how unpredictable he can be, how carefully I have to handle him. I didn't see it at first. The disturbance, the sickness. It's obvious, really. But I was too taken up with the thrill of it. Forbidden, dangerous.

Psychotherapy was never going to be enough. Almost certainly he has borderline personality disorder. Ideally, I'd have referred him for specialist psychiatric help but I didn't want to involve my supervisor. By then it was all too late. When he told me he felt responsible for his stepfather's death, I assumed it was survivor's guilt, a natural regret that he couldn't have done more that night to save him.

Later, after we started seeing each other, he told me more. Words poured out of him, a confession really, even though by then I didn't want to know. He told me anyway. How he hid the Ventolin inhalers. How he could have saved his father's life but decided to end it instead.

Sometimes I catch Tony looking at me. He unnerves me, those lifeless eyes, what lies behind them. As the minutes tick by I can't help thinking... I'm the only person alive who knows Tony's secret. What if he decides that's one person too many?

*4 February 2023*

Dr. Nate Reid's memoir *Hurting* has been a record-breaking success rising up the *New York Times* bestseller list with first-day sales exceeding expectations.

*Hurting* attracted enormous press coverage in the early weeks of its publication following the second high-profile death at his home in West London, two and a half years after his wife, Eva Reid, also died there.

On the evening of his book launch in Marylebone, Dr. Reid had returned to Algos House, his riverside property earlier than expected, surprising an intruder who then viciously attacked him with a knife.

Dr. Reid was forced to protect himself in self-defense only but in the fight that ensued, his assailant was left fatally wounded.

The deceased was later identified as Mr. Anthony Thorpe, an ex-patient of Eva Reid's. According to psychotherapy notes discovered at her home, he was suffering from mental health issues and admitted full responsibility for his father's death over twelve years ago.

Eva's notes also reveal that Mr. Thorpe was due to visit on the evening that she died, offering further evidence that he could have been involved in her death. A second inquest is expected later this year following an initial open verdict, meaning there was insufficient evidence to decide how the death came about.

One theory is that Mr. Thorpe broke into the property, assuming it would be empty in order to find the therapy notes—now in the hands of the police.

This steady drip of scandal and intrigue has, it seems, only helped to drive more book sales. High-profile interviews with Dr. Reid in America and London have also helped to intensify interest. *Hurting* sold more than half a million copies in all formats in the United States, Canada and Britain.

Priya James, Dr. Reid's publisher at Grayson Inc., confirmed this week that another book deal would soon be announced and, despite the news of Mr. Thorpe's death, there will be no change in publishing plans. The next publication has been slated for a January 2025 release.

# EPILOGUE

It is such a long way down. I step toward the balcony's edge. There are hundreds of them packed into the bookshop; the hum and the heat of their bodies pressed close, the clatter of their voices rising up to meet me. My fingers trace where Nate's once were, gripping the mahogany handrail, seeking comfort in its cool worn surface.

Those words float back to me from that evening, words that we wrote together.

No one can really bear the truth that every minute of our life hangs by a thread. However much we think we can script our own existence and try to ensure nothing bad can ever happen to us, it does and it will.

How I labored over those lines, how prophetic they turned out to be. But even the worst outcomes can turn out well in the end, given the right spin and a little imagination.

Now it is my own editor, Tash, who stands up, taps a pen against her wineglass until the clamor subsides. Tash is older than Priya, less driven, more of a listener. I warmed to her as soon as we met, with her elegant mane of silver hair and wise olive green eyes. She has my best interests at heart. I look out at the sea of animated faces, mainly female, below. I speak softly, like Nate, so people crane to listen.

"Thank you so much. First, I want to say I couldn't have done all this without my fantastic editor, Tash, who encouraged me to write something for myself. Kath too, who has been an invaluable consultant on the book. As you may know I started out in publishing as a ghostwriter two years ago and although that memoir was successful, it only really told part of her story. But it did teach me one thing. I needed to write a different sort of ending—for both of us.

"In *All About You*, I wanted to tell Eva's story in a new way, to explore how she paid the ultimate price for a life without pain. I always saw her as the ultimate unknowable woman, cool, elusive, unattainable. She was what someone like me could never be. Yet in coming closer to Eva, I discovered a rare vulnerability. She yearned to empathize with others, to feel whatever they felt and, I think, in the end, she really did. It is in the spirit of Eva's desire to understand that I wrote this book. Let's raise a glass to her."

There are cheers and clapping while Tash tells guests I'll be signing copies on the floor below. I walk down the wrought iron staircase just as Nate did a year ago. These days I try not to think about him and that final evening, but it's more difficult coming back here. In the months that followed, I would wake up haunted by horrific images replaying in my mind. In quiet moments, it's been a struggle to make peace with what happened and how it all ended, but I've come to realize there is no other way.

I jump when Tash touches my shoulder, her smile is rich and warm and reassuring. So unlike Priya's. She's as thrilled as I am that the book is already tipped to be a bestseller.

Tash hands me a glass of champagne, my first in many

weeks, and I figure I deserve it. She tells me that our Spanish publisher can't wait to meet me and after that she'll introduce me to the publicity team from New York. But first I must sign my books.

A long queue curls its way through to the back of the shop. Usually, I can't help reflexively scanning the crowd, looking for the one face I'll never see. But this time I focus only on the blank page and the repetitive task of each signature. It is only when there's a slight lull that unthinkingly I look up. It is the line of shoulders I notice first, not exactly in the queue but standing to the side with his back to me. The nape of his neck and the short hair that's more silvered than I remember.

But when I look again, he's not there. I was imagining it after all. It has happened before, this shadow circling and prickling at the edge of my vision, and I wonder if through sheer force of will I conjure him into being. He's vanished again and something in me deflates, a chasm deep inside yawns open.

The queue tapers and a woman steps forward, beaming, hands me a copy of the book. She is animated, taking up space with the details of her life that at this moment are of no real interest to me. Depression. Divorce. Redundancy. Triumph over tragedy. I should engage but I'm a million miles away. I watch her lips move, words pouring out that register only as white noise. Smile and nod, smile and nod. My face is flushed, my breathing shallow. What I would give for her to finally shut up. Every cell of my being is drawn to what I know can't be there.

"I'm so glad that at last you've found some resolution," I say, managing a smile. She thanks me, catches my eye as she leaves. But I'm elsewhere, fixated on a flicker that settles into an outline, no longer just my imagination. There is the pure rush of the moment, the lurch in my chest as I try to focus only on steadying my hand to sign each book.

He waits patiently for his turn and when at last we're face-to-face, he doesn't smile. Neither do I. We say nothing and instead he frowns a little to himself, an intensely solemn expression so deeply familiar to me, and offers up the open book. I take it and begin to write:

> *To my partner in crime.*
> *Love always,*
> *Anna*

★ ★ ★ ★ ★

# ACKNOWLEDGMENTS

The idea for my book only came to life thanks to the Faber Academy's novel writing course back in 2016. Thank you to fellow Faberities for making it such an inspiring experience—in particular, Laura Church, Emma Goode and CC Baker. Thank you to our brilliant tutor, Richard Skinner, and his memorable advice to "just keep going" has turned out to be one of life's more useful maxims.

I'm indebted to my agent, Judith Murray, at Greene & Heaton and to my publisher, Sam Eades, for both championing the book early on, and to my editor, Grace Towery, at Harper-Collins US, whose insights and suggestions have been invaluable. Thank you to the team at Orion including Sian Baldwin and Snigdha Koirala.

Thank you to old friends who have always been there down the years with support and advice, writing or otherwise; Angela Hagan, Angela Gourley, Steve Johnstone and Greta Sani. Special thanks to Genevieve Fox—I couldn't ask for a better friend and writing buddy.

Thanks to my work colleagues, Harriet Green, Shay Shaitly, Steve Chamberlain, Eva Wisman and Martin Love, for their support and always being up for a Friday baking challenge!

Thank you to both my book groups for being about much

more than just the books—in particular, Sue Lee-Stern, Susi Glyn and Leeanne Vinson. Thank you to my writing group, Clare Longrigg, Genevieve, Bev Thomas, Jennifer Nadel, Susannah Kleeman and Nicole Dunaway, and to early readers Susannah Waters and Hayley Webster.

Thanks to Martin Toseland for his invaluable insights on the art of ghostwriting.

Thank you to my brother and sister-in-law for nurturing an early love of books and cinema at a young age, and my father for his medical advice about everything pain and drug related.

Thank you to my children, Louis, Evie and Amelia, for their encouragement, patience and many invaluable plot discussions! Thank you to my husband, Simon, for everything—I couldn't have done any of it without you.

Thank you to my mother, Sally, who always used to say, whenever I told her pretty much anything, however mundane, "That's a good line, you should write it down." And finally I did.

A final note: two stories in particular got me thinking about the potential of pain in a fictional setting. The first was a story that appeared five years ago about a woman called Jo Cameron who lives in the Scottish Highlands. At 71, she became something of a news sensation after doctors discovered her rare genetic mutation that meant she was incapable of feeling pain. Also writer Nicola Twilley's fascinating *New Yorker* profile of Professor Irene Tracey six years ago, an eminent neuroscientist known as the Queen of Pain with a lab in Oxford where she tests and measures pain, much like the ones Anna reluctantly endures when she interviews Dr Reid.